A

KILLING

TIDE

A Novel

P. J. Alderman

Tumbling
Creek Press

Kingston, Washington, USA

A Killing Tide is a work of fiction. Names, characters, places and incidents either are the product of the author's imagination or are used fictitiously. Any resemblance to actual persons, living or dead, business establishments, events, or locales, is entirely coincidental.

Copyright ©2006-2012 by P. J. Alderman. All rights reserved.

ISBN: 978-0-9838431-0-8

Published by Tumbling Creek Press
Kingston, Washington, USA

First Tumbling Creek Press Printing, January 2012

Library of Congress Subject Headings:
Romance
Romantic Suspense
Thriller
Romantic Thriller
Mystery
Women Sleuths

By P. J. Alderman:

Columbia River Thriller Series:

A Killing Tide

Phantom River

Port Chatham Mystery Series:

Haunting Jordan

Ghost Ship

Acknowledgments

Those familiar with the town of Astoria, Oregon, will note that I have taken literary license with a few building locations and the makeup of the East Marina.

I am indebted to the authors of several excellent books for my research about the Northwest Coast and its fishing communities. *The World of the Oregon Fishboat,* by Janet C. Gilmore, provided me with wonderful details about fishing trawlers and maritime folklife. For general information about Astoria, the Columbia River, and surrounding communities, I relied upon the excellent writings of Timothy Egan, *A Good Rain,* and John Paul Barrett, *Sea Stories: Of Dolphins and Dead Soldiers.*

I am additionally grateful to all the people who made this book possible. Special thanks go to authors Pam Beason and Amy Atwell for their hard work, support, and encouragement through every step of the process.

Prologue

Astoria, Oregon, late winter, evening

Century-old clapboard buildings huddled together on the narrow triangle of land between Marine Drive and the raging waters of the Columbia River. Sixty-knot gusts of wind rattled loose windowpanes; sheets of rain flayed peeling siding. A rusty streetlight groaned, its pool of light dancing on the darkened sidewalk.

The door of the Redemption Tavern swung open, and a man staggered out. Propping himself against the brick alcove, he peered into the night, eyes slitted against the wet. A Pineapple Express, damn their luck, straight out of the South Pacific. Someone'd probably die on the river bar tonight. Someone they all knew.

Shivering, he shoved throbbing hands into his pockets. Goddamn ratfish. Their fins cut like razors. In the last week, he'd flung enough of 'em off the port bow to last a lifetime.

He closed his eyes, swaying. Someone from inside the tavern yelled at him to close the door, but he paid no attention. All he had to do was make it six miserable blocks, then he'd be home with Julie and the kids. He'd take a hot shower, eat a home-cooked meal. Get some sleep.

They wouldn't come for him at the house. Too many witnesses.

His hands fisted, the right one closing around the small snow globe he'd forgotten he'd put in his pocket. Scowling, he held it up to the dim glow of the lamp above the door. A miniature white fishing trawler floated on a pretty blue sea, glittery bits of snow falling all around it. The skipper's sister had given it to him for Bobby.

"Since Bobby's too sick to go out with you right now," Kaz had explained.

His jaw clenched. She had no clue about the kind of trouble he was in, the kind of trouble they were all in. Pretty little bobbles couldn't fix anything, and there weren't going to be any happy endings. With the snow globe still clutched in his hand, he pushed himself onto the sidewalk.

Rain iced his face and ran inside his collar, soaking the front of his wool shirt. A car passed him, splashing greasy water over his boots. He shook a fist at it, but it never even slowed, its taillights disappearing into the swirling darkness.

What a fool he'd been! But he never thought they'd find out, not really. And he'd been desperate.

At least the Skipper should've understood. After all, Gary was his friend—the two of them went way back. A bitter laugh escaped, its sound swept away by the wind. In all the years he and Gary had been together, he'd never seen Gary so angry, so...disappointed.

What have I done?

In the lull between wind gusts, he caught a sound, a faint scrape on the concrete. Spinning around, he peered into the rain-drenched night.

The street was empty, the only movement the quaking shadows of wind-whipped vegetation.

Increasing his pace, he ducked around the corner of a coffee house, and then from under its creaking sign, crossed a patch of grass to stand in the deep shadow cast by the concrete bridge abutment.

He stared into the darkness, fear chasing each breath, then shuddered.

He was so damn tired. Tired of running. Tired of trying to

make things right again.

His head fell back and he looked up, letting the rain batter his face. High overhead, the steel deck of the bridge loomed, its tiny lights winking against the turbulent black sky. Steady streams of water poured off the structure, flooding the grass and soaking his boots.

Sensing movement behind him, he started to turn. Something heavy crashed down on his head, driving him to his knees. Pain exploded, radiating down his spine. Dazed, he shook his head.

Hands grabbed his coat, slamming him against the concrete. Breath soured by beer washed over his face. "Where is it?"

He immediately recognized the low, gravely voice.

Can't tell.

His shoulder rammed against the concrete, his collarbone snapping with a hot, grating pop. *"What did you do with it?"*

He choked and sucked in air. "I'll give it back...just give me a chance." The hands tightened like a vise, and he clawed at his throat. "Wait! *I'm begging you.*"

The pressure on his collarbone increased, and he screamed.

"You'll never find it," he got out, but his words were swallowed by the howling wind. He struggled. "I made sure," he whispered.

The hands loosened, and he fell, facedown.

Was that the ocean roaring? Didn't make sense....He was by the river, wasn't he? He chuckled, but the sound only echoed inside his head. Funny. He'd always figured he'd die crossing the river bar, but never like this. It shouldn't have been like this.

The storm was easing. Calm settled over him as night closed in. *Julie will understand.*

The fingers of his right hand loosened, and the snow globe dropped into the mud. He never even felt the last blow.

3

Chapter 1

Kaz Jorgensen opened the cedar plank door of the Redemption and stepped into its dimly lit interior. A gust of wind caught the door, and she had to use all of her strength to drag it shut.

Hanging her dripping sou'wester on a peg in the entry, she paused long enough to roll the tension out of her shoulders. By the time she'd crossed the river bar, the seas had been running at seventeen feet. Waves two stories high had battered the trawler, making it shudder beneath her feet. It was her first rough crossing since coming home, and she'd nearly been paralyzed by the sense of déjà vu.

Rubbing icy hands on her jeans, she glanced around the smoky, cavernous room, taking a quick headcount. And breathed a quick sigh of relief. As far as she could tell, no fishing crews were MIA from the storm. Her twin brother Gary caught her gaze, frowning and glancing deliberately at his watch. Shrugging, she held out both hands, then started threading her way through the crowded tables.

"You're late," Lucy McGuire said as she approached. "That's the second time this week."

"Hi to you, too." Kaz dropped into the captain's chair across from Lucy, propping salt-encrusted, wet sneakers on the extra chair. "I would've been here an hour ago if some *idiot* hadn't run through my lines." Catching the bartender's eye, she mimicked a drinking motion.

Steve's brow arched, and he nodded.

While she waited, Kaz watched her best friend take a bite out of her Reuben, miraculously managing to avoid dribbling sauce on her designer jeans and expensive charcoal wool blazer. "How do you *do* that?"

Lucy raised a brow. "Do what?" Her detective's shield was discreetly clipped to her waistband, her Beretta semi-automatic barely distinguishable under the perfect cut of her jacket. An intricately designed antique silver clip tamed thick, curly black hair into a discreet French braid.

Kaz just shook her head. The tavern's only waitress appeared at her elbow with her usual—a frosty pint of microbrew and a tablet of ibuprofen. Kaz shot Sandra a grateful smile, then realized she'd gotten distracted from finishing her rant. "I lost a half dozen pots, dammit. Remind me to hunt down the jerk and give him a piece of my mind."

Lucy snorted. "Like you have a prayer of discovering who it was. So how many crabs did you catch?"

"You don't *count* them, Luce. You *weigh* them." When Lucy raised a brow, Kaz sighed. "Okay, the catch was light—a few dozen."

Lucy choked on a sip of beer, waving a hand in the air. "Wow. Big ones or little ones?"

"Oh, shut up." Kaz slumped more comfortably in her chair, raising her mug. "To safe passages."

"Safe passages," Lucy repeated, clinking glasses. "So tell me you didn't just come into port—that you aren't that crazy."

"I'm not that crazy," Kaz replied obediently, swallowing the ibuprofen with another gulp.

Lucy glared. "Dammit, Kaz—"

"I'm handling it."

"Yeah, right."

Time for a change of subject. "So who's the new guy?" Kaz nodded toward the booths along the back wall.

She'd noticed him right away, of course—they didn't get

5

many tourists this far into Uniontown. The Redemption was a working-class tavern in a working-class neighborhood, a little too rough for most with its worn, scarred tables and harsh, mingled odors of fish, grease, and creosote. Then again, the guy didn't strike her as a tourist.

He sat in a booth by himself, eating a hamburger while he read *The Daily Astorian*. Obviously, no one had told him not to order the grilled food. Few locals except Lucy, who had a cop's cast iron stomach, were that foolish. For the first time, Kaz noticed the black German shepherd asleep at the guy's feet. Stretched out on the floor, the dog looked about the size of a full-grown deer.

Lucy followed the direction of her gaze. "That's the new fire chief, guy by the name of Michael Chapman. He made the rounds to introduce himself a couple of days ago—comes from back East. When Richardson decided to retire, this guy applied for the job. The Mayor took one look at his resume and snapped him up."

Kaz frowned. "That good?"

"Yeah." Lucy abandoned the rest of her sandwich and leaned forward, lowering her voice. "He's some kind of a big-time, washed-up arson investigator. The way I hear it, he and that dog of his brought down one of Boston's worst arsonists in decades, some guy who'd set dozens of fires and killed several people." Her expression turned grim. "I *hate* arsonists. They're sick little creeps."

Intrigued, Kaz sneaked a second glance. The guy definitely looked tough enough to bring down a serial arsonist. Dark hair, cut military-short, barely touched his high forehead, and hard features telegraphed a quiet grimness. He had a rangy, muscular build and shoulders wide enough to make any woman's heart skip a few beats.

Definitely good-looking. Rough-edged, like he'd lived hard. "So why do people think he's washed up?" Kaz asked, her curiosity getting the better of her.

"The torch burned down Chapman's apartment, killing his fiancée." Lucy straightened and tossed her crumpled napkin on top of the remains of her sandwich. "Rumor is that Chapman wigged."

"Sounds like he had good reason." Kaz knew all too well what that kind of loss did to a person.

Without warning, he glanced up, his gaze locking with hers.

He had light-colored eyes, maybe blue—she couldn't tell from this distance. But she had a sneaking hunch they'd chill her right down to the bone. His jaw was rock-hard, that much she *could* tell.

She returned his look without blinking, a shiver dancing across her skin. This guy wouldn't welcome her sympathy.

He nodded, the slightest inclination of his head, then turned back to his meal.

"Kind of cute for a burnout, huh?" Lucy's voice cut into her thoughts.

Kaz made a noncommittal noise, disguising her reaction by drinking more beer. "Maybe he wanted to downshift, live with a little less stress," she murmured, not believing it for one minute.

Lucy harrumphed. "If that's true, he'll go stark raving mad the first winter. Guys like him come out here to kick back, to live the supposedly idyllic, small-town life. After the first hundred inches of rain and thousand dollars of counseling to help them cope with all the peace and quiet, they de-web their feet and head back home."

Kaz smiled, her tension easing a little. Living on the north coast of Oregon *did* require a certain kind of fortitude. "Still, if he's got the kind of experience you say he does, maybe Astoria is lucky to have him," she pointed out.

Raised voices forestalled Lucy's reply. Kaz turned in time to see her brother Gary shove his friend Chuck hard against the bar. The room fell silent.

She jumped to her feet, shaking her head at Lucy, who was already half out of her chair, then headed toward them.

"I need your help, damn you," she heard Gary say in a low tone as she neared. His large hands fisted in Chuck's shirt.

She ducked under Gary's arm and placed a hand on his chest. "Hey." Pasting a smile on her face, she glanced over her shoulder at Chuck. "What's going on, guys? You're starting to draw attention."

Beneath her hand, Gary's muscles were rigid with suppressed violence. Their genetic propensity for height had blessed him even more than Kaz—he towered a good six inches over her five foot ten. And whereas she tended toward a willowy frame, a stint as an Army Ranger and grueling years of drag fishing had given Gary a solid, powerful build.

"Yo, guys? You're turning me into a candidate for high blood pressure, here. What d'you say we—"

"Stay out of it, Sis," Gary muttered, not looking her way.

She risked a quick glance at Chuck, whose expression was calm. But then, Chuck *always* looked calm.

"Bad move, what you're thinking, man," he murmured to Gary, his lips barely moving.

A frisson of unease slithered through her. "What's this all about?"

Chuck spared her a chiding look. "Not your business."

"You're making it my business," Kaz shot back softly, "as well as everyone else's." She angled her head toward the room. People's gazes were lowered, but they hung on every word.

"Problem?" The resonant baritone came from behind Kaz. She swung around, her shoulder connecting with Gary's chest, which served to force the two men slightly apart.

The new fire chief stood a few feet away, boots planted, arms hanging loosely at his sides. He was taller than she'd realized, and if the crow's feet around his eyes were any indication, older than she would've originally guessed—maybe around forty. *Formidable* was the first word that leapt to mind. If any more tough men showed up, she'd asphyxiate from the ambient testosterone.

"I'm handling it," she insisted.

Chapman's gaze flicked over her, then he turned back to the men. "You two might want to continue this outside."

"Who the hell are you?" Gary demanded, causing Kaz to wince. He had an almost preternatural gift for irritating the authorities.

"Just a guy who wants to finish his dinner in peace," Chapman said, crossing his arms. The soft wool of his cable-knit sweater glided smoothly over hard muscle. "And I'd prefer that the lady not get hurt."

Kaz frowned. "I won't—"

Gary overrode her. "No one asked you to butt in, pal."

Chapman shrugged and nodded toward his booth. "Zeke—over there—tends to get real stressed out." The dog let out a snore. "I do what I can for him."

"You're a regular comic."

Steve chose that moment to walk up on the other side of the bar. "Take it outside, Jorgensen. I don't want another fight in my bar."

Gary rounded on him, his expression lethal. "You've got no room to complain, *no room*. For all I know—"

Steve's normally pleasant expression hardened, his eyes going flat. "I *said*, leave. Now."

Kaz reached out and gripped his arm. "Gary. Please."

He glared at her for a moment, then jerked away. "Hell, I'm out of here." He tossed some money on the bar. When she reached out again, he glanced down at her, his expression momentarily softening. "Leave me be, Kaz." Then he shot a hard look at Chuck—a look, she realized, that was tinged with fear. "You think about what I said." He snagged his coat off the

9

back of the bar stool and shouldered his way between them.

Chuck slanted a quiet look at her while he paid his bill. "Stick to the sidelines on this one, kiddo." Then he followed Gary out the door.

She stood for a moment in the spot they'd vacated, then huffed out a breath. Turning back to Chapman, she forced another smile. "You know, I really could've handled that."

He studied her without comment. She'd been right—his eyes were light blue, so light they were almost silver. But his gaze wasn't so much unfriendly as simply world-weary.

"Most women would hesitate before getting between two rough-looking men spoiling for a fight," he said finally.

She shook her head. "One of those 'rough-looking' men was my brother."

"Ah." He nodded and held out a hand. "Michael Chapman."

"Yes, I know." His grip was firm, warm, and slightly rough. He held her hand a moment longer than was called for, and she pulled away, taking an involuntary step backward and crossing her arms.

One corner of his mouth lifted at the movement. "Small town—word travels fast, I imagine." He waited.

"Oh, sorry." She introduced herself.

"Kaz." He cocked his head. "Unusual name."

"It's short for Kasmira, a family name—my grandmother's," she explained, then gestured vaguely toward the center of the room. "Well. I should be getting back—"

"I'm not keen on women getting shoved around in bar fights. In the future, you'd be wise to be more careful."

She curbed her impatience. He was new; she probably should cut him some slack. "Gary and Chuck can disagree on something as minor as whether the Cubs have a chance to win this year's pennant race," she explained. "They're *friends*. It wouldn't have gotten out of hand."

"Obviously you didn't think so, or you wouldn't have raced

over to break it up."

Her irritation notched a peg or two higher, her voice chilling. "This is a small town, Mr. Chapman. You'll find folks around here won't appreciate you butting into their business."

A flicker of something, possibly humor, came and went in his eyes so quickly she might have imagined it. "Folks rarely appreciate my butting in, as you put it, no matter where they live," he replied, his tone dry as dust. "Ma'am."

She watched him walk back to his booth, annoyed that she'd let him push her buttons. Protective males made her crazy, and Astoria had an overabundance of them. There had to be something in the water—this guy had been indoctrinated in less than a week.

"Well?" Lucy asked when she returned.

"Not a clue."

"What did Chapman want?"

Kaz jerked her shoulders, still unsettled by him. She was good at handling aggressive men—it'd been part of her job description for the last ten years. But Chapman had gotten her defenses up in less than thirty seconds.

She noticed Lucy was scanning the room, her "cop" expression on. *"What?"*

Lucy hesitated, then shook her head. "You'd better have that talk with Gary, and soon," she said, referring to the discussion they'd had when she'd called Kaz early one morning a month ago and suggested she come home on extended leave from her consulting gig in San Francisco.

Hearing the uncharacteristic worry in her friend's voice, Kaz hadn't even hesitated. She'd packed her laptop, told her business partner she'd handle whatever she could from Astoria, then booked the first flight to Portland. Once home, she'd made excuses to a disgruntled Gary about how she could use the break from her high-stress job, about how she figured she could use the downtime to help him get the family fishing

11

business back on its feet. About how getting back out on the water would be good for her.

He hadn't bought her last argument any more than she had. She'd known coming home would cause old memories to resurface, keeping her awake late into the night. But she'd deal with them—she didn't have a choice. And though she hadn't been able to ferret out yet what was bothering Gary, she was working on it.

"I don't want Sykes back on his case," Lucy said, bringing Kaz out of her thoughts. Jim Sykes, the chief of police and Lucy's direct superior, had never been able to stand Gary, even when they were kids growing up. "And I *really* don't want to be the one to haul your brother in on another assault charge on the chief's orders."

Kaz frowned. "Come on. That's stretching it, don't you think?"

"Two fights in one night? I don't think so. And you *know* this gives Sykes the excuse he needs to yank Gary off his parole."

"Whoa. Earth to Luce. *Two* fights?"

The light dawned. "Right—you weren't here yet, were you? Gary and Ken got into it earlier." Lucy paused. "Now that I think about it, it was the same kind of thing—a serious row that looked like something I might have to break up. But Ken split before it could go anywhere."

Kaz rubbed at an aching muscle in the back of her neck, the uneasiness she'd been feeling off and on returning full force. Ken was usually already home with Julie and the kids by the time she made port, so she didn't see him all that much. Particularly now that his son was so sick.

But he and Gary had always been tight, ever since they'd served together in Iraq. They had a lot of shared history—both from the war and from being out on the water together. Their friendship had had its share of rough patches, but their disagreements had always been short-lived. Gary had always stuck by Ken, no matter what. In fact, both she and Lucy suspected that it had been Gary's loyalty to Ken that had landed him in jail six months back. Which made the fight Lucy was talking about incomprehensible. Kaz sighed. Just like the rest of Gary's behavior lately.

Lucy was waiting for an explanation, and Kaz dearly wished she had one. "Gary's been having nightmares—at least, I think he has," she admitted. "I can hear him pacing in the living room at night."

"Nightmares about what? The war?"

Kaz shook her head. "I don't know. He's hard to read under the best of circumstances. But still, bar-fighting has never been his style."

"Yeah, well, could've fooled me." Lucy's expression was grim. "And Sykes was here earlier—he saw what went down with Ken."

That wasn't good news. If Sykes thought Gary was a danger to the community, he wouldn't hesitate to throw him back in a cell.

Kaz mentally reviewed what Gary had said to Chuck and Steve at the bar. Or not said, to be more accurate. She gnawed on her lip. "Look, you know those guys'll argue about just about anything..." Her voice trailed away as she took in Lucy's stubborn expression. "Okay, okay. If it'll make you happy, I'll go hunt Gary up and ask him some extremely pointed questions."

Lucy looked relieved, far more than Kaz would've thought was warranted. Which made her even twitchier. "Of course," she added, trying to inject a lighter note, "I'll have to take a rain check on the pool game."

"Yeah." Lucy sighed. "I should get back to the station anyway."

Kaz glanced around the room, schooling her expression so

that she didn't show the worry that was gnawing at her gut. None of the fishermen would make eye contact with her. And now that she thought about it, they'd been unusually silent out on the water earlier that afternoon. The typical radio chatter had been missing—along with the camaraderie. "Hmmm?" She realized Lucy had been talking to her.

"I *said*, you just don't want to get trounced again at eight-ball and owe me double or nothing on last night's bet."

"Like hell." Kaz kept her tone light as she found a few crumpled bills to drop onto the table for her beer.

Lucy snagged her wrist as she walked past, her expression uneasy. "Just watch your back, okay?"

Michael Chapman leaned back in his booth and watched the Jorgensen woman leave. Thick, waist-length, blond hair, a slim, athletic body, and soft, chocolate brown eyes. And attitude—tons of it.

He grimaced. He hadn't paid much attention to women the last couple of years—a sad fact his friends in the Boston Fire Department had pointed out repeatedly—but Kaz Jorgensen had caught his attention and held it. And after talking to her, he could sympathize with the reactions he'd seen on the faces of the other men when she'd arrived. A few had watched her with wistful expressions, a few with barely concealed irritation. But the rest had looked relieved, perhaps even exasperated— probably fishing buddies who'd been worried about her. He'd bet she drove them crazy on a good day, taking chances they privately labeled foolish. She'd certainly caused *him* a qualm or two when she'd waded into the middle of a brewing bar fight— one that looked as if it might get real ugly, real fast.

Most of the patrons were typical of any waterfront tavern— hard-working, decent people. He'd been looking for just that kind of place when he'd come through the door, and he hadn't been disappointed. He'd looked forward to relaxing, getting a handle on the locals.

The atmosphere in this place, though, was beyond tense. He'd already been sizing up a few hard-looking locals and monitoring the brewing fight when the blonde had jumped in. She was damn lucky, even if one of them *was* her brother—she easily could've gotten roughed up.

He grimaced, reaching down to rub Zeke's stomach. The dog moaned appreciatively in his sleep. Christ. He'd learned his lesson, hadn't he? He had no business wondering what secrets these people were hiding.

He'd moved out west to find some measure of peace in his life, not to take on someone else's troubles. All he had planned for the next few days was to move his belongings, which had finally shown up several days late, into the Victorian fixer-upper he'd purchased for Zeke and himself on the east side of town. To renew his acquaintance with a few carpentry tools.

Shoving aside his half-eaten burger, he pulled out his wallet, adding an extra five for tip. As he did, he glanced around the bar, noting the closed expressions. Felt the undercurrents. And, in spite of himself, was intrigued.

Those guys hadn't been fighting about anything as minor as Kaz Jorgensen had wanted him to believe. This town had secrets...too many secrets.

Chapter 2

Kaz arrived at the family's vintage 1900's bungalow above town to find the house dark, the driveway empty. After a moment's thought, she reversed onto the street and headed back in the direction she'd come. When Gary needed space, he sometimes slept on the *Anna Marie.*

She drove down steep hills, skirting the historic downtown district, then turned east on Marine Drive, passing shadowed, abandoned warehouses that were remnants of a more prosperous era. Even though the rain had let up, the clouds were moving low and fast, and she had to hold the wheel firmly against the gusting wind. Gary was nuts to be sleeping on board—even moored, the boat would be pitching hard.

But then lately, Gary *had* been acting nuts.

When Lucy had called sounding worried last month, Kaz had assumed she'd spend her annual two-week vacation the way she always did—hanging around the waterfront and working on the never-ending list of boat repairs. And while home, she might try to feel out what was bothering Gary. But immediately upon her arrival, she discovered a family business on the verge of bankruptcy, and a stranger inside the skin of her brother.

If anything since she'd been back, Gary had become even more reclusive, more prickly. Admittedly, since she'd had to spend so much of her time out on the *Kasmira B,* she hadn't had that many opportunities to sit him down for a real talk.

But he hadn't made himself available, either. She'd even begun to wonder if he was actually avoiding her.

Gary had a tendency to hole up like a wounded animal when he was hurting—he'd taken "time-outs", as he called them, more than once since he'd returned from Iraq. His recent behavior was out of character—he typically wouldn't avoid her, and he wouldn't pick fights in bars. He'd withdraw instead—heading for the hills where he could be by himself.

And she was certain the fight six months ago had been an aberration. But if Jim Sykes used the fights tonight to revoke Gary's parole, she *would* be concerned about his state of mind. He'd never be able to handle more jail time, not after what he'd been through in the war.

Spying his truck on the wharf of the East Mooring Basin, she heaved a sigh of relief and turned in, pulling in behind it. It was locked up tight, so she headed toward the docks. Using the palm of her hand, she slapped the chain-link gate that opened onto the docks, running into it when it refused to budge.

She took a step back, perplexed. Someone had chained it from the inside. What idiot would do *that*?

Then she heard an odd, percussive, whooshing sound, and the wheelhouse of the *Anna Marie* exploded into flames.

Lucy drove to the new police headquarters located on the east side of Astoria, having second, third, and even twentieth thoughts about having encouraged Kaz to come home. She'd hoped Kaz would be able to ferret out what was going on with Gary. Instead, the persistent prickling on the back of her neck was telling her she'd put Kaz in danger.

Astoria had changed—it wasn't the same town they'd all known from their time growing up here. In recent years, they'd experienced an influx of rich vacationers who had bought up many of the old Victorian homes, using them as weekend getaways. The newcomers brought with them too much

17

disposable income, as well as a thirst for parties where the flow of controlled substances went unchecked. In reaction, "We Ain't Quaint" bumper stickers had quietly shown up on many of the locals' trucks, and not-so-quiet clashes between the old and the new had become more commonplace.

From the looks of it, Gary had landed right in the thick of those culture wars. Lately, his behavior had given Lucy some really bad moments late at night. And though she'd be the first to admit he'd been giving her bad moments ever since high school, this was different. Whatever he'd gotten himself into, she now realized she didn't want him involving Kaz. Which was why she dearly wished she'd minded her own business and never placed that call.

Gary was a big boy, and he could take care of himself. In fact, it was about damn time he handled his problems on his own. He needed to be shaken out of the rut he'd been in ever since the war—needed to acknowledge that the aftereffects of being a POW *hadn't* made him unfit company, for the fishermen *or* for the right woman. Lucy snorted and pulled into the left-turn lane, hitting her blinker. Yeah, right. He'd admit to *that* the day pigs flew over the Columbia.

Lucy pulled into the brightly lit parking lot, suppressing a pang of homesickness for their old headquarters in the heart of Astoria's historic downtown district. Progress, she reminded herself, was good. Smiling hello to Joanne, she used her keycard to open the secure door to the squad room.

"Everything quiet?"

"Yep," Joanne replied, with no hesitation in the rapid clicking of her computer keys. A single mom with three young boys, Joanne was fond of telling anyone who'd listen that her job of police dispatcher was merely relief duty.

The door closed behind Lucy with a hollow click. The place was empty except for her partner, Ivar, who sat at his desk, studiously working his way through a stack of files. A mug steamed gently at his elbow, and soft classical music played on a boom box confiscated from the evidence room.

Lucy dropped into the desk chair facing his, sniffing at the pale green liquid. "I hope that vile-smelling crap is for poisoning some perp, or else I'll have to request a transfer to the state police."

"Green oolong tea," Ivar rumbled in his soft, deep voice without looking up. "Full of antioxidants. You should try some."

"Over my dead body."

He nodded while he calmly made a note in the margin of the page. "A real possibility, since you insist on eating red meat." Setting his pen down, he leaned back, lacing his hands behind his head and stretching his legs out so far that his feet crowded hers. He eyed her with his typical air of quiet aplomb.

Her partner was tall, thin, pensive, and when he bothered to speak at all, laconic. In the five years Lucy had been teamed up with him, she'd never once seen him lose his cool. Which actually made him the perfect foil for her, because she lost her cool as often as possible. In fact, she considered a well-honed rant a work of art.

"Chief would like to talk," he informed her now.

"Any idea what he wants?"

"Nope."

"Any chance I can delay this and go home for a good soak in the tub?"

Ivar shifted his gaze over her head in warning, and she glanced around to find Jim Sykes approaching her desk. He'd changed out of the tux he'd had on earlier for some kind of political fund-raiser. His "day" suit was baggy and rumpled, and he looked as if he'd been living in it for too long.

Sykes was an okay boss, mostly staying out of their way and letting them do their jobs but providing support when they needed it. She might not agree with how he'd handled Gary's prosecution, but to be fair, Gary had set himself up for a fall when he'd landed that punch. With Sykes standing no more than ten feet away that night, Gary might as well have handed him an engraved invitation to arrest him. The hotheaded idiot.

Sykes settled his large frame heavily against the edge of her desk. "I'm hearing rumors about the fishermen," he said without preamble. "That whole community is tense—they're hiding something."

Lucy sneaked a peek at Ivar, who wore a surprised frown. She'd heard hints of something big going down, but she hadn't heard about any connection to the fishermen. And she had yet to discover anything concrete. So far, the only people talking were a couple of small-time junkies who were trying to bargain their way into their next fix.

What surprised her was that the rumors had made it up to Sykes' level—few locals felt comfortable confiding in him.

"I'm making you the primary on the investigation," Sykes informed her. "See what you can dig up."

She hesitated, taken aback. She was the rooky detective on the force, so surely, this assignment should go to Clint Jackson or one of the other, more experienced detectives. Besides, this didn't feel like a solid investigation—at least, not yet. "I don't know if that's warranted, Chief. Why don't I do some unofficial poking around and—"

"What I'm hearing indicates otherwise," Sykes interrupted. "You may not want to believe that your friends might be involved in anything illegal, McGuire, but my sources say they are."

"They're decent folks, just trying to make a living," she said quietly.

"Yeah, and until the government makes good on its buyout promise, that living is damn poor. I need you to use your contacts within the community to find out what they're up to. We don't want this thing exploding in our faces."

She glanced at Ivar again, to see his reaction. He was still frowning. So maybe that was what this was all about—the fact that her contacts with the fishermen were better than Sykes'.

Before she could frame a suitable response, Joanne poked her head into the room.

"Chief—"

"Not now, Joanne," Sykes said over his shoulder, then stood. "Something's going down, I can feel it. Take Ivar with you, question the fishermen. Get results."

"*Chief!*"

"Dammit, Joanne! *What?*"

Michael Chapman was driving east on Irving Avenue, only a block from his new home, when the two-way radio crackled to life. He eased his foot off the accelerator and listened intently.

Swearing, he cranked the steering wheel hard, pulling a U-turn in the middle of the street and throwing Zeke across the back seat. He stomped on the gas, searching for a through street that would take him down to the waterfront.

For one stunned moment, Kaz simply stared at the roaring inferno. Then she threw herself at the gate, jerking it back and forth. *"Gary!"*

The flames leapt higher.

Backing up, she vaulted, hitting the top half of the gate with enough momentum to drag herself over, then ran down the ramp.

"Gary!" She glanced around for someone, anyone. The docks were deserted. *"Fire!"*

The entire deck of the trawler was burning now, flames roaring off the bow and around the winch, aft of the wheelhouse. She strained to catch a glimpse of her brother, but all she could see silhouetted against the orange glow were the boat's mast and boom. A gust of wind shifted the flames toward her, and she fell back from the searing heat, flinging an arm up to protect her eyes.

"Gary!" she tried again.

The wind switched again, propelling the flames toward their other trawler, the *Kasmira B.* Kaz took advantage, leaping onto the *Anna Marie's* deck. Flipping open the nearest seat cover, she reached for the fire extinguisher.

Gone.

The flames whipped toward her again, and she dove behind the wall of the wheelhouse.

She pulled herself into a crouch, coughing, then tried to look through the open door to see if the passage to the engine room and galley was clear. Twice she had to pull back.

The boat's aged timbers crackled. The wall beside her, when she touched it, singed her fingers. She pounded on it with her fist. *"Gary!"*

No answer.

Edging around the corner, she assessed the stairs. Flames were burning down one side of the risers, but they were still partially clear. Pulling the hood of her coat over her head, she dove into the darkness below.

Landing hard on the engine room floor, she rolled onto her stomach, the scrabbled on all fours away from the flames that were burning next to the equipment. Inside, the roar was muted, but the heat was stifling. The timbers overhead hissed in the relative silence. Varnish from the ceiling plopped onto her coat, and thick, black smoke hung in the air.

Sweat poured off her, and a strong metallic flavor coated the inside of her mouth, making her gag. Her face and hands were unbearably hot, and her skin felt as if it was melting. She couldn't see more than a few inches into the smoky gloom.

In desperate need of air, she took a cautious breath. The bitter, chemical odor of hot carpet assaulted her. She crawled through the galley door. More flames, though smaller, ran in a line across the floor and were hungrily eating at the galley wall. With one hand stretched out in front of her, she crawled toward the forecastle where the berths were. *"Gary!"*

The timbers overhead hissed and groaned in the silence.

Kaz stood hunched over, then felt blindly along the berths. She tripped over something, landing hard on her hands and knees, then got back up.

Dizzy.

She shook her head. She had to keep going.

There.

Her hand touched a boot, then clung to a jeans-clad leg. Sobbing, she shook him.

He didn't move.

Yanking hard on his jacket, she managed to roll him. He fell heavily onto the floor, wedged on his side against the storage locker. She couldn't budge him, and she seemed to be moving in slow motion.

No. Can't black out.

Gripping the heels of his boots, she threw her weight backward. He slid a few inches toward the stairs. She sank onto her knees beside him, head hanging, ears roaring.

Hands grabbed her from behind and yanked her to her feet. He floated out of the haze above her, an apparition in a black oxygen mask, black coat with yellow stripes, and boots. When he pulled off his facemask, she saw that it was the new guy.

...Chapman, that was his name.

"We've got to get out of here!" he yelled.

No.

She heard a roar and looked up. Blue flames streamed across the ceiling from the engine room, reaching for her. Chapman dropped beside her, dragging her down, and covered her face with his arms. "Hang tight, they'll hose it down." He brought his face close to hers, pushing his mask over her mouth, and she gulped the oxygen greedily. Water rained down, scalding her scalp. She heard someone whimper and realized that it must be her.

Water began to fill the cabin—she was lying in several inches of it. *Gary's facedown in this.* She shoved at Chapman, hard.

He grunted and shifted sideways, and then rolled her with him, pulling her out of the stream of the hose. She pointed toward Gary. "My brother," she managed, but her voice broke.

"...cave-in! Move it!" He pulled her to her feet and dragged her toward the stairs.

Kaz fought him, but he simply wrapped an arm around her middle and walked backwards, hauling her with him. She rammed her elbow into his solar plexus, and he slumped forward, his grip loosening.

Staggering toward the berths, she fell over Gary's body. She heard Chapman swear, but then he seemed to catch on. He ran a hand along both berths next to her, then knelt and hauled Gary up over his shoulder. Above him, the ceiling sagged with a splintering *crack.*

Taking hold of her arm, he threw her toward the stairs. "Dammit, *move.*"

He propelled her up the stairs and through the door as burning timbers fell behind them, showering them in roiling sparks.

He didn't let go of her until they were off the boat and several yards away. She dropped to her knees on the dock, coughing and retching. Firemen raced past them, dragging hoses.

Chapman laid her brother down several feet away, ripped off one of his gloves, and felt for a pulse. Then pulled back an eyelid.

She crawled toward Gary. *No, no, no.*

Behind her, the rest of the deck collapsed. Sparks flew on the night wind, and from the adjacent dock, the sea lions barked excitedly.

Before she could reach Gary, Chapman pushed up his mask and threw out an arm to block her. She shoved it aside.

He turned then and gripped her shoulders, hard. His face was grim. "I'm sorry. He didn't make it."

She sobbed, pushing at him with both hands. "I have to go to him—" She froze, staring over his shoulder.

The man lying on the dock wasn't her brother. It was Ken Lundquist, their crewman.

Chapter 3

Kaz sat on the back steps of an aid car, breathing oxygen from a mask attached to a portable tank. Her throat was raw, her skin hot and prickly. Flashing lights from emergency vehicles illuminated the wharf and marina in rhythmic sweeps, hurting her eyes. Occasional gusts of wind caused the boats' rigging to clank like gunshots, adding a syncopated unreality.

To keep the growing crowd at bay, Chapman had roped off the wharf with yellow crime scene tape strung between sawhorses and the wooden railings. Fire hoses twined around each other as they snaked down the steel grate ramp leading to the *Anna Marie*.

Kaz used a trembling hand to wipe her eyes and felt grit smear across her cheek. In spite of the heat from the fire, she couldn't stop shivering.

In the three generations her family had been on the water, they'd never lost a crewman, never had a fire on one of their boats. The importance of fire safety had been drilled into her at an early age—she and Gary never took chances. *Never.*

Perhaps electrical wiring had deteriorated—somehow sparking near the fuel. The *Anna Marie* was rigged for drag fishing and frequently out of port, so she hadn't been on the trawler lately to assess its state of repair. Still, it would have been suicidal for Gary to let something as critical as bad wiring go unnoticed—a fire at sea was every waterman's worst nightmare.

Kaz frowned as a new thought occurred to her. Ken *never* spent time on the trawler when it was in port. He usually had a beer or two at the Redemption and then went home early to Julie and the kids, particularly now with Bobby so sick from the chemo treatments. So why had he been on board at this time of night?

She needed to talk to Gary, to see what he knew. Setting aside the oxygen mask, she stood and scanned the crowd, hoping to catch a glimpse of him. Nothing. Surely he knew about the fire by now. Why wasn't he here? Increasingly uneasy, she begged a cell phone off the EMT.

No answer at home. She left a message on his cell phone, then disconnected.

Hugging herself, she turned back to the fire scene just in time to watch the *Anna Marie's* spool of fishnet and winch disappear in an explosion of flames.

After ordering the nozzle man to redirect his hose to the bow of the trawler, Michael turned and studied the Jorgensen woman. Her naturally pale complexion was washed of all color, and she looked unsteady on her feet. He wasn't surprised, given what she'd just been through.

Civilians always thought they could handle a fire, but they couldn't, dammit. In any blaze, there were enough toxic chemicals to take out even the strongest person. His jaw clenched. He doubted he'd ever forget the breathless panic he'd felt when he'd seen her dive into those flames.

He didn't like what he was seeing with this fire. It was burning way too hot. That would've screamed 'suspicious' to him, even if he hadn't hauled a body out of the hold. According to one of the firefighters, Kaz and her brother co-owned the boat. And the brother was on parole for assault—the near-brawl Michael had witnessed in the tavern evidently hadn't been out of character. He'd also seen Gary Jorgensen going at it with the guy who was now lying on the dock, dead. And his sister was the first person on the scene of a suspicious fire.

He frowned as he noted a look of renewed determination on her face that spelled trouble. When she started walking toward the dock, he stepped into her path, placing a hand on her arm. "Sorry, but you can't go any closer."

She gave him a brief, impatient glance, her expression distracted. "She's taking on too much water. You'll sink her."

Touching her was like touching a door with a raging inferno behind it. Disconcerted, he stepped back, removing his hand. "I'm keeping an eye on the water level," he assured her, only to have her shake her head.

"I need to talk to the firemen myself."

"Can't let you do that." He started to pull out a pencil and a small pad he kept with him for taking down notes. "Why don't we go over what happened here tonight."

Her expression was perplexed. "That's ridiculous—I have the right to protect my boat."

"She's a crime scene, for now. No one goes near her except authorized personnel."

"Excuse me?"

"That fire was deliberately set." Her face blanched of all remaining color, and he shot an arm around her slender waist. "Whoa. Maybe you'd better sit—"

"That can't be," she whispered, staring in the direction of the docks.

He studied her closely. Most people weren't that good at acting, but he'd seen all kinds. "I'm afraid it's a very real possibility."

After taking several deep breaths, she seemed to pull herself together, stepping away from him. Recognizing the pride and fierce self-control behind the move, he let her go.

"When will you know for sure?" she asked, her voice sounding more composed.

"After I go over the areas that burned, find the source of ignition."

She raised a slender hand to push her hair away from her face. When he saw the red, watery blisters that had formed along the outside edge of her palm, he reacted without thinking. His hand shot out, clasping hers, and he gently turned it so that he could examine the burn. "You need to have this taken care of," he said, his voice more gruff than he would've liked.

She glanced down and shrugged. "It doesn't hurt."

"It will once the adrenaline wears off." He forced himself to let go of her and pointed at the aid car. "Have the EMT put a dressing on it. And keep taking oxygen—smoke inhalation is nothing to mess with."

He waited for her to head in that direction, but instead, she turned her back on him and watched the fire, her shoulders hunched, her arms folded.

He shook his head. Stubborn, and a control freak to boot. He needed to get some distance—she was a suspect. At the very least, she could be her brother's accomplice.

It was one hell of a coincidence that she'd been first on the scene—he couldn't ignore that. And the bottom line was that he had an investigation to run.

Down at the dock, Lucy knelt beside the corpse, taking pictures while Ivar made notes and drew sketches. Jim Sykes stood a few feet away, observing. Her eyes burned, more from the effort to hold back the tears than from the smoke in the air. Ken had been a good man.

They didn't get many murders in Astoria—this was only her second since she'd been on the force. The first one had happened last year, when some tourist had beaten his wife unconscious inside their motor home, then gotten liquored up and set the whole mess on fire, himself included. That scene

29

had been gruesome, but this was far worse.

As she moved back to let Greg Ewald, the medical examiner, do his job, Lucy sneaked a glance at in the direction of the wharf. Kaz looked like she was hanging in there, but it was hard to tell from this distance.

"This makes it pretty hard to ignore those rumors I've heard," Sykes said, breaking into her thoughts.

"Sir?"

"About the fishing community," he explained impatiently.

Lucy held her tongue. She wasn't ready to point any fingers or jump to any conclusions, not yet. The chief, however, had been on a warpath ever since he'd arrived. Crimes like murder and arson didn't happen in his town. From all appearances, he was taking this very personally.

Ewald straightened, having completed the in situ examination. He said something quietly into his tape recorder and then pulled off his surgical gloves, motioning for the EMTs to bag the body. "Going to be tough to get an exact time of death," he told her. "The fire retarded the rate of temperature loss in the corpse. I took a kidney temp, but—" He shrugged.

"Any preliminary determination on the cause of death?" Lucy asked, earning herself a glare. Ewald hated giving prelims. But dammit, she needed *something* to work with.

"Most likely blunt force trauma to the back of the head." Ewald's tone was truculent. "He's got grass stains and mud on his shoes and jeans—you catch that?"

"Yeah. The grass stains could've happened at any time, but it also might mean that the body was moved."

"They look fresh to me."

"Let's not get too exotic with the theories," Sykes interrupted. "Jorgensen probably followed Ken here after their argument in the Redemption and killed him. It's his boat, and he's our most likely suspect. Procedure says we need to concentrate on finding out whether he did it."

Light rain fell steadily now, and the fire was almost out. Kaz was shivering so hard that she knew she'd have sore muscles by morning.

Chapman stood down on the dock, silhouetted against the orange glow of the dying fire. The flames reflected off his face shield, looking for one crazy moment like the comforting flames in a fireplace, seen through a window. Then he flipped his shield to speak into a portable radio, and the image dissolved.

The fireboat, the *Harry Steinbach*, which had been hosing down the other boats, turned a fog stream from its deck guns onto the *Anna Marie*. Chapman stopped a patrolman carrying a camera and pointed at the crowd. Then he headed back toward her, talking into the radio unit. "...don't hit inside the wheelhouse. I don't want the evidence washed away if we can avoid it." His deep voice had a calm, soothing quality to it.

But Kaz couldn't count on Michael Chapman to be either soothing or helpful. He thought the fire had been set on purpose. And she'd be willing to bet, based on the way he was keeping an eye on her, that he thought she might be involved.

Of course, the idea was patently absurd—Lucy could vouch for her, or for any of the fishermen, for that matter. But Chapman was a newcomer—he didn't know them. What was it she'd told Lucy earlier in the tavern? That they were lucky to have him? Those words might be coming back to haunt her.

She'd been dead-on in her earlier assessment of him, though—the man all but radiated a force field of authority. The volunteer firefighters, most of whom barely even knew him, were jumping to carry out his orders. She knew those guys—they weren't prone to take orders from anybody, much less a newcomer. Then again, he *did* seem to know what he was doing—the men had worked quickly and efficiently to put out the fire and protect the other boats.

31

She let out a sigh. The fact was, she should be grateful that Michael Chapman had arrived on scene so quickly. If he hadn't, she could be lying down on the dock next to Ken. Tonight made the second time in her life that she'd narrowly escaped death. And this time, she couldn't claim any of the credit for her survival—she owed her life to Chapman's quick thinking.

Which made her beholden to him, and she didn't like that one bit. She was inexplicably drawn to him, and that scared her, because he wouldn't be on her side in all of this.

He was slowly scanning the crowd of onlookers and jumble of fire, police, and aid vehicles, those knowledgeable eyes of his cataloguing and filing away everything he saw. What was he looking for? Or whom?

She followed his lead, working her way through the crowd, then froze. Chuck was standing off to the left, his calm gaze trained on her. He cocked his head slightly, sending her a quick, silent message she couldn't decipher, then stepped back, immediately swallowed by the surging crowd. She strained for another glimpse of him, but she saw nothing. If Chuck was around, then so was Gary. He had to know she was there, and yet he wasn't coming forward. Before she could sort through the significance of that, Chapman walked over to her.

"Is that your truck over there?" he asked.

She looked in the direction he was pointing. "It's my brother's. He frequently leaves it parked here." She was careful not to glance at the place where Chuck had been standing.

"So your brother was here tonight."

She hesitated, then shook her head. "I don't know where he is."

Chapman's pale gaze lingered on her for another moment, his expression giving away nothing. Then he turned and motioned to Clint Jackson, the cop who was keeping the crowd back. "One of you guys will want to impound that truck."

"Hey!"

At her reaction, he replied over his shoulder, "Standard procedure. Your brother is a possible person of interest."

"You're kidding—you think *Gary* would set this fire?" She waved her arm toward the docks. "The *Anna Marie* was built by my grandfather, named after our mother. Gary is a third-generation waterman."

"Anyone is capable of murder under the right circumstances. Setting a fire to cover it up is the easy part."

"Murder." She pressed a hand to her roiling stomach. "You think Ken was killed."

"Yes."

"And you believe Gary killed him," she repeated dully.

He turned to her, his expression all business. "Your brother was seen arguing with the deceased earlier this evening in the tavern."

Kaz shook her head. "You've got it all wrong."

"I'm told your brother has a record for assault."

"If you knew the circumstances—"

"And in an arson investigation," he continued as if she hadn't spoken, "it's standard to check out the owners of the property."

"Look." She strove for calm. "I'm sure you're used to things working differently in the city. But around here we take into account what we know about someone before we go around accusing him of something he isn't even remotely capable of!"

Chapman raised an eyebrow. "Your brother seemed plenty capable of violence in the tavern."

God. He had it all worked out. Except he was wrong, he had to be. "What makes you so sure the fire was deliberately set?"

"I smelled gasoline when I first came on board. That, and the pattern of the fire—"

"We don't keep gasoline on board the *Anna Marie*—she runs on diesel. It's crazy to keep gasoline on board any boat."

33

He opened his mouth to speak, then sighed instead. "You don't have to educate me about the potential hazards on a boat, Ms. Jorgensen. And the fact that someone used gasoline to start the fire when there was none on board makes it look even more deliberate."

He was right. She stared at the now smoldering trawler. My God. Someone *had* planned this.

"You were the first person on the scene, correct? You saw no one else, no one perhaps running away from the *Anna Marie*?"

"No. The marina is usually deserted this time of night."

"So why were *you* here?"

She hesitated. She needed to be very, very careful with regard to how much she revealed. At least for now, until she could find Gary, talk to him, and straighten out this mess. With the odds stacked so heavily against him, she couldn't take the chance that she'd provide information that could worsen his situation. "I wanted to talk to Gary," she said finally.

"Why did you think he'd be here?"

"I didn't find him at home, and Gary sometimes sleeps aboard the *Anna Marie*. But before I could get to the boat, the fire exploded."

He glanced up from the notes he was taking. "Did the explosion knock you down, or was it more of a whooshing sound?"

"The latter," she said after thinking about it. "I realized that Gary might be on board, so I yelled for help and then ran to the boat."

"You called the fire in?"

"No. I didn't have my cell phone with me, and I didn't want to take the time to go back to the car to get it."

"*Someone* called it in. Who, if no one else was here?"

"I don't know," she replied coolly. "Perhaps someone who has a view of the mooring basin."

He studied her, his expression turning speculative. "When I got here, the gate was chained shut, and I had to use bolt cutters. The other gates along the wharf aren't locked. Did you do that?"

"Of course not!" Then she remembered. "Someone had chained it from the inside. I didn't have time to deal with it....I climbed over."

"So you thought your brother was down below."

Chapman was relentless, and he wasn't going to give up or go away until she gave him the answers he wanted. "Yes. The wheelhouse door was open, and when we're in port, we keep it locked. We have expensive equipment on board—radios, a depth finder, radar—"

"Who has keys?" Chapman interrupted.

"Just Gary. And me, of course."

"All right, what happened next?"

She repressed a sigh and told him about trying to use the fire extinguisher, about finding it gone. "We never move it, except twice a year to check that it still works."

"Probably tossed overboard." He made a note. "I'll have a diver check."

She pulled her coat tight around her, feeling the cold all the way to her bones. It had begun to rain harder, adding to her discomfort, and the wind was picking up again, chopping the rain into drenching sheets.

Wrapping her arms tighter around her waist, she inhaled the acrid odor of the smoke that clung to her clothes and hair. A new thought occurred to her. It had to be common knowledge that Ken was rarely on the boat when it was in port. So had Gary been the real target and Ken just an innocent bystander? Whirling, she started walking toward her SUV.

"Wait up," Chapman said, catching her arm. His hand was startlingly warm, his grip firm. "We're not done here. And you'll need to go to the hospital for tests."

"I'm feeling fine," she protested.

Gripping her shoulder, he urged her toward the ambulances. "I'll have one of my men take you."

She dug in her heels, staring pointedly down at his hand. "You most certainly will not."

A look of exasperation flashed across his face, but he dropped his hand. "You really should go to the hospital, Ms. Jorgensen. You could collapse any time in the next couple of days from whatever you breathed when you were down in the hold."

"I have other priorities that don't include spending the night at the hospital being subjected to a lot of unnecessary tests."

"And I'll need your clothes," he added, ignoring her explanation.

She gaped at him. *"What?"*

"You were first on the scene, remember? And you *are* part-owner in the family fishing business, are you not?"

"If you're suggesting—"

"—that I'll need to test your clothes for accelerant. Standard procedure."

She really was beginning to hate that phrase. She started to retort, but broke off as Lucy, Ivar, and Jim Sykes walked up the ramp. Ivar came over to stand beside her. He didn't say a word—just used one of his big hands to rub gently between her shoulder blades.

Lucy walked up on Kaz's other side and slipped her arms around her, hugging her. "Are you okay?" she asked, sounding a bit tenuous herself.

"Yeah, mostly." Kaz tried to smile and failed, then nodded to Jim Sykes, who was shaking hands with Chapman.

"So," Sykes said, turning to Kaz. "One of your boats out of commission, your crewman dead, and your brother possibly the prime suspect."

Chapman frowned slightly at Sykes, which struck Kaz as odd since he seemed to be thinking along the same lines. "You know Gary wouldn't do this, Jim," she replied as calmly as she could manage.

"Are you planning to issue a BOLO on him?" Chapman asked Sykes.

Kaz looked from one to the other, not comprehending.

"We need to talk to Gary," Ivar explained to her in his soft rumble. "Find out what he knows."

"Possibly armed and dangerous," Sykes confirmed.

"Hey," she snapped. "No way—"

Lucy spoke up. "Chief, I don't think—"

Sykes held up a hand. "Jorgensen has violated his parole, and he should be approached with extreme caution. It's in this community's best interests, as well as his, to bring him in off the street as soon as possible."

"That's *way* out of line," Kaz retorted.

Ivar gripped her shoulder gently. "With respect, sir—"

"You've known Gary all your life, Jim," Kaz protested. "And you know damn well he'd never hurt Ken."

"Yeah, but I also know that his military training alone, with or without a firearm, makes him a deadly force." Sykes' tone hardened. "Your brother has been a walking time bomb ever since the war, Kaz. You need to stay out of this, and let us handle it."

"Why should I?" she shot back. "What I'm hearing so far doesn't give me any confidence that you'll look for the person who really did this."

"Kaz," Lucy said quietly. "Trust us to do our job. We just need to talk to Gary."

Kaz shut up. She had to find Gary before anyone else did. If they tried to arrest him, she couldn't predict what he would do. And there had to be another explanation for all this—Gary simply wasn't capable of arson or murder.

Chapman had been standing back, observing all of them, his expression intent. For some reason, he didn't look any happier than she was.

His next comment, however, showed that he hadn't softened his stance. "So, Ms. Jorgensen. Your clothes. You can either go to the hospital with an official escort or give them to me here." His lips quirked. "Your choice."

Chapter 4

At dawn the next morning, Michael stood with Zeke on the north jetty of the mooring basin, waiting for the state lab technicians to finish their work on the *Anna Marie*. Pale sunlight pierced charcoal clouds, illuminating the rippled spines of sand bars on the Columbia. Gulls screeched as they fought over the morning's catch, and on the docks, sea lions barked, their frenzied discussions broken only occasionally by the watery chug of a diesel motor as another fishing trawler headed out for the day.

Michael warmed his hands on his coffee cup while he gazed across the vast stretch of the water. Although he'd been in town less than a week, each new day brought moments of beauty so stunning they took his breath away. The river's surface was misleadingly tranquil—here and there, a small eddy the only indication of the turbulence that lay hidden beneath. Softly framed by forested, evergreen hills, illuminated by the choreography of sunlight and clouds, the river fooled most visitors. Only those who lived in its shadow understood that such daily theatrics came at a heavy price.

Initially, Astoria had evoked memories of summers on the Maryland shore. Driving into town that first day, he'd noticed what everyone else saw at first glance—the steep hillsides with weathered clapboard houses clinging to them, the mooring basins with their neat lines of docked fishing trawlers, the sharp smells of the waterfront. Those long ago summers had been a happier time in his life, a time when he'd felt a bone-deep satisfaction from helping his cousins bring in the day's catch.

But after less than a week of talking to Astorians, his impression of the town had quickly changed. On the Maryland shore, danger came from the storms that blew in from sea. One at least had warning. Here, danger was hidden in the submerged, shifting sandbars, and in the treacherous current of an unforgiving river that could reduce your boat to toothpicks in a heartbeat. Michael had come away from his summers out on the Atlantic Ocean with a healthy respect for the open water. But the Columbia...these waters made him uneasy.

He took a sip of coffee, its steam partially obscuring his view of a crab boat moving downriver. A slight breeze off the docks carried the scent of wet, charred wood from the *Anna Marie* in their direction. Zeke looked up at him, his expression eager as he whined softly.

"Yeah, I know, boy," he murmured. "You can smell it all the way up here, can't you?"

After an exhausting night of battling high winds and rain, Michael had gone home to shower and change clothes only an hour ago. Thanks to a small pump donated by the nearby boat works, the *Anna Marie* was now sitting much higher in the water, no longer in danger of sinking. And although the weather was calm, more storms were on the way. Which meant he had to hustle, because he wanted every damn bit of evidence off that boat.

Zeke whined again, and Michael drank the last of his coffee, grimacing at its bitter taste even while he was relieved to have the distraction. He'd had better coffee in Boston, for Christ's sake. This was the Pacific Northwest, renowned for its damn coffee. So why was it he couldn't find a decent cup in this town?

The techs from the state crime lab were packing up and preparing to leave. He looked down at Zeke. "Okay, boy. You ready to rock and roll?"

Zeke barked and jumped in a circle around him, nipping at the hem of his sweater.

Michael pulled a pad of paper out of his pocket. "So here's the deal, pal," he said as they walked across the wharf and down the ramp to the dock. "You've got to be careful not to fall through the deck in a couple of places. We need to check out the wheelhouse, and getting there's going to be a little dicey."

"Mawroooo, rooo," the dog responded in his unique combination of moaning and dog talk. His expression was baleful.

"I'm not insulting you—it's just that you're not always so nimble of paw, you know?" The sea lions that had been lazing on the dock slipped into the water, and Michael had to grab Zeke's collar to keep him from going in after them. "Not a good idea, big guy. They'll have you for breakfast. Didn't you see the warning signs up on the wharf?"

He nodded good morning to the lead technician. "You guys do a thorough sweep of the wheelhouse and the flying bridge?"

"Yeah." The kid yawned. "We might've found a hair off the guy; if we're lucky, it will have the follicle attached. With all the soot, there's no way to tell the color until we get it back to the lab. Of course, it could belong to the owners. Or is one of the owners the torch?"

"Always a possibility."

The tech grunted. "Figures. We also dusted the lock for fingerprints, like you asked. Nada. But there's a hunk of melted metal that could be what's left of the ignition source."

"Good. I'll have more for you once I dig out the forecastle and galley. What's your timeline on the hair?"

"We should have a preliminary opinion on the match to the vic by later this afternoon. DNA, you know the routine—like

41

sometime in the next century, unless you've got clout." He grinned at Chapman. "Since you're new in town, I figure I've got plenty of time."

Michael tossed the dregs of his coffee into the water and crumpled the paper cup in his fist. "Put a priority on it. I want this guy yesterday."

The kid held up both hands. "Hey, man, I was just kidding."

"And if you've got any DNA saliva collection kits, I need them."

Mumbling something about no sense of humor, the tech fished around inside his voluminous carryall and produced the tubes. "You know to keep these refrigerated, right? And I'll need chain of evidence forms. I don't want to be sitting in court six months from now explaining who had access to the evidence and could've contaminated it."

Michael slipped them into the inside pocket of his jacket. "I'll handle any problems that come up in that area."

"It's your funeral, man."

He waited until the crime van had backed off the wharf, and then held back the tarp at the edge of the deck. "Here you go, Zeke. Jump!"

The dog looked at the decking, then at the dark, brackish water visible between the edge of the dock and the trawler's burned-through railing. He sat down on the dock, looked up at Michael, and yawned.

"Christ, dog. Down-shifting has turned you into a wimp."

"Rooooo, raaoow."

Michael picked him up and transferred him to the boat, earning an enthusiastic licking for his efforts. Familiar with the routine, Zeke sat and waited patiently for his next command.

Once Michael had completed a scaled drawing of the fire scene, he pulled on surgical gloves. He and Zeke picked their way around the gaping hole of charred timbers over the hold and forward to the wheelhouse. Inside, the equipment was badly melted, the wheel charred black and partially disintegrated, the room scorched. Where the fire had burned hottest, the paint on the ceiling was blistered. But the walls were still intact, which meant that the fire had burned here only briefly before spreading quickly to other sections of the boat.

Even after being up all night, which impaired his sense of smell, Michael still had no doubt as to what odor he was picking up. "Okay, pal, are you getting what I'm getting?" He gave Zeke the command to go to work.

The shepherd criss-crossed the room, sniffing eagerly, then focused on a spot at the base of the wheel. He lifted one paw in a positive signal. Michael knelt beside him, studying the floor. Pulling out a pair of tweezers, he picked up a bit of cloth and held it to his nose. Gasoline. Placing the cloth inside a small, clean paint can, he tapped the lid shut, then continued his perusal. A short distance away, as the technician had indicated, lay a melted clump of metal, the remains of a piece of wire, and another smaller, scorched lump—possibly some kind of cheap timer. Michael pulled a large Baggie out of his jacket and carefully put the whole mess inside. Then he sat back on his heels and surveyed the area.

He'd lay odds he was looking at what was left of a small space heater, its electrical chord, and a simple timer. The guy had probably stuffed the heater with gasoline-soaked rags. When the timer had turned the heater on, firing up the electrical elements...kaboom.

"Our torch seems to have known what he was doing, huh Zeke?" Michael murmured. "Now isn't *that* a bad sign."

Marking the location of the ignition source on his diagram, he stood up, his eyes tracking the burn flow pattern down the stairs to the engine room and out the door to the foredeck. He stared at the decking, the hairs on his neck rising. He'd seen flow patterns hundreds of times, but this one....The pencil he was holding snapped in two, and he swore at himself. *Don't go there*. So some burn patterns had become, for him, emotional triggers, like Rorschach inkblots. He'd cope, dammit.

He rubbed the back of his neck with a shaky hand and made himself run through possible scenarios. Maybe a fight had erupted and gotten out of hand. The arsonist had hit the victim too hard, accidentally killing him. That fit Jorgensen's MO— he'd thrown a punch six months ago that had broken a guy's jaw.

Michael frowned and glanced around. Most people use whatever is handy to start the fire, maybe old rags and gasoline. Not a space heater. Had the Jorgensens actually kept a space heater on board? He supposed it was possible—it had to get damned uncomfortable out on the water during the winter. But in his experience, most crab boats had an oil heater down below for the crew. You simply didn't waste precious battery power on a current-hogging space heater.

As for the gasoline, Kaz Jorgensen had told him the night before that she and her brother didn't keep any on board. Which made starting the fire not so easy. To use diesel, Gary would've had to siphon the tanks. And according to Kaz, they typically brought the boats in on empty, which meant siphoning would've been a bitch and a half. Besides, he and Zeke had identified gas, not diesel.

Michael straightened and studied the layout of the mooring basin. The problem was, it would have been a hell of a lot easier to get rid of the body by dumping it in the river from the jetty. There was a nice, swift current, and last night, there'd even been a convenient storm as cover-up. Even if the body hadn't been washed out to sea, it probably would've gotten snagged under a dock somewhere downstream, which meant that it would've been days before it was discovered. Or it would've come ashore, possibly as far downriver as Warrenton. Either way, dumping it in the water was less risky than leaving it on board the *Anna Marie*.

And why, if Jorgensen was the torch, had the guy been willing to burn his own boat? Had he needed the money? Or was he just tired of struggling to keep the family business alive, had decided to cash out, and Lundquist had been in the way? Michael made a note to check into the Jorgensens' finances.

It was fully light now, and he noticed that more fishermen were arriving. The crabbers would want to use the window between storms to lift and rebait their pots. Someone—he couldn't remember who at the moment—had said that the fishermen crossed the bar just before the tide turned, on the slack tide. That way if they got into trouble, at least the tide would carry them out to sea before their boat was reduced to a pile of debris on the rocks or run aground on the sandbars. Michael grimaced. Hell of a way to make a living.

Several fishermen cast curious glances his way, but no one approached him. Those guys knew what was going on, he'd bet on it. He'd have to interview them later, but he had no illusions as to their willingness to cooperate. He shrugged, returning to the task at hand.

"Okay, Zeke, what about streamers?" He pointed to a burn mark that flowed away from the wheelhouse door and around to the deck. "If I'd been in this guy's place, I would've poured gasoline from here to the deck, where I dumped a shitload of it, then I'd continue around the corner and down the stairs into the engine room. What d'you think? Have I got it right?"

"Mawroooo."

"If I'd known you had conversations with that dog of yours, I might not have hired the two of you."

Michael glanced over his shoulder. Wallace Forbes, Astoria's mayor and his new boss, was standing on the dock. "Don't try to come on board, sir."

"Wouldn't even think of it. Just stopped by to see how things were coming along."

45

Forbes was typical of politicians everywhere, dressed casually to put his constituents at ease, persistently cheerful, and always careful about what he gave away in a conversation. He wasn't a bad sort, necessarily, just the product of the electoral environment. Michael had never had much use for politicians, but he'd learned to live with them.

"Zeke is helping me confirm that this fire was deliberately set," he said by way of explanation.

"From what I hear about that nose of yours, you already knew that," Forbes observed.

"Never hurts to have a second opinion."

"Now *those* are words to live by." Forbes pulled a cigarette out of a monogrammed silver case, tapped it a few times, and lit it. "So tell me you also know *who* set it."

Michael hesitated. "Fires have a way of burning up a lot of the evidence, and the weather last night was particularly foul. But with any luck, I'll find something useful."

The mayor nodded and looked out across the docks. He waved to the crew of a departing trawler. "Is there any possibility that it wasn't Jorgensen?"

"He had motive, as well as opportunity," Michael said, uneasy with giving the wrong impression. "But there are a few unanswered questions."

Forbes' gaze turned shrewd. "Like what?"

"I'd rather not say until I complete a thorough investigation."

The mayor watched him for a long moment through eyes half-shut against cigarette smoke, then let loose a chuckle. "Word has it you used to drive your superiors nuts."

Michael didn't respond. Forbes hadn't stopped by on a casual morning stroll along the waterfront, not at the crack of dawn. And he wasn't there to give Michael grief about his reputation as a maverick, which he had to have known about well before he'd made the decision to hire.

46

Michael's buddies in the Boston Fire Department had told him Forbes had checked him out. Thoroughly. He hadn't just conducted a routine, cursory check—he'd made it a point to talk to anyone who would volunteer information about Michael. And while Michael resented it, he respected the Mayor's thoroughness.

Forbes sighed. "You know, I've known the Jorgensens for most of my life. Knew their parents, too. Anna and Tim died in a freak storm—let's see—that would be fifteen years ago now. The twins would've been eighteen at the time. It was hard on them, real hard. Gary enlisted, ended up a Ranger in the Army—in one of those elite units that does things the rest of us would rather not know about." Forbes shook his head. "Now Kaz, though, she went south and got herself one fine college education. Made a go of that consulting business of hers. People round here don't let on, but they're awfully proud of both of them."

He paused while he flicked some cigarette ash into the water. "Kaz was with her parents that night, you know. She barely made it to Sand Island, a nasty pile of shifting sediment just this side of the bar. She couldn't save her parents, and that's eaten at her. She hasn't been back, other than for her annual visits, in years. That is, not until about three weeks ago, when she showed up and started working the crab pots."

Michael remained silent, wondering where all of this was leading. The mayor might think that Gary'd had a couple of bad breaks, but that didn't mean the guy hadn't finally snapped. And the fact that Kaz had come back to town for an extended stay right before the fire occurred wasn't exactly a point in her favor.

Forbes was smiling fondly, his expression distant. "She's a pistol, though, isn't she?"

"Yes, sir," Michael's reply was a little too heartfelt.

"The irony is, folks around here thought Kaz was the most

47

gifted female skipper to ever work the North Coast. She has this eerie sixth sense about the river bar. The fishermen used to just follow her across, knowing that if they did what she did, they'd make it home to their wives." Forbes watched the boats pulling away from the docks for a long moment, then sighed. "Fishermen are a superstitious lot—after being gone for so long, she'll have to prove herself all over again."

He turned his shrewd gaze on Michael. "Heard you went in after her last night before you had backup in place."

Small towns. Michael wondered who had talked. He flipped his notebook shut and slipped it into his pocket. "I assessed the situation, made the decision to go in."

"I'd hate to think that business in Boston is still affecting your judgment."

Michael's voice turned cool. "You knew my reputation. It's a little late to be having second thoughts."

"True enough." Forbes reached over to pat Zeke's head. The dog endured it with one slightly curled lip. "You know, people move out here for a number of reasons. Some of them just can't handle being in the city any more—the peace and quiet is easier on their nerves. Some simply don't fit in anywhere else, and the folks out here are more forgiving of that than your average urban dweller." He paused. "I'm willing to bet you came out here for similar reasons."

Michael stared back, his expression impassive. "Was there anything else you wanted, sir?"

Forbes chuckled. "I also heard you are a real hardass." When Michael didn't reply, he shrugged, then continued, "There've been a few run-ins between Gary and Jim Sykes in the past. Jim didn't grow up with the same advantages as the Jorgensens. His home life—excuse my French—sucked. Drunk mother, abusive father. More often than not, the only good meal Jim got was at school. But he's worked hard, risen above all that." Forbes paused to draw on his cigarette. "A couple years' back, Jim broke up a burglary ring here on the North Coast that'd been driving us all nuts. Men were afraid to go to work and leave their wives, for fear the women would come home from the grocery store and walk in on a robbery in progress. Jim changed all that, and folks around here are grateful.

"I guess what I'm trying to say, Michael, is that if you do right by us on this case, the townsfolk aren't going to forget it. They'll be on your side from here on out. We stick by our own, no matter what."

"Yes, sir." Forbes was letting him know they'd overlook his checkered past, he realized, his mouth twisting. Just like they had with Sykes.

"Well." Forbes brushed his hand across the edge of the *Anna Marie's* scorched railing, then rubbed the soot between his fingers. "I'm sure you're busy, so I'll be on my way."

"Thanks for dropping by, sir."

"Somehow, I doubt you were all that happy to see me, son," Forbes observed, his tone wry. He turned to go, then stopped and looked back. "Michael."

"Yes, sir."

"I don't think I have to tell you how much I appreciate having your expertise on this. I know you'll do everything you can to solve the crime fairly and impartially, and to bring the right person to justice."

Michael nodded. He hadn't missed the tension among the cops last night, with two of them flanking Kaz and sending a not-so-subtle message to the police chief that they wouldn't tolerate any subjectivity on his part. And Michael had also been neatly warned—no outsider would be allowed to run roughshod over one of their own.

But unless he was mistaken about the intent of this little visit, the mayor was willing to use him—the newcomer—to ensure that those friendships and loyalties weren't a hindrance to the investigation. He could've told Forbes not to worry. No one ever got in the way of his investigation—at least, not for long.

"Well, then," Forbes said, nodding. "I'll leave you to it."

Michael knelt and rubbed Zeke's chest while he watched the mayor walk away. He had a confusing fire scene, a beloved town daughter who was up to her neck in intrigue, and a boss who didn't trust the motives of his own police force.

"Well, well, well," he murmured. "This town is looking less quaint all the time, huh, boy?"

"Raaaoow."

Chapter 5

Kaz lunged up in bed, clawing her way out of the nightmare and gasping for air. She scrambled into a crouch against the headboard, the harsh rasp of her rapid breathing disturbing the early morning quiet. Shuddering, she stared at the familiar furniture and knickknacks of her childhood bedroom, barely registering them.

It was just the dream. She repeated the phrase over and over inside her head, like a mantra. She lifted a shaky hand to shove damp hair back from her face and made herself look again at each of the sturdy pieces of walnut furniture her grandfather had built for her, to take in the pale morning light filtering through the sheer lace curtains of her south-facing window.

The nightmare had been occurring more often since she'd come home, and it didn't take a rocket scientist to figure out what had triggered it this time. Years of hearing the local legends about ghouls hunting for the skulls of drowned sailors, followed by the shipwreck when she was a teenager, and now last night's disaster—she would've been surprised if she *hadn't* had the dream.

Usually, the ghoul turned out to be whoever was hassling her at the moment—in this case, Chapman.

She pulled the comforter around her and climbed stiffly from bed. Out of habit, she walked over to the window to gauge the weather. The skies were gloomy, the clouds gray and threatening to drop their moisture. But the wind was light, and for now, the rain held off. In the distance, she could actually see patches of weak sunlight over Young's Bay. She hugged the quilt close to ward off the chill seeping through the windowpane. Was Gary out there somewhere, standing at someone else's window, gauging the weather just like she was? Was he all right? Or was he running from a killer?

She wouldn't let herself even think about the other possibility—that somehow, he was involved. Not Gary. Not the quiet, gentle kid she'd grown up with. Not even the hardened, disillusioned man—the stranger—he'd become. She refused to believe it.

After Chapman had dropped her off around 3 A.M. and confiscated her clothes, she'd called every friend of Gary's she could think of, waking them up, which hadn't made her popular. No one knew where he was. Or, at least, no one was *admitting* they knew where he was. She'd checked his bedroom, but he hadn't slept in his bed. And his camping gear and Army revolver were gone. The missing revolver had her the most worried—Gary *never* carried his gun.

Knowing there was nothing else she could do before first light, she'd pulled on one of Gary's Seahawks jerseys, hugging it around her as she'd dropped off into a fitful doze—only to awaken from the nightmare less than an hour later, feeling as if she were drowning.

She shook herself out of her reverie. She should be out looking for Gary—not dreaming about a past that she couldn't change. Or about a burned-out arson investigator, for that matter.

Michael Chapman thought Gary had run, and that by running, Gary had as much as admitted he was guilty of arson and murder. But Gary had other reasons to run.

For twenty agonizing days during the Iraq war, she and the rest of Astoria had watched and waited for the Iraqis to release

Gary and four other POWs after his unit had been captured during a covert op. He'd finally come home, quiet and withdrawn; the rest of his unit hadn't made it out alive. He'd never talked about what he'd endured, but the experience had changed him into a remote stranger who had trouble sleeping through the night, who no longer spent any length of time confined inside.

Chapman intended to prove that Gary had set the fire—she knew that as surely as she knew the tides. And Jim Sykes—well, Jim would do whatever it took to keep his town clean. If that meant throwing Gary in jail, he wouldn't hesitate.

Lucy had related how people in Astoria thought Jim Sykes walked on water ever since he'd busted up a burglary ring. But Sykes' overzealousness on the job made Lucy a tad uneasy.

"He's taking 'by the book' to a whole new level," she'd told Kaz.

Since Gary was the most obvious suspect, Kaz had no illusions that Sykes would waste time investigating anyone else. She was the only person, with the possible exception of Lucy, who was in a dicey position, who wouldn't readily accept that Gary was guilty. So the responsibility lay with her to prove them all wrong, Chapman *and* the police.

She needed a plan, and fast. Planning was her forte—she'd built an entire career around her organizational skills. It was time to put those talents to good use outside the corporate boardroom.

She sighed, turning away from the window and heading for the bathroom. Getting the smell of smoke out of her hair and off her skin would be a first step toward feeling up to facing the day. The quick shower she'd taken last night before falling into bed hadn't even made a dent. So first, a long, hot shower. Then caffeine. She *definitely* needed lots of caffeine.

A half hour later, Kaz stood in her cheery turn-of-the-century kitchen, watching the coffee drip with excruciating slowness into a glass carafe while she listened to the sounds of the house waking up around her—the ancient furnace in the basement kicking on with a *thump*, the *whoosh* of air through the cast iron heating grates, the *creak* of the walls and floors as the wooden structure warmed up.

She'd missed the old place. It represented home to her in a way that her condo in Stinson Beach never would. Her great grandfather had built the Mission-style cottage for his young bride in the early 1900's, handling all the finish carpentry himself. The house wasn't luxurious by anyone's standards, but its high ceilings, built-in, glass-fronted cabinets, and mahogany crown moldings made her condo seem cold and sterile by comparison.

Each of the rooms of the Astoria house held decades of memories, images of times when the family had still been together. Good memories, memories to cherish. In the last decade, she'd led a full and productive life down in San Francisco, but she'd been too focused on building her consulting business, and she'd let her relationships with family and friends suffer. Maybe she could be happier here than she'd been down south...no, that was crazy. It was insane to think moving home permanently would fill that empty place deep down inside her. Wasn't it?

There was a loud pounding at the back door, jolting her out of her thoughts. She jumped a foot.

Michael Chapman stood on the other side of the glass, his gaze watchful. Zeke stood on his hind legs beside Chapman, both paws on the window ledge, looking in. The dog grinned, his tongue lolling out the side of his mouth. Chapman wasn't nearly so cheerful, but neither did he look as ghoulish as he had in her nightmare.

Rubbing damp hands against her jeans, she walked over and flipped the lock. Zeke pushed against her leg, wagging his tail, and she leaned down to let him sniff her hand. "Don't you two have a home of your own to go to?" she asked Chapman. It was the first time she'd said something out loud since she'd awakened, and the words came out raspy. Obviously, the abuse her throat had gotten the night before hadn't helped her vocal chords.

"I went home after I left you for a change of clothes." Chapman handed her the morning paper that she had yet to retrieve off the lawn and sniffed the air appreciatively. "You going to share some of that coffee?"

His Bostonian accent was stronger this morning than it had been last night, and he looked as tired as she felt—he probably hadn't gotten any sleep at all. Although she didn't need the diversion of having him underfoot, she simply didn't have it in her to refuse him the coffee. As far as she was concerned, coffee was one of the major food groups and should be featured prominently in international human rights laws. She pointed to a chair and then opened a cupboard door to retrieve a second mug.

He sat down at her oak pedestal table, slouching comfortably, his long, jeans-clad legs stretched out in front of him. His hair was damp and casually disheveled—he'd evidently showered on that trip home. But he hadn't taken the time to shave. A day's growth of beard darkened his strong jaw line, making his pale gaze seem even more piercing by contrast.

Zeke collapsed at his feet with a moan, resting his chin on his paws. They both looked disgustingly relaxed and comfortable with their surroundings—a couple of confident males. Chapman's gaze was sharp, though, as was his dog's. The laid-back attitudes were a pose, meant to encourage her to relax her guard. She frowned and turned away to deal with the coffee.

Carrying the steaming mugs over to the table, she came to

the point. "So why are you here?"

"I brought your clothes back. They're clean of accelerant."

"You didn't have them long enough to send them to a lab," she pointed out, taking a chair across from him and sipping from her mug.

"Zeke sniffed them. His nose is as good as any gas chromatograph, and he didn't find anything. I didn't see any reason to send them to the lab."

"So I'm no longer a suspect?"

One corner of Chapman's mouth quirked, drawing her gaze there. He had a very nice mouth, one that encouraged fantasies. And okay, she might need to revisit the whole Freudian dream-scenario issue. Then she realized the direction her thoughts were taking, and froze. *My God.* She wasn't actually *attracted* to the man, was she? How insane was *that?*

If he noticed her momentary distraction, he didn't comment on it, saying only, "It means I don't think you set the fire while you were wearing those clothes."

She barely managed to refrain from letting her impatience show.

He pulled a large manila envelope out of his jacket. "I'd like you to look at some pictures of the crowd from last night and tell me who you recognize. Whether you see anything out of the ordinary, like a boat moored in the wrong location, a car that isn't usually there—that sort of thing."

She sat up a little straighter, even more on guard. "Why don't you show them to the harbormaster?"

"I'm headed there next. But this is your community—you've known the fishermen for a couple of decades, at least."

"I only spend a couple of weeks here each year—I haven't lived here for the last ten years."

He waved a hand, overriding her objection. "You might notice something or someone that the harbor master wouldn't." Pulling the photos from the envelope, he spread

56

them across the table. "Arsonists are pretty messed up in the head. Whoever did this might've hung around to watch."

So this was what he'd had Clint Jackson doing last night during the fire. Although still wary, Kaz was curious in spite of herself. She propped both elbows on the table and leaned forward.

Each photo had been taken to show a section of the crowd, and he'd arranged them on the table, from left to right, as she would've seen the crowd from where she'd been standing on the wharf. Sipping her coffee, she studied them one by one.

Michael leaned back, taking the opportunity to observe her. She looked exhausted, wrung out. Her hair hung in long, golden ropes down her back, still damp from her shower, and her face, stripped clean of any makeup, was still unnaturally pale. She wore a royal blue football jersey that was three sizes too large for her, jeans worn thin enough at the pressure points to have his imagination working overtime, and fluffy red wool socks.

She looked sexy as hell.

Don't go there. Focus on the job. Yeah, right.

He frowned. There were shadows under her eyes, and hollows beneath her cheekbones. Anxiety had stamped deep creases on either side of her mouth. She'd finally bandaged the burn on her hand—the stark whiteness of the gauze stood out in contrast to the angry, reddened skin. It bothered him more than he wanted to admit that she might be hurting.

She studied each photo, moving methodically from left to right, her concentration absolute. She might not have lived in town in recent years, but she had to know most of the people in the pictures. Odds were she'd grown up with them, gone to school with them. The question was whether she'd be up front with him about whom she recognized. Or whether she'd lie.

The knuckles on the hand that held her coffee mug whitened. She was staring at the photo on her far left.

"See something?" he asked.

She started, almost as if she'd forgotten he was there. He smothered a grin of self-deprecation—here he couldn't seem to keep his eyes off her, and she didn't even remember he was in the room. Not good for the ego.

"These guys are all fishermen," she said abruptly, pointing to another of the photos and reeling off several names that he managed to jot down on the back of the envelope. "You'll recognize some of them from the tavern last night."

"And none of them were at the mooring basin when you arrived," he clarified, forcing himself to concentrate on the business at hand.

"No, I told you, the marina was deserted."

He propped a boot on top of one of the claw-foot legs of the table, cocking his head while he studied her body language. She was holding back on him, dammit. "But you recognized someone else just now," he pushed. When she didn't respond, he rubbed a hand over his chin. He knew he had no right, at this point, to expect her to trust or confide in him, but it rankled, just the same. "Ms. Jorgensen—"

"I thought I might've recognized someone, but I was mistaken."

"Withholding information in a criminal investigation is a prosecutable offense."

Her jaw set. "There's no one in these photos that I consider capable of arson or murder."

He leaned forward, picked up the photo she'd been staring at and tossed it directly in front of her. "Leave the judgments up to the authorities—tell me who you saw."

Her soft brown eyes flashed at him. "I saw no one."

He waited her out, using the silence to try to unnerve her. The phone rang shrilly, startling both of them. She got up to answer it, but whoever it was must've hung up.

Michael picked up the photos and carefully stacked them. "I

understand that you want to protect your brother," he said, giving her time to reconsider, "but it's unnecessary. If he didn't do it, I'll find out who did."

"Maybe, maybe not."

He started to snap at her, then sighed. "Look, if you're worried that I don't conduct thorough investigations, then let me set your mind at ease. I don't jump to false conclusions—I let the evidence tell the truth."

"I only have your word on that," she pointed out, sitting back down. "And frankly, I'm worried about your hidden agendas."

"I don't have any hidden agendas," he said, letting his voice reflect his irritation. "Although from what I've seen so far, everyone else in this town does. I'd say that you're engaging in a bit of psychological transference, wouldn't you?"

Kaz stiffened. Even as her temper spiked, a part of her—the part that had spent ten years in corporate political battles—was impressed. He knew when to bide his time and when to go for the jugular. His interrogation skills were excellent. She would be wise not to underestimate him.

"You could've had Lucy return the clothes," she parried. "The harbormaster could've answered any other questions you have. You just wanted another shot at me, didn't you?"

A muscle ticked in his jaw. "We're on the same side," he pointed out. "We both want to catch whoever did this."

"That remains to be seen."

His intense gaze never wavered. "Talk to me about the financial aspects of the fishing business."

Frowning, she got up to refill their mugs. And to stall. "What do you want to know? It's a tough business—it always has been."

"Are the marine stocks depleted out here the same way they are on the East Coast?"

"Yes." What was he getting at? "But the government just

59

announced a buyout plan that, along with a reduction in fishing licenses, allows some fishermen to exit gracefully."

"Is your business profitable?"

She shrugged. "Historically, some years yes, some no." Then she clued in. "If you're trying to imply that Gary or I would set fire to the boat to collect the insurance, you're way off base. Our boats represent a way of life to us—neither of us would ever burn our legacy. Besides, the insurance would never cover the total cost of replacement."

"Maybe. Then again, maybe your brother had an immediate need for cash."

"Gary's needs are simple, he lives on very little," she retorted. "And he could've opted to be bought out, which would've given him plenty of cash. He didn't—he chose to stay in. Those who do can look forward to double the catches they've had in recent years."

"As long as the government doesn't change its quotas," Chapman pointed out. "And the government never moves that fast—Gary might've needed cash faster than he could get it from them."

"He could always ask me for a loan if he needed it."

"I know." Chapman was implying that he had already checked out her finances. She hated knowing someone was poking around in her life. "But would he?"

She shifted uneasily, not admitting how perceptive the question was. When she'd suggested to Gary a week ago that she fund the worst of the repairs on the boats, he'd pitched a fit.

"You'd be throwing good money after bad," he'd told her.

When she didn't answer, Chapman got up to put his coffee mug in the sink. Then he walked back to the table and leaned across it, both hands braced on the surface so that she had to look up into his hard gaze. "You know where your brother is. I want to talk to him."

She shoved her chair back abruptly and stood. Keeping her back to him, she made a production out of assembling the ingredients for a protein shake. "You're wrong—I don't have a clue where he is."

"I find that hard to believe."

"And even if I did know," she continued, turning to face him, her arms crossed, "I wouldn't tell you. You're not going to use me to get to him. Gary doesn't deal well with figures of authority. My guess is that he's trying to find Ken's killer, not running from the law."

"If you believe he has nothing to hide, then convince him to come in and talk to me, tell me what he knows."

She was shaking her head before he finished. "Gary wouldn't trust a stranger."

Chapman had come over to stand beside her at the counter, purposely invading her personal space. Trying to rattle her. "I can have you arrested for obstructing justice. If you know something you're not telling me, I won't hesitate."

She sent a cool look his way while she measured out protein powder and put it into the blender. "You don't frighten me, Mr. Chapman."

"Yeah, but I sure as hell bother you," he said softly, leaning closer. Close enough that she could smell the spicy fragrance of the soap he'd used in his shower. "Now, why is that, I wonder?"

"Don't flatter yourself." She added yogurt to the blender, mixing the two ingredients together, then tossed in a couple of handfuls of frozen fruit. She leveled a steady look at him, tapped the lid on, and flipped the switch. The blender started making a loud, grinding racket.

After a second, Chapman reached out, hit the Off switch, and slanting an amused glance her way, fished out the spoon she'd left in.

She closed her eyes for a moment, feeling the heat creep

into her cheeks. Then she busied herself pouring the shake into two glasses, holding one of them out to him. With any luck, his portion had some metal shavings in it.

He rinsed the spoon off in the sink, using the towel lying on the counter between them to dry his hands. Taking the glass from her, he set it on the counter, then removed a long tube containing a cotton swab from his jacket pocket.

She backed up a step. "What's that?"

"The lab techs found a possible DNA sample on the boat this morning. I'll need yours to rule you and your brother out."

She thought rapidly. Anyone would tell her that she was crazy to comply without consulting a lawyer, but she doubted she could find one on such short notice. The only lawyer she knew in town was the one her parents had used as executor of their will, and he'd retired years ago. Not that he would know anything about criminal law anyway.

She could call Phil, the lawyer she'd been dating for the last couple of years in San Francisco, but that would take a day or two—Phil wasn't known for returning calls he considered a low priority. And ever since she'd told him she wasn't ready to commit to marriage, she'd definitely been a low priority.

"I can go get a court order compelling you to give me a sample, or we can get this over with right now," Chapman said, apparently reading her thoughts.

She hesitated a moment longer, then shrugged.

He moved closer and held up the swab. "Open up." She complied, and he ran the swab expertly along the inside of her cheek.

His hand paused, the swab resting lightly on her lower lip, and she looked up, right into his heated gaze.

She could hear his heightened breathing, sense the strong, steady beat of his heart. His shoulders blocked out the light coming from the window behind him, creating a zone of intimacy around them.

His gaze dropped to her mouth, and her breath hitched. *Bad sign.*

They both took a cautious half-step back.

His expression curiously grim, he put the swab inside the tube, sealing it and replacing it in the pocket inside his jacket.

She slowly released the breath she'd been holding and picked up her glass, taking a sip of it. Her hands were shaking. "When can I get access to the *Anna Marie?*" she asked, trying for a normal tone of voice. "I need to get her dry-docked."

"Soon. I'm almost done processing her for evidence." He drank a couple of sips out of his glass, probably out of politeness, then set it down on the counter. Walking over to the table, he picked up the envelope of photos. "You might want to think about the fact that someone who has killed once usually doesn't have a problem with killing again."

She cocked her head. "Does that mean you think someone other than Gary did this?"

"Anything is possible," he conceded. "And one of those possibilities is that you could be in danger. Why don't you let me tag along, help you find your brother?"

She tsked. "That was smooth, but I'm not quite that gullible. Or that rattled."

He merely shook his head. "Then I'll be on my way. Thanks for the coffee and...everything," he said, smiling slightly. "Where do you buy your coffee, by the way?"

"My partner mails it to me from California."

"Figures." He gave Zeke a hand command and turned to leave, then stopped. "Do you keep a space heater on board the *Anna Marie?*"

She barely kept herself from reacting. "No, why?"

He shrugged. "Just thought I'd ask—it's not important."

After the two of them left, Kaz stood for a moment in the silence of her suddenly empty kitchen, waiting for her system to level out. Okay, she needed to reassess. She'd been ambushed by the strength of her response to him. But it was just a little unwelcome chemistry, that's all. She could handle it. Handling men on a personal level had never been her strong suit, as Phil was always quick to point out. But she'd deal with Chapman.

She sighed and rubbed her forehead. And maybe, just maybe if she repeated that to herself enough times, she'd start to believe it.

She had no illusions that she'd seen the last of Chapman—he'd probably made it only as far as her curb and would hound her every move. Or simply sic his dog on her.

He'd been more accurate than he knew. She *did* have a good idea of where Gary had probably gone to ground. Well, at least, the general area. And she knew whom to ask—if he had a phone, she already would've called him.

After he'd ducked out of her view the night before, Chuck must've stood at the back edge of the crowd, watching. She'd recognized him in the photo and was still a little surprised he'd allowed himself to be seen. Someone had had a hand on his shoulder—a hand that bore a ring she'd know anywhere. The gold, embossed signet of Astoria High School, Class of '88. Gary had been there, watching from a distance.

How long did she have before Chapman showed the photos to Lucy, who'd have no trouble identifying that blurred image? Or before he asked Lucy about the space heater, which she knew that Gary regularly stored in his truck and used in the wheelhouse on long drag-fishing trips?

An hour, maybe two.

Picking up Chapman's glass, Kaz downed the other half of the protein shake. She could use the boost, and right now, a few metal shavings were the least of her worries.

Chapter 6

After stopping for gas, Kaz drove west on Marine Drive, then veered off along the north shore of Young's Bay. The tide was out, exposing deeply carved, milk chocolate-tinted ridges of mud at the bay's edge. Tufts of bright green grass and burnt-orange reeds topped each ridge, and where water had drained away, silvery lines etched the shiny surface of the mud. The lines deepened into gullies that eventually dumped into the section of the bay where calm water could still be found, reflecting the gray sky above. As Kaz drove, she spotted at least a dozen great blue herons wading in the shallows. Eagles, plentiful in the winter months, fished from the ends of old logs and rotted piers.

She kept an eye on her rearview mirror, hoping to spot anyone tailing her. A mile back, she could've sworn she'd glimpsed Clint Jackson in a patrol car. All Gary needed, at this point, was for her to lead the cops right to him. There was no one behind her now, though.

Chapman remained her biggest worry. She thought she'd lost him, but maybe not. She could kick herself for not noticing what make and model of car he drove.

Crossing the Wallooskee River, she drove through farm country until the highway started winding into the foothills toward its ultimate destination, the old logging town of Mist. After another ten minutes, she came to the Elk Preserve.

People who wanted a lot of privacy and very few visitors had homes near the preserve, well hidden in the forest. The foothills of the Coast Range had been logged at least twice in the last century, and some of the more recently clear-cut areas resembled pastures full of nothing but dead stumps—stump farms, the locals called them. The older cuts, which had happened before logging companies had been obliged to replant, had grown stands of mixed, native forest as nature had intended.

Chuck Branson had eighty acres of older forest, up a now-defunct logging road on the southeast edge of the preserve. He'd moved out there after Desert Storm, buying the land out of the money he'd earned fishing in Alaska. For the first two years, he'd lived in an army tent while he, Gary, and Ken had built his cabin from the trees on his land. The sign at the entrance to his property read, IF I DON'T KNOW YOU, YOU SHOULDN'T BE HERE.

He meant it.

His gate was chained shut with the kind of padlock that would take C-4 to breach, so Kaz parked her SUV in front of it and climbed over.

The woods glistened in the morning light, and a tiny winter wren warbled shrilly from a nearby bush. Up ahead, a doe and her yearling browsed. As Kaz passed by, they watched curiously but didn't bolt into the brush.

Sounds traveled oddly in the woods, muffled on level ground, yet amplified up ravines through the trees and underbrush. From his front porch, Chuck could hear a twig snap a thousand feet away. He wasn't fond of surprises—it hadn't been serendipity that had led him to build his cabin at the top of the ravine. And he had, Kaz was certain, been tracking her since she'd crossed onto his property.

Although she hadn't heard him, the hairs on the back of her neck had already been standing up when Chuck suddenly materialized beside her, halting her before she was even halfway to his cabin.

His Chicago Cubs sweatshirt had seen better days, and was matched by worn, baggy army fatigues and battered combat boots. In his left hand, he balanced the gleaming stock of a shotgun so that its barrel leaned against his shoulder. Chuck had always had chiseled, blunt features, and he rarely made the effort to soften them by smiling. His pale brown hair, shaved close to his skull, heightened the sense of danger that he exuded.

"War games?" she asked lightly, nodding at his weapon.

"Patrolling the perimeter."

"Why? Worried that someone will find out Gary's here?"

He took his time answering, pulling out a hand-rolled cigarette and lighting it. "That's none of your business," he said gently.

"He's my brother."

Chuck shrugged. "He doesn't want your help."

"Tough." She lifted her chin, ignoring the hurt his comment caused. "He's got it anyway."

Chuck didn't respond, waiting with an eerie kind of stillness he'd perfected in the military.

"I saw you at the fire last night," she persisted, hoping to get an explanation of the message he'd been trying to send.

He drew on his cigarette, then removed a bit of tobacco from the tip of his tongue with two blunt fingertips. "You could've been hurt, going onto the boat like that."

She shrugged. "I'm still in one piece. Unfortunately, the same can't be said for Ken."

"He was a good man, but he made mistakes."

"Are you saying that Ken was killed because he was in some kind of trouble?" But Chuck merely shook his head. She hugged herself, trying to shake off her unease. "Where did you go after you left the tavern last night? I wanted to talk to you."

He looked amused. "Checking on my alibi, Kaz?"

She ignored that. "What were you and Gary arguing about?"

"I believe we told you to butt out." He took another drag on the cigarette, then looked off into the distance. "Had a date with the lovely barmaid Sandra."

Kaz hadn't noticed Sandra in Chapman's photos, and she certainly hadn't heard Sandra and Chuck were an item. Chuck didn't form attachments easily—Gary and Ken being the only exceptions she knew of. That made his explanation improbable at best.

"Lucy told me Gary argued with Ken before I got to the tavern. Do you know anything about that?"

"It was nothing."

"Not according to Lucy. She says Gary was pretty angry." Kaz waited, but he didn't comment further. Her frustration ratcheted higher. "Chuck, I have to talk to Gary."

"He'll contact you when he needs to."

"So you *do* know where he is."

"Didn't say that."

"Oh, for...quit being such a damn spook!" she snapped.

He smiled slightly, a hint of affection showing in his hazel eyes. "But I'm so good at it."

Well, he was right about that. Her breath expelled on a half laugh, but she quickly sobered. "Look. I get that you're loyal to Gary—that you feel you owe him. But have you considered that you might not be doing him a favor this time? If I'm going to help him, I need to find out what he knows."

"You know better than to think Gary had anything to do with Ken's death."

"Of course I don't," she quickly assured him, "but the cops are on a mission to pin this on Gary."

This bit of news had Chuck frowning. "Then Gary would be right to lay low, in my opinion."

"Is that what he's doing—laying low?"

"Not necessarily."

She controlled the urge to scream. "The cops won't give up, you know that. This is too big—Sykes can make a name for himself by bringing down Ken's murderer. Show that he's dedicated to keeping the community safe."

Chuck fieldstripped his cigarette, rubbing the bits of tobacco between his thumb and index finger, his expression contemplative. "Gary doesn't need or want your help," he said finally. "He wants you to stay out of it. You could be in danger."

Angry, she made a chopping motion with one hand. "That's not important right now."

"Yes, it is." Chuck suddenly focused his intense gaze on her, and she had to work hard not to show her uneasiness. Sometimes he seemed to look right into her soul, as if he knew things about her even she didn't know.

She'd never understood Chuck, not even back in high school. He was a ghost, a shadow on the perimeter of her life, always waiting, always watching. "So you've talked to Gary," she tried one more time.

"I talk to Gary all the time, you know that."

"Since the fire last night," she clarified impatiently.

"I didn't mean to imply that."

She threw up her hands. "Fine. At least tell me that he's all right, that he's not in danger."

"He's fine. Gary can take care of himself."

His answer gave her some measure of relief. Taking a shot in the dark, she asked, "Do you know how many days of supplies he had with him? What area he headed into?"

Chuck gazed at her, his expression giving away nothing. "If he wants to get seriously lost up there, you won't find him. *I* couldn't even find him."

That much was true. Gary had training in wilderness survival and evasion. And he knew the foothills of the Coast Range intimately.

She paced the small clearing in which they were standing, earning herself a scolding from a stellar jay in a nearby alder tree. "The new fire chief thinks Gary killed Ken and then set the fire to hide the crime."

"That's ridiculous, and you know it." Chuck shifted the butt of the shotgun to the soft cushion of leaves at his feet. "Gary renounced violence after the war. He wouldn't hurt anyone, not even a cockroach. He was protecting Ken six months ago when he punched out Svensen."

"Well regardless, Gary's the prime suspect. I've *got* to talk to him, find out what he knows, and figure out a way to prove he didn't do it." She continued to pace, feeling like she was jumping out of her skin. Perhaps she'd needed to back off on the caffeine.

"There are a lot of cockroaches in this town."

She halted, staring at Chuck, chilled. "What did you say?"

Chuck rubbed the barrel of his shotgun with an index finger, his expression hard. "They need to be wiped out before things can get better."

She'd always tried hard, since Chuck was Gary's friend, not to ask herself what he was capable of. He'd been a Ranger, like Gary and Ken, and the three of them had been tight ever since the war. But the rumor was that Chuck had also contracted out to the CIA as a sniper. "What—precisely—are you trying to say?"

"Never mind. Go home, that's all. Lock your doors, don't get involved. Gary won't appreciate it if you do."

She shivered uncontrollably. What was going on in Astoria? Had her hometown changed that much in her absence?

She inhaled the crisp, clean mountain air, drawing it deep into her lungs, but it did nothing to allay her anxiety. "At least tell Gary to get in touch with me."

Chuck looked noncommittal.

"Please."

70

He hesitated, then nodded. "We'll see." He grasped her arm in an almost courtly manner and turned her downhill, toward the gate. "I'll walk you back." He waited politely while she decided whether to acquiesce—an illusion, since he was leaving her no choice. Then he escorted her off his property, melting into the woods once she was safely on the other side of the gate.

Kaz climbed into the SUV and jammed the keys in the ignition. Then she leaned back, staring blindly at the dense green wall of vegetation in front of her. Nothing, she realized, was as it seemed. It was as if everything she'd thought was real was simply part of a well-constructed façade, created by friends to protect her from a harsh reality they'd decided she couldn't handle.

She shook her head, starting the SUV. She was wasting time.

She backed up, then on a sudden hunch, turned uphill past Chuck's place toward one of the area's more primitive campgrounds. Towering, old growth firs with trunks almost the size of redwoods shaded the small area, their canopies shutting out any light that would've allowed undergrowth to flourish. The forest floor was littered with pine needles and old, fallen rotting logs, cleared here and there to provide level spaces in which campers could pitch their tents.

Parking on the side of the road, Kaz glanced around to ensure that the campground was empty, then got out of the SUV. After orienting herself, she stepped a few yards into the woods on the north edge of the property, to where an ancient Douglas fir had fallen and was now functioning as a nurse log to newer trees and ferns.

She knelt in the decaying woodland debris behind the log and studied the space beneath it. As she'd suspected, there were faint signs of recent digging. Removing some small branches and twigs that had been used to camouflage the

71

entry, she used her hands to scoop soft dirt and rotted bits of bark out of the way. There was a small cave, not much more than an indentation in the ground, which would easily be mistaken by most campers as some animal's den. Except that it wasn't—it was one of the many hidden locations Gary used to store supplies up in the hills, in case he needed to disappear into the backcountry for a few days. He'd made a habit of maintaining his "stashes", as he called them, ever since Iraq. She'd always thought his behavior excessively paranoid, but now she was simply glad he'd planned ahead.

Feeling with one hand along the cool dirt walls all the way to the back, she prayed that a fox or a raccoon hadn't decided to take up residence. The cavity was empty—of both animals and supplies.

She sat back on her heels, dusting off her hands. So Gary really was on the run, as she'd feared. Why? Chuck obviously believed in his innocence, as did she. So why would he run? To avoid being jailed on the parole violation? She didn't think so. More likely, he'd stand his ground with Sykes, daring him to take action. No, something more was at stake. Either he was running because he was guilty, or because he was regrouping before going after the killer himself. Both possibilities scared the crap out of her.

She stood and studied the surrounding woods. They were silent, too silent. The birds had stopped singing, and no small critters rustled in the brush, foraging for their meal. The back of her neck tingled in warning.

Was someone watching her? It couldn't be Gary. If it were, the animals wouldn't have taken cover—they knew he wouldn't harm them. Animals had a sixth sense that way.

Breathing shallowly, she stood where she was, casually scanning the vegetation around her, straining for a whiff of scent, for anything that would identify the intruder. But after a few long moments, the birds came out of hiding, and Kaz's sense of someone watching her faded away. She let out the breath she'd been holding. Maybe the intruder had been of the four-legged variety. Or maybe she'd been overreacting.

She glanced around one more time, still harboring the faint hope that Gary might be nearby. But she knew any effort to find him would be fruitless. Chuck was right—Gary was too good to leave behind any trail, even if she knew which direction he was headed in. Frustrated, she returned to the SUV.

Once she was on the highway, she reviewed the events of the night before. To be guilty of killing Ken and setting the fire, Gary would've had to leave the tavern and head directly to the marina. After all, she hadn't been more than forty-five minutes behind him. And Ken had to have been on the boat already— there wasn't enough elapsed time for them to meet elsewhere, go to the boat, and argue—all before Ken was killed and she'd witnessed the first explosion of fire.

So why had Ken been on the boat? What had he been up to? It all came back to that. She had to find out where he'd been and what he'd been involved in. It was her only hope of figuring out why Gary had run, or of proving his innocence.

As she passed the Elk Preserve, a nondescript, dark green sedan passed her going in the other direction, and she glanced over, recognizing Michael Chapman behind the wheel. Seconds later, shots rang out, and her window exploded.

Chapter 7

Kaz ducked, raising both hands to protect her face from flying shards of glass. The SUV veered immediately toward the ditch. Yanking the wheel back, she felt the back wheels slip, then find purchase on the shoulder as the vehicle barely missed plunging into the marsh that bordered the road.

She held on as she careened around a sharp curve, then she brought the SUV to a skidding stop. Cutting the engine, she sat in the sudden silence and shook.

Tires screeched behind her. She heard a door slam, then running footsteps. Fumbling with the door handle, she jumped out just as Chapman reached her.

He gripped her shoulders hard. "Are you all right?"

"Yes." She dragged in air, trying not to hyperventilate.

Evidently unconvinced, he checked her over for injuries.

She batted at his hands. "I'm *fine*—he missed me."

Chapman turned loose of her, a muscle working in his jaw. He carefully searched the surrounding fields, then asked in a calmer voice, "Which direction did the shots come from?"

"Inside the preserve, I think." She pointed across the road.

He reached inside the cab of the vehicle, brushing the glass to the floor, then placed both hands on her waist and lifted her back inside. Ignoring her sputtering protest, he shut the door. "*Guard*," he told Zeke, then headed in the direction she'd indicated.

He jogged toward the preserve, his heart still pounding. For a split second, he'd thought she'd been killed. He forced himself to slow to a walk, to gulp in deep breaths.

Opening the gate to the preserve, he stepped inside. Closing his eyes, he listened for the sounds of someone's retreat—the faint crackle of dried grass, the snap of a twig. All he heard were the birds chirping and the wind rustling the dead stalks of grass. The shooter was long gone.

The tension in his shoulders eased, and he began his search.

About fifty yards down, just inside the fence line, he found what he was looking for—a small area of trampled grass. The son of a bitch had followed her out to Branson's, then patiently waited, hidden in the tall reeds, for her to drive back by. At the right moment, he'd simply aimed and taken his shot. And come damn close to killing her.

Dropping to one knee, Michael studied the ground. The shooter had been careful—no spent shell casings, no cigarette butts or candy wrappers. No evidence. A professional, then.

Michael stood and looked at the surrounding grass. He could just make out, from a bent reed here and there, a trail through the meadow toward the back of the preserve. No doubt the shooter had parked on the far side of the preserve, so that he could escape undetected. Michael wanted to follow his trail, to see if he could find any evidence that could be used at a later date, but he'd already left Kaz alone for too long. He'd come back later, and he'd find something, even if it was only a partial footprint.

No one was that good.

By the time she spotted Chapman walking up the road, Kaz had already spent a good ten minutes chastising herself for not insisting that she accompany him.

The look on his face, when he saw her still standing next to the SUV, petting Zeke, was one of extreme irritation. "Don't you ever listen? I told you to stay in the car."

"Why? Whoever it was, they're long gone." Her point was reasonable but didn't seem to have much impact. "Look, it was probably some idiot hunter. The preserve has problems with poachers—"

She huffed as he moved her aside and leaned inside her car. After a few seconds, he took out a pocketknife and used its blade to pry something out of the ceiling.

He examined it closely, then pulled out a plastic baggy and dropped it in. "I'd guess fifty-caliber." He held the bullet up for her to see. "Know any hunters who go around shooting elk with a sniper rifle? I don't."

Her knees turned to rubber, and she braced a hand against the side of the SUV. Drawing a breath, she opted for humor. "Well, at least he was a lousy shot, so that leaves out all the people I know."

Chapman's expression turned thoughtful. "Not necessarily. Maybe he wasn't trying to hit you, even though he came damn close. Maybe this time was a warning."

She hugged herself. "But I don't have anything to do with this. And if he thinks this will permanently scare me off—"

Chapman snorted. "Anyone who knows you wouldn't be likely to make that mistake." He ran a hand through his hair, disheveling it. "This incident is an example of *exactly* why I told you to leave the investigating to the authorities. Civilians always get hurt when they get in the way."

She ignored the comment, changing the subject. "So what are you doing out here? Following me? Don't you have something more important to do, like gathering evidence off the *Anna Marie* so that I can get her dry-docked?"

"No thanks to you, I was able to deduce that Chuck Branson is one of your brother's best friends and is, in fact, the second man you were talking to in the tavern. So, as part of the ongoing investigation, I thought I'd see if he knows where your brother is." Chapman's tone turned sardonic. "I gather I'm not entirely off base, seeing as how you're within a mile of his place."

She shrugged. "Chuck won't tell you anything. Not if he wouldn't tell me."

"Would Gary pull a stunt like this?" Chapman asked abruptly.

"Of course not!"

"It makes sense. He has the training, and he knew he wouldn't hit you, so he fires a warning shot, hoping to get you to go away."

She shook her head. "You're so far off base—"

"He has a history of run-ins with the police, and a record for assault. Just how well do you really know your brother?"

She barely managed to contain a wince. Chapman had hit on her greatest fear—that she didn't really know her brother as well as she thought. That Gary might have turned into someone capable of doing exactly what Chapman was suggesting. She folded her arms. "The man Gary punched out that night wouldn't even press charges—Sykes was the one who prosecuted. And Gary and Sykes have history. But why bother explaining? You've already got Gary tried and found guilty."

Chapman made a dismissive motion with his hand. "What about Chuck?"

She thought about it for a moment. "I don't know," she admitted. "Chuck's...well, weird. I think he's got some CIA stuff in his background."

"He's sure as hell got something spooky going on—his records are sealed."

"Gary, Ken, and Chuck were all in the Army together. There's no way Gary or Chuck had anything to do with Ken's death—they were all too tight."

"They could've had a falling out. You haven't been around much lately, so how would you know?" When she didn't answer, he continued. "You came out here hoping to talk to your brother, didn't you?"

She tensed. "Chuck and I just talked about what happened last night." That much, at least, was the truth.

"Does he know where your brother is?"

She shrugged. "If he does, he isn't saying."

"If Gary asked, Chuck would help him. And that could've been what they were arguing about in the tavern last night, am I right? That Gary wanted Chuck's help," Chapman pressed. "And that's why you drove out here, isn't it? To see if Gary was hiding out here."

"Yes, all right?" she snapped, feeling goaded. "But Chuck refused to tell me anything, other than he'd had a date with Sandra after he left the tavern. So I guess you can cross him off your list of possible suspects."

"Who's Sandra?"

She realized he'd have no way of keeping the locals straight at this point. "The waitress at the Redemption."

"I'll check into it." Chapman rocked back on his heels, his hands shoved in the pockets of his jeans, a stance that emphasized his lean hips and wide shoulders. His gaze was far too perceptive for her peace of mind.

"If you believe someone is shooting at me, that means I can't be on your list of suspects anymore, right?"

"Maybe not, but you're sure as hell on my list of uncooperative witnesses."

She shrugged; she could live with that. "Sooner or later, you'll have to consider that whoever killed Ken might not be Gary—that Ken could've met someone else on the *Anna Marie* for some reason we haven't yet uncovered."

"I'm keeping an open mind."

She doubted it, but the conversation was getting her nowhere. Yanking open the door on her SUV, she got inside. With the kind of winds they got on the coast, taping plastic over the broken window would last about five minutes—she'd have to drop the car off at the dealer's to have the window replaced. Which meant dealing with another insurance claim.

She sighed and closed her eyes for a moment. The adrenaline was beginning to wear off, leaving her punch-drunk with fatigue.

As if on cue, it began to sprinkle. More weather was moving in; the sky to the southwest looked dark and threatening.

Pushing the door shut behind her, Chapman leaned both arms on the edge of the window. The man appeared to get a kick out of invading her personal space, a habit that should've annoyed her. "I'll follow you to the police station so that you can report this," he said.

Which would put her in the position of being questioned by the cops, and delay her even further. "It's a waste of time to bother the police with this."

"They should fill out an incident report and have it on file, in case anything else happens to you, so that they can establish a pattern."

She didn't like the sound of that, but she shook her head. "I prefer to keep this to myself."

He watched her for a long, silent moment with those silvery blue eyes, then nodded once, the movement abrupt. "I get it. You don't want to put your friend Lucy in an awkward spot about what you were doing out here." He laughed, but there was no humor in it. "You people really do stick together, don't you?"

"Okay, yes, you're partially right." She wished he weren't quite so astute. "Lucy's been my friend since grade school. She doesn't need Jim Sykes breathing down her neck about a conflict of interest."

He shook his head. "Why don't I follow you to the mechanic's and give you a ride home? That is, if you don't give me the slip between here and there."

Narrowing her eyes, she reached down and started the

engine, putting the SUV into gear. "Don't bother. The dealership is less than a mile from my house—I can hoof it."

"I'll give you a lift," he repeated firmly. "If you're at home and without transportation, I figure that limits the amount of damage you can do to my investigation for the next few hours."

She was amused. "You forget that I've lived here most of my life. I won't be without a car for any more time than it takes to make a call or two."

Gunning the engine, she pulled onto the highway, gravel and dirt spurting from beneath her tires. When she glanced in the rear view mirror, he was still standing there, his hands in his pockets and his dog at his side, watching her.

Chapter 8

Lucy hung up the phone and eyed the Kleenex box on her desk, which Ivar judiciously moved out of reach before she could hurl it at the far wall of the squad room.

"Tell Papa," he said.

"I could've used the stress relief," she pointed out.

Ivar merely waited.

"Okay, fine. We've got no exact time of death." She picked up a pencil and tapped it rapidly on her desk blotter. "The heat from the fire makes it impossible to pinpoint by body temperature any closer than a range of about two hours."

Ivar flipped through his notes. "Ken left the bar around 8:00 last night. Kaz found him on the boat a little over one hour later."

"So that's our timeframe for the murder," Lucy agreed, then held up a hand. "But wait, it gets better. Ken had bits of concrete embedded in one cheek, and mud and grass on the heels of his boots."

"Hmmm."

"Not a lot of boats are made of concrete," she offered up.

"Body was moved."

"Give the man a gold star." Lucy flopped back in her chair, causing it to squeak in protest. "We don't even have a murder scene."

Ivar's long, narrow face took on a brooding look, which meant he was headed into his silent mode. She *hated* his silent mode. For long stretches of time, she couldn't even get monosyllabic responses out of him. Unrewarding in the extreme. Not to mention that she was convinced it wasn't healthy for any human being to be *that* quiet.

She drank warm soda out of the can that had been sitting on her desk for...she couldn't really remember how long. Hopefully, the caffeine didn't disappear along with the carbonation.

Jim Sykes chose that moment to walk in the back door carrying a latte, which he took into his office. She wasted a couple of seconds fantasizing about forcibly removing the java from his office, not all that concerned for the consequences to her career.

Heaving a sigh, she forced herself back to the subject at hand. "Okay, I've got a theory: The killer did him on the boat, then dragged him off the boat, hunted around for some concrete to scrape his cheek with, then dragged him back on the boat." Ivar snorted, and a new thought occurred to her. "Dammit! This whole thing—"

"—doesn't make sense." She swiveled around in her chair. She'd last seen Chapman around 2 A.M., right before she'd headed off to the hospital for the preliminary autopsy. There were deep grooves of exhaustion bracketing his mouth, indicating he hadn't gotten any more sleep than they had.

"The killer knew what he was doing when he started the fire," Chapman said as he settled into the chair beside her desk, propping one boot on his knee. He gave them a quick run-down on the ignition method. "Who in this town would have that kind of knowledge?"

"Half the men in this town have military or Coast Guard background," Lucy replied. "There aren't a lot of options growing up here—signing up for a stint is pretty common. Get three squares, play with lots of neat toys, and then get your schooling paid for after. I considered it myself." Ivar rolled his

82

eyes, and she kicked his foot.

"Jorgensen would know a thing or two about setting a delayed fire," Ivar said. "So would Chuck Branson. Both are ex-Rangers, and Rangers are trained in diversionary tactics."

Lucy shifted uneasily in her chair. She'd been having a hard time—throughout the long night and all morning—wrapping her brain around Gary as a possible suspect. She didn't like the fact that her loyalties were impossibly divided. And knowing Gary, he'd be amused by her moral dilemma. The jerk. "I could say the same about anyone with a stint in the military police or the Coast Guard," she argued. "They both have to be able to spot and investigate arson." She looked at Chapman. "What about your own backyard? Arsonists, many times, are volunteer firefighters, right?"

"I'm checking that out, but none of them have an obvious motive. Do you know the cause of death?"

"Not officially. Unofficially, someone bashed his skull in from behind." She drank the last of her soda while she brought him up to date on the forensics.

"Interesting."

"Yeah. Why kill him elsewhere, then move the body onto the *Anna Marie* when there's a perfectly good river with the Current from Hell a few steps away?"

"I'd wondered the same thing." Chapman steepled his fingers. "On the one hand, we don't know that he was killed close to the river, so we can't assume that it would've been convenient to dump him there. Still, going to the trouble to put him on the boat doesn't compute."

"Need to take soil samples and concrete scrapings," Ivar said.

Lucy cocked her head. "Ken usually walked home from the Redemption," she said, thinking out loud. "So we start at the tavern and work in a radius out from there."

"What about insurance money as a motive?" Chapman

asked. "Maybe Jorgensen burned the boat for profit."

"Nuh-uh." Lucy had no doubts on that score. "Gary loved that boat—he'd never burn it. Besides, he left the tavern at least a half hour after Ken did, so if Ken was killed and then moved to the boat, Gary didn't have the time to do the crime."

"Unless the murder occurred close to the mooring basin," Ivar pointed out.

"So you're suggesting what?" Chapman asked Lucy. "That there's a possibility that someone might be framing Jorgensen?"

Lucy sighed. "I don't know *what* I'm suggesting, because I can't think of a reason for anyone to frame Gary, either."

"As theories go, it's farfetched." Chapman dropped his foot to the floor and leaned forward. "You know these people, grew up with them. What would get Jorgensen to the point that he'd be desperate enough to kill?"

"If you'd asked me that question up until six months ago, I would've laughed you out of the room," Lucy answered. "Gary's been acting weird for awhile now. And, yeah, I've been wondering why. But I still can't believe that he'd kill someone."

"He's got the training."

She shook her head. "Since he came home from the war, he's renounced violence. That bar fight was an exception."

"He didn't strike me as the passive type when he was getting ready to bash Ken's face in last night in the Redemption."

Chapman was right, and it bothered the hell out of her. "The point is," she said stubbornly, "I'd stake my reputation on the fact that Gary wouldn't kill anyone."

"What reputation?" Ivar rumbled.

"Shut up," she suggested, then gave the matter some more thought. "We're nowhere on this unless we can find the real murder scene."

"Evidence collection from the boat is almost complete," Chapman said. "And if Lundquist really was killed elsewhere, that suggests we won't find much else. The galley and forecastle were pretty much trashed by the fire."

"I can pull together a list of people who might have the knowledge to start a time-delayed fire and check their alibis," Ivar offered.

"Good." Chapman stood, looking down at Lucy. "You ever going to impound Jorgensen's truck?"

"It's still at the wharf?" She swore under her breath. "Brenner!" A uniformed officer stuck his head into the squad room. "Try to pick up Gary's truck sometime this century, will you?" She turned back to Chapman. "Anything else?"

"Only that this guy is no slouch in the brains department. He made damn sure the area on the boat where Lundquist would've been found burned both from above and below. He left the hatch open to ventilate the fire, and soaked the decking with gasoline, which ensured that the entire deck in that area would collapse."

Lucy snapped her fingers. "Damn, I forgot. Get this— according to Ewald, there was evidence of severe bruising on Ken's body, already partially healed. Which means he'd suffered at least one beating in recent days."

"What about the normal amount of knocks he would've taken out fishing?" Chapman asked. "The waters around here aren't exactly smooth sailing."

Lucy shook her head. "Too much bruising, and in all the wrong places. Whoever administered the beating knew what he was doing. He inflicted the most damage where it wouldn't be seen—around Ken's kidneys, and on his back and ribs."

"And where it would also cause the most pain—the kind of beating that sends a message," Chapman's expression was thoughtful. "So we've got a carefully planned arson and a victim who was possibly in some kind of trouble with people who don't play nice. Did you talk to the wife?"

"Yeah, nada, but she's acting scared. We've subpoenaed

Ken's bank records, and we're looking into any calls he made from his home or his cell phone. Maybe we'll get lucky."

"What about the bartender? Could he have overheard something?"

"We interviewed him this morning but didn't get much out of him. Steve makes a point of turning a deaf ear."

"A lot of unanswered questions," Ivar mused. "Too many illogical events to assume the easiest solution. Need to gather all the evidence in one place, then study it carefully."

"I agree," Chapman said.

Lucy rolled her eyes. "I tell you what—you two pick through the little bits of stuff in the collection bags and cans. I'll take a drive and see what I can find by the tavern. I need some fresh air."

But Chapman clearly wasn't through with her. "Kaz is obviously intelligent, and if Gary was a Ranger, he's also no slouch."

"What's your point?"

"That Jorgensen had motive—the argument in the tavern; means—access to the boat and the knowledge to start the fire; and opportunity—his truck was found at the wharf."

Lucy concluded she wasn't all that happy with Chapman's one-track mind. "When's the lab work coming back from the boat?"

"Some later today, the rest in a couple of days." He pulled a manila envelope out of his jacket and tossed it onto her desk. "Photos of the crowd from last night. I'd appreciate it if you'd take a look at them."

"Fine." She broke off as her phone rang. "Yeah." She listened a minute, and then said, "Yeah. Give me fifteen." She hung up and gave Chapman her coolest look. "Just so you know, Kaz had nothing to do with this."

"You may be right, but if her brother did, she'll go down with him."

"Meaning?"

"She's withholding information from me. Obstruction of justice."

Ivar nodded. "Sounds like her."

"Hey," Lucy objected.

Ivar shrugged. "She'd do anything for Gary, you know that."

"She wouldn't break the law unless she had a very good reason."

Ivar remained silent then, when Lucy glared, spread both hands.

"Just so I'm not working totally in the dark here," Chapman said, his tone taking on an edge, "do you two want to volunteer anything about your relationships with the primary suspects in this case?"

"We're just friends," Ivar quickly assured him.

"And that's all?"

"Look, we all want the same thing—to find the bad guy and bring him in," Lucy said. "Murders don't happen in our town, and Ken was a friend."

A look passed between the two men that Lucy couldn't decipher, and after a moment, Chapman nodded as if satisfied and stood up. "I've got a lot of work to do before dark," he said, and turned to go. "And I figure I've got maybe twenty-four hours before your friend is on my case about dry-docking her boat." He stopped, one corner of his mouth lifting. "Then again, I don't really have even that long, do I? Once you let Kaz borrow your car, she'll be mobile again."

Lucy flushed.

"Call your friend off, before she gets herself hurt," he suggested.

"She won't listen to me on this one." His brows arched, and she sighed. "Kaz feels responsible for Gary, feels an obligation to help him."

"The shipwreck fifteen years ago," he guessed.

She gave him a quizzical look, and he explained about the conversation he'd had with the mayor.

"Kaz believes she should've been able to save her parents that night. She's felt guilty ever since," she explained.

"Could she have?"

Lucy shook her head. "There were gale force winds that night, and storm surge well over thirty feet. Most of the waves were at least fifty feet, crest to trough. For you landlubbers, that's a five-story building. The miracle is that *she* survived. But the way she sees it, Gary's had a harder time of it, partially because of losing their parents."

"And you don't have any influence over her."

"On a lot of things, sure, but not this."

"Then let's arrest her as a material witness."

Lucy hooted. "That'd last about as long as one phone call to her lawyer ex-boyfriend in California. He'd have her out on bail within a couple of hours."

"Then see to it that you keep her out of my way, or I *will* have her arrested." He nodded at both of them and walked away.

"Well, well," Ivar said.

"What?" Lucy asked.

"Chapman and Kaz. Bad timing, though."

"*What?*" Lucy wondered if her partner had been ingesting too many herbs. "He didn't even sound like he liked her."

Ivar looked amused. "And your point is?"

"Oh, right, crazy me." She gnawed on the idea. "You've heard the stories, right? About how Chapman was placed on administrative leave after the fire that killed his fiancée? And that there was some question as to whether he could've saved the arsonist in the fire six months later?"

"Yup. You telling me you're upset about a serial arsonist who got himself dead?"

"Of course not."

88

"So?"

"So Kaz already has enough problems on her plate without Chapman adding to them."

"Especially if she's being her typical, driven, nosy self," Ivar said, his tone wry. "I noticed you didn't tell Chapman about the rumors Sykes has been hearing regarding the fishermen."

Lucy shrugged. "We don't know whether that's connected to the fire, or even if there's any truth to what the chief has been hearing. I didn't see any point in sending Chapman off in that direction."

"Get real. No one controls where that guy goes but him."

Chapter 9

It was still early afternoon, but as Kaz walked home from the car dealership, the weak winter light was already showing signs of fading. It would take two days to order the window for the SUV and have it installed. With Gary's truck impounded by the cops, she hoped Lucy came through fast.

A patrol car was parked across the street from the bungalow, and she changed course, heading for it. Clint Jackson. So he probably *had* been following her.

"He's not here, Clint," she said when the cop lowered his window. "Go home."

"Now, Kaz, you know I can't do that. My orders are to keep the house under surveillance."

"Why? If Gary sees your car, he'll be gone before you even have a clue he's around."

"Maybe, maybe not." Jackson rested an arm on the edge of the window. "Your brother's not God—we'll get him sooner or later." He bared his teeth in a cold smile. "Collaring your brother could be a damn good move for my career –I'm in line to make detective this year."

Kaz smiled back just as pleasantly. "If memory serves, I used to baby-sit you, didn't I?"

"Go to hell, Kaz."

She walked back across the street. Okay, so not all the cops on the force were like Lucy and Ivar. Some were assholes. If Jackson caught up with Gary before Lucy and Ivar did....Her stomach knotted.

The phone was ringing as she entered the house through the kitchen door. She jogged into the living room to answer it, only to have whoever was on the other end hang up on her. Just what she didn't need right now—some oblivious idiot calling the wrong number, over and over. Her tolerance for idiocy was at an all-time low, starting with her own.

Being attracted to Michael Chapman was the ultimate in stupidity, and reckless, besides. She couldn't understand her apparent inability to function intelligently around him. All she had to do was take one look at that rugged physique and curly dark hair, and all her brains flowed out onto the floor and rolled around like just so many marbles.

She yanked open the refrigerator door and stood there, staring inside. Gary was her only remaining family. His future and happiness were at stake, maybe even his life. And here she was, getting sucker-punched by good looks and a pair of pale blue eyes shadowed by hints of a tragic past—something for which, of course, she'd have way too much empathy. She expelled a breath. *Get a grip.* She couldn't afford to be distracted, no matter how powerful that distraction proved to be.

She gave up on the meager contents of the fridge, grabbed a handful of saltines, and walked back out the kitchen door. Waving cheerfully at Jackson, who flipped her off, she cut across the neighbor's side yard to walk the six blocks downhill to Julie and Ken's house. It was past time that she paid her respects and asked Julie what she could do to help out.

The Lundquists' home was in the Uniontown neighborhood, an older, working-class section of Astoria filled with narrow, multi-story Victorian homes jammed onto a steep hillside above Marine Drive, the main highway through town. Homes in Uniontown might be more modest than their cousins further uphill, but they still commanded a stunning view of the river and the bridge connecting Oregon to Washington. Julie and Ken's house looked neglected, its shades drawn tight. The yard was not as neatly maintained as it had been a couple of months ago. Kaz couldn't hear any sounds from inside but rang the doorbell anyway. After a moment, the door opened.

Julie stood in the doorway, wearing a simple black blouse and black cotton slacks. Her pale brown hair was scrubbed back from her thin face into a ponytail, her hazel eyes bloodshot and red-rimmed. "Kaz." Her tone was lifeless.

"I'm sorry," Kaz offered, spreading her hands in a futile gesture. "I don't even know what to say."

Julie stared at her for a moment and then stood aside. Kaz stepped over the threshold and then halted, her eyes widening. The house was a mess—books and papers strewn about the living room, cushions from the couch ripped open and lying on the floor, lamps toppled and broken. What used to be a pile of paperwork—probably hospital bills—now lay in a haphazard line of loose pages flung across the carpet.

"What in the world?"

"Someone broke in while I was at the funeral home." Julie swiped at a tear, then asked bitterly, "What kind of person robs people while they're arranging for a memorial service?"

"You called the police?"

"No."

Kaz looked around the room, her gut screaming at her. The destruction had a methodical feel to it—someone had been searching for something. "You have to call them, Julie. I can help—stay here with you, if you want. But you need to report this."

"No!" Julie snapped. She seemed to collect herself, drawing a breath, then said more calmly, "No more cops. They were here all morning, asking questions I couldn't answer." Her gaze shifted.

Kaz frowned. "Then let me help you clean up."

"I don't need your help." Julie bent down to retrieve a broken toy and a stack of children's books, keeping her expression hidden. "So why are you here, Kaz? If it's to ease your conscience about what Gary did, then—"

"No, that's not it at all," Kaz replied, surprised. When she tried to help by kneeling to pick up a sheaf of bills, Julie snatched them from her hands. "Julie, had Ken been acting any differently lately? You know, angry, maybe? Or desperate?"

Julie laughed without humor and waved a hand at the dilapidated furniture and threadbare carpets. "Look around. Who *wouldn't* be feeling desperate?"

"I meant, well, more desperate than just the day-to-day stuff."

"The day-to-day stuff is a pile of bills we can't pay, Bobby's chemo treatments, a furnace that decides when and how long it will work..." Julie stared down at the shards of a broken glass lampshade at her feet.

"How *is* Bobby?" Kaz couldn't imagine what it was like to watch a small child struggle with the side effects of chemo. To live daily with the fear that you might outlive your son.

"Bobby's fine," Julie replied, her tone abrupt.

"Gary mentioned that Bobby was having a tough time with side effects."

"That's over or, at least, better."

Kaz took in her closed look, her rigid posture. "Can I help out with the medical bills? Or perhaps babysit when you have to go to Portland?"

"No, look—" Julie stopped and ran a nervous hand over her thin ponytail. "I appreciate it, really I do. But my mom is paying for Bobby's treatments, and I don't want your help, Kaz."

"But—"

"Having you around is a reminder, okay? Of what your family has taken away..." She turned to Kaz, resolute. "Perhaps you should leave."

"Julie, Gary didn't do this, I *know* he didn't."

"I'm sure you'd like to believe that, being his sister and all." Julie nodded. "But Gary hasn't been okay for a long time now. Ken stuck with him out of loyalty, and because no one else would crew for him."

"That's not true," Kaz said, shocked. "I know Gary can be difficult at times—" She took in Julie's mulish expression and changed tactics. "Did Ken tell you what he and Gary had been arguing about?"

"*No,*" Julie said. "Look, Kaz, there's nothing I can do to help you. Ken never said a word to me, other than to mention here and there when Gary had been a jerk on the water that day."

"At least tell me whether Ken came home last night," Kaz pressed.

"No." Julie's face crumpled. "The last time I saw him was early Saturday morning, before they left port. Then I had to go down to the morgue to identify him."

"I'm sorry," Kaz said again, feeling helpless. She turned to go.

"Kaz." Julie's sharpened voice stopped her.

Kaz glanced back.

The young woman trembled with rage, her expression fiercely determined. "If Gary *didn't* kill Ken, then I want to know who did. You find out who the hell did this to my children."

Lucy bounced a tennis ball against the far wall of the squad room while she waited for Ivar to summarize his stack of notes into what she figured was the Master Note he wanted to have with him when they went out to investigate possible murder sites. She'd already rolled her eyes, paced, and tried her best to annoy him in inventive ways, but he wasn't budging. If he spent even five more seconds writing in that neat little script of his, she was going to club him to death with the butt of her service revolver. "You about done?"

"You've already asked me that three times." He never glanced up from his task. "Why don't you go drop off your car for Kaz?"

"I already have, which you would've noticed if you weren't so driven to organize your life to death."

Jim Sykes emerged from his office. She snagged the ball mid-air and dropped it into her drawer. This afternoon, the chief was wearing a tailored, dark blue wool suit, tasteful tie, and spiffy, tasseled loafers. "Where the hell does he get the money for those kinds of clothes?" she muttered out loud, envious that his clothes budget was clearly more substantial than hers.

Ivar glanced up. "Inheritance. His aunt died about a month back."

"Huh."

Seeing them, Sykes rerouted from the coffee pot over to their desks. "McGuire. Status?"

She brought him up to date. "Brenner should have the truck heading for the impound right about now. If there's anything in it, we'll find it."

"What about Jorgensen? Any sign of him?"

She shook her head. "Clint is staking out the house, but so far, no go. We talked to Gary's fishing buddies early this morning, but no one's seen him."

"Talk to his friend Chuck Branson and see if you can pick up any clues. If Jorgensen's headed into the hills, we're better off bringing in the dogs before the scent gets diluted by all this rain."

Lucy made sure she didn't show any alarm. "I don't think

95

we're at the point where we need tracking dogs, Sir."

"Murders are typically solved in the first 48 hours, McGuire, if they're going to be solved at all. And we're already—" he glanced at his watch, which looked as expensive as the rest of his outfit, "—almost twenty hours into the investigation. I don't want anyone dawdling."

"I've still got a number of people I can talk to, who can get a message to Gary so that he can turn himself in, if it comes to that."

"Good." Sykes shoved both hands into his pockets and stared at her. "The Jorgensens are good friends of yours. You got a problem with that? 'Cause if you do, I need to know right now so I can reassign you."

Lucy hesitated. She *did* have a problem with it, but she also wasn't willing to let anyone else on the detectives' squad be charge of the investigation. No matter how difficult it was for her, it was far worse for Kaz and Gary. And it was her fault that Kaz was involved at all.

And the truth was, Lucy couldn't handle having Gary's fate rest in anyone else's hands. Not that she was the world's greatest detective, but she'd never be able to keep her nose out of the investigation, so she might as well make sure it was run fairly, even if that meant she had to be the one to slap the cuffs on Gary. "No, sir. No problem."

"Good." Sykes turned to go, then stopped. "So why are you two still here? Don't you have a murder scene to locate?"

Lucy managed to contain her glee as Ivar hurriedly gathered up the rest of his notes.

Chapter 10

Kaz walked back up the hill to pick up Lucy's car, deep in thought. Julie's attitude had been puzzling—one minute unfriendly, the next nervous and almost afraid. And though Kaz hadn't expected a particularly warm reception, she hadn't realized Julie would assume Gary was guilty. Julie knew how tight he and Ken had been. If she was convinced Gary murdered her husband, did the rest of the town believe that as well? It was a depressing thought.

Kaz didn't believe for one minute that the Lundquists had been the target of a random burglary. Someone had been looking for something. What if Ken had put that 'something' on the *Anna Marie*? And he'd gone back to retrieve it? Had the murderer followed him there?

Kaz reached the edge of her yard. So someone thought that Ken had something valuable, maybe even worth killing for. And Julie possibly knew what it was. Given Gary's argument with Ken in the tavern, it was a safe bet that Gary also knew. But what could it be? The only items Gary and Ken ever handled that were of any value were a few fish.

Eighteen hours after the fire, she hadn't found Gary, and she wasn't any further along in figuring out who had Killed Ken and set the fire. In fact, she was more confused than ever. Some super sleuth she was turning out to be. Clearly, she should stick to consulting with Fortune 500 executives. Even with all their political agendas and power plays, they were turning out to be downright straightforward in comparison to her hometown friends.

She glanced at her watch. They were starting into flood tide, so the fishermen were coming into port soon. They had to know what was going on, what Ken had been mixed up in. Those guys kept track of their own.

Lucy's street car was a shiny black Jeep Cherokee, complete with roll bars, which she rarely pulled out of her garage. The city provided her with a patrol car when she was on duty, and weather permitting, she biked to the police station to stay in shape. Kaz retrieved the keys from underneath the floor mat, climbed in, and cranked the ignition. The engine growled to life, attesting to the excessive amount of horsepower under the hood. The clutch had a different feel than the one in Kaz's SUV, and she burned it more than Lucy would've liked as she backed out of the driveway.

In less than ten minutes, Kaz had parked on the wharf at the mooring basin. Many of the boat slips were still empty, but there was a line of trawlers coming upriver. Her timing was good.

Someone had pulled back the crime scene tape from the parking area so that it now only surrounded the *Anna Marie*. The cops were there with a tow truck, working on Gary's pickup. She tossed Brenner her key to the pickup so that they wouldn't have to jimmy the locks. If she couldn't manage to help Gary in any other way, she could at least keep his repair bills to a minimum.

As she headed toward the docks, she spied Chapman and Zeke on board the burned trawler. Gathering more evidence, no doubt. He kept poking around in her and Gary's lives, and she resented the hell out it. It was all she could do to keep herself from marching right over there and demanding that he let her on board.

Several of the fishermen who'd already made port noticed her approach, and they didn't look happy to see her. She grimaced. Her status seemed to have gone from 'buddy' to 'outsider' in less than a day. Then again, maybe they'd never considered her their buddy; maybe she'd been deluding herself.

Karl Svensen stood at the bow as his crewman brought the trawler up into its slip. "Karl," she called when he drew close enough to hear her. "I need to talk to you for a moment."

"Well, Kaz, that doesn't mean I want to talk to you." He shoved aside a stack of crab pots. "I'm busy."

Karl was the fisherman who had refused to press charges six months ago, even though Gary had broken his jaw. Kaz had never been able to ferret out what the argument had been over. The usual rumors had circulated—one had it that they'd fought over a woman; another, over fishing territory. But Kaz had always believed that Gary had been protecting Ken, which was what Lucy also believed.

Kaz deliberately raised her voice, hoping others would hear. "*Someone* here must know what Gary and Ken were arguing about at the tavern last night."

"We don't tell tales out of school," Svensen retorted. "This doesn't concern you, Kaz."

"The *hell* it doesn't!" She was heartily sick of hearing that. "*My* brother is the one the cops want to pin this on." She looked each one of the crew in the eye, and they dropped their gazes, flushing with embarrassment. Yet no one was forthcoming. "You're Gary's friends," she stressed. "Do you really want him to take the rap for this?"

"Gary hasn't been an easy person to get along with in recent years, Kaz." She turned toward Bjorn Ewald, the captain of one of the larger trawlers and the medical examiner's brother.

Bjorn was a mountain of a man, well over six feet, with red hair and a bushy beard. And he had a huge family to match—

99

eight children at last count. When Gary needed extra crew, Bjorn sometimes lent out one of his teenage sons. Personally, Kaz had always liked Bjorn.

"Maybe not," she acknowledged his comment. "But that doesn't make Gary a murderer." She turned back to Svensen. "Who was standing next to Gary and Ken last night? You, Karl? They were standing near where you always sit."

Svensen uncoiled the bowline and jumped onto the dock to tie off. "Who told you that?"

"So you *were* there."

He shrugged. "I didn't want to tell you, because I knew that if you found out about the argument, it'd upset you."

"Knowing what I'm dealing with is better than not knowing anything at all. What were they arguing about?"

"All I heard was that Gary was real upset with something Ken had done. Ken told him that he hadn't had any choice. And Gary got even madder, told him that if he didn't fix it, he'd be sorry."

Karl's eyes kept darting toward the other fishermen. Was he lying? "Did you talk to Ken?" she asked.

"No."

"Witnesses in the bar say that you weren't exactly uninvolved," she said, taking a shot in the dark.

He climbed back on board his trawler and started stowing gear. His expression was no longer even marginally friendly. "Even if I know more than I've told you, I'm not saying anything else."

"Where were you last night around eight-thirty? You weren't in the bar, I would've seen you."

"Butt out, Kaz."

"I can't do that," she said evenly. "My brother is about to take the fall for something he didn't do."

Karl's smile was cold. "Are you sure about that? I'd rather face down forty-foot waves than your brother, given the mood he's been in. And like I said, I heard him threaten Ken."

Her anger bubbled to the surface. "Are you willing to swear to that in court? Because that's what it will come down to."

He shrugged. "No skin off my nose. You Jorgensens have never done any favors for me."

"I'm not looking for favors, Karl. I'm looking for the truth."

"Yeah, well, I've already told you everything I'm going to, so why don't you take a hike so I can get straightened away and go home to the wife?"

"Fine. If you remember anything else, would you please give me a call?"

"I won't."

She stood there a moment longer, rubbing her forehead to ease the headache that was starting to pound, then turned to leave. Bjorn came out of his trawler's engine room, rubbing grease off his hands with a rag. "Don't pay any attention to Karl," he said, his voice low so that it wouldn't carry. "He's grumpy because his catch has been so light lately."

Kaz searched his face, but all she saw was concern for her. Bjorn hated to see people at odds. "Are you sure that's all it is?"

His expression turned wary. "I don't know anything, if that's what you're asking."

"Don't know, or won't say?"

"Kaz..."

She made an angry gesture with her hand. "Never mind. When push comes to shove, you guys don't seem very willing to help one of your own."

"That's not true, and you know it."

"Do I? I'm asking a lot of questions, but no one's giving me any answers."

"You were gone a long time."

"I'm still part of this community, dammit."

"Give it time—the guys will come around. You've already made a difference on the insurance and other stuff you've

101

helped the guys with, and they know it. But people are slow to trust around here in recent years."

Kaz stared out across the river, her hands on her hips. "Yeah, well, time's up. Gary needs help *right now*, and you guys aren't exactly riding to his rescue."

"Has it occurred to you that the best thing you can do is to stay out of it?"

"I don't believe that."

Bjorn fiddled with the netting on a crab pot, then seemed to come to a decision. "The rumors are true," he said in a low voice.

Kaz felt a chill ripple down her spine. "What rumors?"

"Some of these guys are involved. You've got to stay out of it, Kaz. You could be in real danger. Let the cops handle it."

"Who's involved?"

"No way. Even if I knew for sure, I wouldn't tell you. I won't be the cause of you ending up badly hurt, or worse, dead. Ken was *killed,* Kaz. And these guys think he was murdered to send a message."

"Is Gary involved?" she asked, her voice harsh with urgency. "Do you know what Ken was into?"

Bjorn shook his head. "Look, I've already said more than I should have. I'll check your crab pots for you, if you want. That's all I can do, for now."

She stared at him, frustrated, then shook her head. "I'm scheduled to go out tomorrow, but thanks for the offer."

Kaz turned to make the return trip to Lucy's 4x4, then veered toward the *Anna Marie* instead. When Chapman noticed her approach, he came over to the dockside railing. Silhouetted against the late afternoon light with his face in the shadows, he looked every inch the tough investigator—hard, maybe even a little dangerous. This was a man who kept going until he got the answers he wanted, no matter how long it took or who got in his way. Normally, she appreciated—even respected—that kind of tenacity. Normally.

Something stirred within her at the sight of him. She ruthlessly squelched it. No sane woman would ever get involved with a man like Chapman. He was carrying around a boatload of baggage, just like she was. That alone made him someone she should be wary of. And if he decided to, he could put Gary away for life.

"I need to come on board to start assessing the damage, make a plan for repairs," she told him, taking the offensive.

He shook his head. "Not an option. The boat is still a crime scene."

She stared across the river, trying to control her runaway emotions. So far, the day had little to recommend it. And she was having a hard time, all of the sudden, holding it together. Maybe she was still suffering from the effects of smoke inhalation. That might be why she was exhausted and felt...fragile. God! She hated feeling this way.

"I've spent the last ten years creating solutions to problems and implementing them." She tried to control the tremor in her voice. "It's what I'm good at. Waiting, on the other hand, is something I don't do well."

"Imagine my surprise."

She gave him a sharp look, her tolerance for sarcasm at an all-time low. "The business can't afford to have one of the trawlers out of commission for any length of time," she said through gritted teeth. "I need to get on the *Anna Marie*. Now. And I don't think you have the authority to keep me off her for very much longer."

Chapman studied her thoughtfully; she really, really hoped he couldn't see how tightly she was strung. He seemed to come to some kind of decision. "I could use a helper for gathering evidence. That would get you on board—but not give you totally free rein. How's that sound?"

"Do you even need to ask?"

He held up a hand to stop her from jumping on board. "You'll do *what* I say, *when* I say it, and you'll do it *exactly* the way I tell you to. Agreed?"

"Deal."

An hour later, they were standing on soggy, blackened carpet in the galley of the *Anna Marie,* working as quickly as they could to beat the approaching darkness. Zeke was watching from the burned upper edge of the deck with what Kaz could have sworn was an expression of self-pity. He wanted to be involved.

"What are we looking for?" she asked Chapman, poking through bits of charred timbers and ashes.

She needed a distraction, so that she didn't break down and cry. She'd never considered herself the sentimental type, but seeing the destruction on the *Anna Marie* up close was hard. Huge sections of the deck had burned through and collapsed into the compartments below. Netting from the spool resembled a melted mass of goo on the floor of the hold. And the beautiful woodwork that she'd hand-sanded and painted in the family colors, now resembled charred sticks.

The wheelhouse was still standing, but the floor of the flying bridge above was buckled and unstable. All the equipment— radar, short-wave radios, sonar—was gone. And that was just the inventory of what had to be repaired and replaced. Who was going to restore the essence of the *Anna Marie?* She'd been a companion on thousands of trips, part of so many of the good memories Kaz and Gary shared.

Chapman straightened and held out a shiny object. "This is the type of item I'm looking for." She struggled to remember what they'd been talking about. "It's the padlock from the door between the engine room and the galley, correct?" he asked.

She leaned closer, then nodded. It was in remarkably good condition—she would've thought it would've melted in the high temperatures.

"It was probably protected by the falling wood to some extent, and the fire would have burned with less heat down here than up top where the accelerant was," he said, reading her mind.

She examined the padlock more closely in the waning light.

"What?"

"See these scratches?" She pointed to the marred surface around the keyhole. "Those weren't there before." The significance of those scratches hit her. "Wait. That means whoever opened it didn't have a key. So it couldn't have been Gary."

Michael nodded slowly. "Possibly. Unfortunately, it doesn't exonerate him."

"What do you mean, it doesn't? It's clear proof!"

"Ken could've done this—he didn't have a key. Correct?"

"But what possible reason did Ken have to get into the hold of the boat late at night? And for that matter, what reason could he have that he didn't want Gary to know about? All he had to do was ask to use his keys."

"Not if they'd been fighting. And these scratches could've been put here any time in the last several weeks—maybe on a day when Gary forgot his keys. But it certainly opens up the possibility that someone was after something."

Perhaps the same *someone* who had broken into the Lundquist home. She started to tell Chapman her suspicions about the burglary, then held back. She was afraid he would think Gary had done it. This could all be used against him to build a case against him. Her shoulders sagged.

Chapman bagged the padlock and put it in a briefcase he'd brought to the boat. His tone holding a hint of sympathy, he said, "I'll have it checked for fingerprints; maybe we'll get lucky." He turned to study the area surrounding the berths. Most of the decking had fallen onto that area. "Which berth did you find Ken in?"

Kaz thought back, reliving those first moments as she'd tried to find Gary, choking and blinded by the thick smoke. She shuddered. "I landed about here," she said, pointing. "Then I crawled..." She turned, her finger following her path of the night before. "...it has to be the starboard berth. I pulled him out of the bunk and he fell against that storage locker."

Chapman paused, then nodded. "That matches my memory of where I picked him up." He picked his way around the winch, which had landed in the center of the galley when it had fallen through the deck, and started removing burned timbers from the berth.

Kaz moved over to help him, but he waved her back. "Stay back—I'll hand wood out to you, and I need you to stack it neatly in one pile. Then I'll get the lab guys back out here to go over everything."

She huffed a little but did as he directed. They worked for several minutes in surprisingly companionable silence, with Zeke whining every once in a while, becoming more and more impatient with his inactivity.

After Michael had cleared the worst of the timbers, he knelt down and surveyed the area without touching it. "We're in luck," he said quietly. "A lot of the berth is still here—just scorched. And I could be wrong, but I'm not seeing any obvious bloodstains."

Kaz craned her neck to look over his shoulder. Why did he think bloodstains were so important?

"Head wounds bleed a lot," he said, answering her unspoken question. "And there was a lot of blood on Ken's clothing. If there are no correspondingly large bloodstains on the berth, then it confirms the cops' theory that Ken was killed elsewhere and moved onto the boat. And that's premeditated arson."

Kaz stared at him, her throat closing. "No matter what else

Gary could've done, he's incapable of planning to burn the *Anna Marie*," she managed. Chapman looked at her, his expression both grim and...pitying.

She turned away, walked over to the stairs, and sat down among the soggy debris. "I know you don't believe me, but deep down, Gary has a good soul. What he had to do in the Army tore him apart inside. He didn't do any of this—I *know* it."

Chapman opened his mouth to speak, but his cell phone chirped. He reached into his pocket, pulled it out, and flipped it open. "Chapman...yeah, I'm down at the boat right now...interesting. I'll come by in a bit—I want to see for myself." He disconnected and turned to Kaz. "Let's get moving. I've got to drop by the police impound lot, and we're done here until I can get the lab guys back."

She wanted to ask him about the call, but seeing the closed expression on his face, she didn't even bother to try. "When can I dry-dock the *Anna Marie?*" she asked instead.

"Not yet."

Chapter 11

By the time Kaz pulled into her driveway, twilight lurked on the edges of the clouds. The wind had picked up, splattering occasional raindrops against the windshield. Below her in the downtown district, the outlines of old brick buildings stood silhouetted against the fading light. Out on the river, running lights glittered on the fishing trawlers, illuminating their wakes as they chugged upstream. Two large freighters were anchored for the night off the waterfront, their towering hulks dwarfing the other vessels.

A car door slammed, and she glanced in the rear view mirror. Lucy had driven up and parked behind her. Kaz climbed tiredly out of the Jeep and followed her into the kitchen.

Lucy hunted through the refrigerator, pulling two bottles of beer out and handing one plus a pizza box to Kaz. "I figured you'd forget to eat. Where're the paper towels?"

Kaz pointed to the far counter and then sat down, placing the pizza box in the middle of the table. She propped her elbows on the table and scrubbed her face with both hands, attempting to get her brain to function. "I need to keep the Jeep for a couple of days. Don't ask why."

"Why?"

"If I tell you, you'll yell."

"I've just spent two hours scraping concrete and digging in the mud. Make my day—I could use someone to yell at right about now."

Kaz sniffed. "I'm no punching bag."

"Yeah, but as my friend, it's your duty to be there for me." Lucy handed her a slice of pizza on a paper towel. "Rumor has it that your SUV is at the dealer's, missing a window. Since you're still among the living—though not necessarily sounding like it—I won't ask if you were in danger."

"That would be good."

"Kaz..." Lucy shook her head. She took a large bite, and her eyes closed. "There *is* a Higher Being, and she believes in the sanctity of junk food. Don't you want to know *why* I was digging in the mud?"

Kaz stared at her slice of pizza, trying to work up an appetite. "Is it okay to tell me?"

"Of course not—I'll have to kill you right after dinner." Lucy gave her a quick rundown. "My big find of the day was a snow globe."

Kaz shot out a hand, grasping Lucy's arm before she could take another bite. "Describe it."

Lucy rolled her eyes. "Geez, Jorgensen. It was a little glass ball—you know, with the little bits of snow inside?"

"A white fishing trawler on a blue sea?"

"Whoa." Lucy quickly sobered. "Tell me how you know that."

Relief flowed through Kaz, almost making her giddy. "I gave it to Ken last week, for Bobby."

"Yesss." Lucy pumped her fist in the air and reached for her cell phone. "Ivar? Listen up: Pull the concrete and mud samples from under the bridge. Make them top priority. And meet me there in a half hour." She hung up. "You know what this means, right?"

Kaz nodded. "If Ken was killed by the bridge, Gary couldn't have done it—he didn't have enough time. The murder scene is on the other end of town from the *Anna Marie*."

"Exactly." Lucy gnawed on her lower lip. "So we see if we can link the mud and concrete from the bridge to the samples from the autopsy. If it's a match, we're one step closer to proving Gary didn't do it. But we'll need more than that to convince Sykes." She took another bite of pizza. "How're you holding up?"

Kaz put her slice down, reality sinking back in. And with that, the gnawing sense of desperation that she'd been feeling all day long. "Gary's holed up somewhere, Luce, and I can't figure out why. If he didn't do this, then someone may have been trying to kill *him,* not Ken. And so far, I'm doing a damn poor job of helping him."

"My guess is that if he needs help, he knows where to find it. Gary's got people all over who'll help him and keep quiet about it."

"Julie Lundquist told me that no one but Ken was willing to crew for him anymore, and the guys at the marina indicated pretty much the same."

"That's pure bunk. And Gary's got buddies from the military in several of the neighboring towns. The fishermen may not be real happy with him right now, but I think that's related to what's going on."

Kaz's panic subsided a little. Lucy was right—Gary knew several vets who lived up in the hills, which meant he had access to supplies for as long as he needed to hide out. Long enough for Kaz to ferret out who could've done this. She should've realized that herself, which was one more sign she wasn't firing on all cylinders. If she could get some sleep and then keep digging for answers—

Lucy gave her a scowl. "I do *not* like the look on your face. You need to take a step back and let me handle this."

Kaz kept silent.

"I mean it," Lucy insisted. "I need to conduct the investigation by the book—it's Gary's best hope of coming out

110

of this cleared of any wrongdoing." She pointed a finger smudged with tomato sauce at Kaz. "And you need to quit letting guilt about what happened fifteen years ago color your judgment."

Kaz shook her head. "Gary hasn't had the breaks I've had. And I haven't been here for him."

Lucy snorted. "He got himself into this, he can get himself back out. I was wrong to ever make that phone call to you."

"You know he won't last even one night in jail."

"He should've thought of that before now. Hell, he should've thought about that six months ago when he punched out Svensen for dissing Ken."

"Do you think the two incidents are related?"

Lucy looked thoughtful, then shook her head. "...nah. How could they be? Too much elapsed time." Her expression became grim. "I saw the photos from the fire."

Kaz's stomach clenched. "Did you say anything to Michael Chapman?"

"I've managed to avoid him for the last couple of hours."

Abandoning any pretense of eating, Kaz kicked back from the table, staring out the window at the garden that Gary had maintained for her all these years, which now looked bedraggled in the late winter rains. "Chapman's all but convinced Gary did it—he's just looking for evidence to convict, at this point."

"Yeah." Lucy sighed. "That was my impression, too. He thinks you're withholding evidence from him. Are you?"

Kaz hesitated, then shrugged. "Nothing important."

"If you know *anything,* you should tell us." When she didn't respond, Lucy glared at her. "I don't believe this—you're keeping *me* in the dark? You won't let me help?"

"Chapman outranks you—"

"Like that's ever stopped me before. That guy gets in my way, I'll mow him down."

Kaz chuckled and held the cold beer bottle against her forehead, trying to ease her headache. "This is where I'm supposed to be grateful you're armed and have poor impulse control, right?"

"Hey, that's why I joined the force. I figure if I lose it and shoot someone, they probably had it coming."

"Just as long as the person you shoot isn't my brother."

Lucy sobered. "You know I wouldn't do that. I could never hurt Gary."

Kaz studied her friend's face, seeing the truth there. She'd always wondered, in the back of her mind, whether Lucy had a thing for her brother. But if she did, she'd kept it well hidden over the years. Which wouldn't exactly be in character.

Lucy wiped her hands with a paper towel and picked up her beer. "We executed a search warrant at the Lundquists' today. God! That was hard."

Kaz frowned. "What were you looking for?"

"Anything related to the crime—it was a general warrant. The place was a mess. I thought Julie usually kept it pretty neat and clean."

"She does. Someone tossed it."

"What?"

Kaz shifted in her chair, realizing what she'd given away. "I went up there earlier, to pay my respects—"

"And to pry information out of the poor woman."

"—right. And she told me she'd been burgled. Wouldn't let me call you or help clean up. What are the chances of a burglary—"

"Happening coincidentally the day after Ken was killed?" Lucy shook her head. "Slim to none."

"Yeah, that's what I thought. I wonder what they were after."

Lucy picked up another piece of pizza and contemplated it. "Do you think Gary broke in and had a look around?"

"I hope not." Kaz considered, then shook her head. "I don't think so."

"So," Lucy mused, chewing slowly. "What could Ken have that someone would want? Something small enough they'd tear apart the house looking for it? Shit. This case gets weirder by the hour."

Kaz stood up and got them another beer. Beer seemed to be all her stomach was accepting without staging a rebellion. At this rate, she'd be on Pabulum with alcohol chasers by morning.

"What's your take on Chapman so far?" Lucy dug into her third slice of pizza, obviously having no such problems.

Kaz hesitated. "Why are you asking me?"

"*Hell.* Ivar is right—you two have a thing going."

"We do not! Chapman's too stubborn and overbearing and—"

"Sexy?" Lucy leaned forward, dropping her pizza. "Please tell me you are *not* interested in this guy."

"It's just chemistry. No big deal."

"I'm serious. We don't know jack about him, except that he lost it on some arson investigation back East. Well, okay, and that he's related to the Boston Police Commissioner."

"Whoa." Kaz took a moment to absorb that little factoid. "You told me he was an arson investigator. You didn't say anything about him being associated with the police."

"He isn't. But the latest info that's floating around on him is that the police commissioner was his guardian during his formative years. His parents were killed in a car crash, or something, and the commissioner was a family friend who stepped in to keep him and his brothers out of foster homes."

"Where do you *hear* this stuff?"

Lucy shrugged. "Ivar told me, and he heard it from somebody on the force, who probably heard it from someone in the Mayor's office...you know how this shit gets around."

"So Gary and I are up against an experienced arson investigator who just happens to have deep ties to law enforcement." Kaz shook her head, closing her eyes as depression settled over her like a wet bank of fog. "Just shoot me now."

"The point being," Lucy continued in a stern tone, "that it wouldn't be smart to get involved with Chapman right now, or even—speaking from a purely one-night-stand-no-attachments point of view—jump his bones." She twisted the cap off her beer and lobbed it into the trash. "Not, mind you, that he doesn't have very nice bones. And not that you'd ever be practical enough to consider sex as a recreational sport instead of the first step toward Happily Ever After."

"Phil would argue that my failure to commit was the reason we broke up," Kaz pointed out, experiencing the twinge of guilt and sadness that surfaced whenever she thought her ex-boyfriend. "I'd say that makes me commitment-phobic, not the other way around."

"Yeah? Well, Phil's a twit. A good lawyer, maybe, but definitely a twit."

A laugh sputtered out of Kaz. "Come on. He's a nice guy."

Lucy just snorted. "Chapman's definitely *not* a twit, but until we have a chance to see how this guy really handles himself..." She gave Kaz a reprimanding look.

"Okay," Kaz admitted. "So I looked a little more closely at Michael Chapman than usual, but that's all. I'm not dead, but I'm also not crazy."

"Since when?" Lucy shot back, then harrumphed. "So tell me what you really think of him."

Kaz took a moment to think about it. "He doesn't know the people involved," she mused, "so it's easy for him to think that Gary's the obvious suspect. Whether he'll keep digging if there are unanswered questions..." she waggled her hand to indicate that she thought he might go either way. "For some reason, my gut is telling me that he's honorable, that he'll work to find out the truth. But you know how good my instincts are when it comes to men."

"The track record from hell."

"Hey."

"Well, it's not like any of those 'suits' you dated down south—including Phil—had any redeeming qualities, other than their ability to pay for tickets to the symphony."

"Oh, come on."

"And, of course, you've been deluded for the last ten years as to what constitutes quality of life," Lucy added, "or else you wouldn't have even stayed down in La-La Land.

"Nice to know you have such a high opinion of me and my chosen life style," Kaz said, her tone dry.

"*Prior* chosen life style. Now that you're back, I don't see you packing your bags and heading back any time soon. Am I right?"

At the moment, Kaz couldn't even think about a permanent move back home. It was a decision she had no idea how to make, or even when she would be able to make it. Her partner was doing a good job so far of handling the business issues that had cropped up, but sooner or later, she'd have to go back. Even if she'd noticed since coming home that it felt right, somehow, to be here, she couldn't take the time to sort it all out.

Oblivious to Kaz's inner turmoil, Lucy rolled right on, her expression turning more business-like. "I'll keep an eye on Chapman. But stay away from him, and let me handle him."

"That won't be easy. He thinks he can get to Gary by following me around."

"Gee, I'd say the man isn't dumb. You *do* know where Gary is, right?"

Kaz hesitated. "Maybe."

"If I were Gary," Lucy mused, "I'd head for the high country around Saddleback Mountain. He's camped in that area for years, and he knows how to lose himself up there. And up near the peak, it's damn near vertical, which would discourage all but seasoned climbers from following him." When Kaz didn't say anything, Lucy nodded and stood up, closing the pizza box and carrying it over to the door. "Try not to get shot at again while you're in my Jeep. It isn't paid off yet."

"Thanks for the pizza and conversation," Kaz said, meaning it.

"Yeah, I can tell you were wild about the pizza." Lucy shook her head. "Let's just get through this, so we can get back to our nightly pool game. I'm starting to go into withdrawal."

Later that evening, Kaz's phone rang for the umpteenth time that day. She'd already taken a long bath and finished her third beer, which had gone straight to her head. Miles Davis was playing "Kind of Blue" in the background, and she was stringing her seventh crab pot while she tried to formulate her strategy for the next day. She was beyond exhausted, but still jumping out of her skin. She glared at the phone, ignoring it.

It rang again.

"Dammit!" It was probably another hang-up. But whoever it was, they weren't giving up—the phone continued to ring shrilly.

Sighing, she dropped the spool of steel mesh wire inside the crab pot's iron frame, then stood and started hunting for the portable in the mess of newspapers and printouts on the coffee table. On the eighth ring, she unearthed the unit and punched the little green button. "Yes, hello."

There was no sound on the other end, except for someone breathing. After a long moment, she heard a click, and then a dial tone.

Suddenly uneasy, she carefully placed the phone on the coffee table and backed away from it.

Chapter 12

Downtown at Astoria's main fire station, Michael tossed his pencil on top of his notes and sketches relating to the investigation. He reached down to pet Zeke, who snored peacefully from his favorite place under the desk.

The station was quiet in the evening. Since the Astoria Fire Department was made up largely of volunteers, the firehouses weren't manned around the clock. Instead, on-call firefighters kept their gear with them.

Michael liked it that way. It gave him undisturbed time to think through the complexities of an investigation. To get inside the arsonist's head, to feel the guy's excitement as he'd lit the match or set the timer.

He read through his notes once more, frowning. So far, the forensic evidence was inconclusive. The lab techs were comparing the human hair they'd found to the victim's, and the unofficial word was that it probably wasn't a match. The hair was blond, a possible match to either Kaz or Gary. But Astoria had a huge Nordic population, so that was hardly conclusive. DNA tests weren't yet complete, so Michael wouldn't know for certain for another day or so.

He'd spent the dinner hour interviewing the fishermen as they came into port, and he'd come away with one overriding impression—that they were afraid. What could possibly have these fishermen—who braved some of the world's most dangerous waters—*that* spooked? And talking to Lundquist's widow and the bartender at the Redemption had been even less illuminating.

Michael had a whole town full of people who weren't talking. Even if he cut them some slack for being wary of outsiders, their reaction was still extreme. This town had a secret, one that caused people to clam up tight. He'd seen real fear in the eyes of the fishermen and the bartender. Something—or some*one*—was putting a lot of pressure on them.

The detective in charge of the case, McGuire, was acting like she had a good idea of what was going down, but even *she* was holding out on him. And the other one, the tall, thin quiet one, seemed to be content to take most of his direction from McGuire. So much for cooperation between the departments. Who was McGuire protecting? The Jorgensens, the fishermen, or all of the above?

He picked up his sketch of the fire and stared at it one more time. Pools of gasoline had been dumped on both the fore and aft decks, resulting in the caved-in sections over the hold and the forecastle. The crewman's body had been lying directly under the largest pool of gasoline, virtually guaranteeing that the deck would cave and burn the body. There was no doubt in Michael's mind that the arsonist had intended to leave very little forensic evidence behind.

Michael smiled grimly. The torch had miscalculated there— he hadn't foreseen Kaz's determination. If she'd shown up a few minutes later, they'd be matching dental records, or DNA from bone marrow, to ID Lundquist. She was also damn lucky to be alive, and the thought of what could've happened if Michael had arrived only a few minutes later was still giving him waking nightmares.

The torch had also poured streamers down the stairs and through the engine room to the galley, breaching two locked doors. Lundquist's wife had verified that no one except Kaz and her brother had keys to those doors. Both locks showed signs of having been tampered with recently, which might be a point in Gary Jorgensen's favor.

Tipping the scales in the other direction, however, were the records on Jorgensen's military training, which had finally arrived a few hours ago via email. Although most of the material had been deleted for security purposes, the type of training he'd received had been clearly documented. Jorgensen could've set that fire in his sleep, with very little forethought or planning. And if he'd had quick access to a space heater, then Michael could no longer argue that the method of ignition required advanced planning. Jorgensen could've simply killed in a rage and then covered it up.

But at this point, Michael had more inconsistencies and unknowns than he had evidence. Like the fact that Lundquist's body had been moved after he'd been killed, possibly from a location that wouldn't have given Jorgensen the time to do the crime. Like those two scratched locks. And it was those inconsistencies that were giving Michael heartburn.

Then again, maybe his heartburn was caused by Kaz. The more time he spent around her, the more he was starting to care about her. Okay, certainly the way she looked invited him to indulge in a few fantasies. But the way her mind worked— *that* was the real turn-on, and that *was* scary. She was smart, savvy, and...not boring, he realized. Kaz was...fascinating. Challenging. *Hell.* The woman was part of the investigation. End of story.

She knew more than she was letting on—she'd seen something in one of the photos. And if McGuire had seen what Kaz had, she wasn't letting on. He'd gone over and over the snapshots, but he couldn't figure out what—or who—had caught Kaz's attention. Dammit, he didn't trust her. And what had him truly worried was that he wasn't sure his libido cared.

He sighed, leaning back in his chair. What was it about

119

moving to a new town that made a person think about new possibilities? Possibilities that he'd never let himself consider in recent years? Ever since Jessica's death, he'd avoided long-term relationships. Anyone close to him could become a target, and that was reason enough, to his way of thinking, to steer clear of commitment. If his actions on this investigation ended up putting Kaz at risk, he'd never be able to live with himself.

He knew his buddies back East thought he'd crossed the line the night he'd finally run to ground his fiancée's killer. Michael would never be able to prove that he'd acted honorably. Going into the warehouse alone had been a mistake, because there'd been no witness to corroborate his version of what had really gone down inside that burning building. The guy had had a death wish—he'd had no intention of going back to jail. Michael would have to live with the rumors for the rest of his life.

He scrubbed a hand over his face and picked up his cell phone, speed-dialing, then waiting for the pick-up on the other end. "Hey, Mac. Still playing politics?"

His long-time friend and police captain in Boston snorted. "Every chance I get. You know how I love kissing ass. Especially your surrogate papa's."

David Waltham, Boston's Police Commissioner, hadn't been happy when Michael had informed him of his plans to move to Astoria. After trying unsuccessfully to change Michael's mind, he'd started targeting Mac, his theory evidently being that Mac could convince Michael to come back home.

"So when *are* you moving back, pal?" Mac asked, breaking into Michael's thoughts. "We've got a pool going on how long you're gonna last out there in the boonies, and I need some insider information here—I could use the cash."

Michael smiled. The guys hadn't changed—if nothing else came to mind, they'd bet on when the first raindrop hit the sidewalk outside. "You're gonna lose this one, Mac. I'm not coming back."

"Oh, man, do *not* tell me that. I'll have to quit my job or else get myself fired."

"You want me to tell him to lay off?"

"Hell, no. I'm getting a kick out of it. For once, the commissioner isn't getting his way. It's about damn time."

Michael couldn't argue with that. He'd be forever grateful that David had stepped into the void left by his parents' deaths, but that didn't mean that the years he'd lived in David's house had been easy ones. Waltham was smart and powerful, and he had one of the most forceful personalities Michael had ever come up against. It wouldn't hurt David to lose a few battles now and again.

"I need a favor, Mac."

He heard his friend sit up in his chair, probably taking his feet off the jumble of papers that always littered his desk. Michael envisioned the serious, all-business expression that had transformed Mac's easy-going looks. When Mac took notice, no one could beat his laser-like concentration. "Name it."

"I need you to check around quietly, see if you can find out who's been checking into my background."

Mac let out a low whistle. "What the hell's going on, buddy?"

"Just a little arson and murder, timed a little too conveniently." He waited while Mac swore, then continued. "It could be nothing—I'm just being cautious."

Mac harrumphed. "Like your instincts on this crap are ever wrong." There was a moment of silence. "You all right?"

"Yeah."

"Maybe the commissioner is right—maybe you *should* come home."

"Quit worrying," he reassured his friend. "I'm up against someone who's clever, that's all. Just get me that info, and I'll be fine."

"If you say so." Mac sounded dubious. "Hey. Maybe I should take a trip out there, check the place out."

"And here I was thinking the commissioner was the only one acting over-protective."

"Okay, okay, I can take a hint." Mac sighed. "You got a name you want me to run through the computers?"

"Not yet. But send me some coffee beans."

"You're shitting me."

"Two pounds of my special blend, from the shop in Faneuil Hall."

"Christ. Do I need to send them by overnight messenger?"

"I'm not made of money. Send it priority mail—I can wait that long." Just. Michael already planned to dip into Kaz's stash whenever he could until his own arrived. But he didn't mention that to Mac—he didn't want his friend getting curious. The next thing he'd hear was that they were betting back in Boston on how soon he'd be getting laid.

He talked to Mac for a few more minutes, catching up on some of the gossip back home, then ended the call with a promise to check back in a day or two.

He leaned back in his chair, thinking about how badly he needed the break he'd counted on but wasn't getting because of this case. When it was over, he promised himself, he'd use some power tools. Knock out a wall or three. Then he'd be back to normal. That is, if he could figure out what constituted 'normal' these days.

He heard a car door slam outside. The chief of police, Jim Sykes, loomed on the other side of the glass door. Michael waved him in, and the police chief opened the door, walking into Michael's office.

"Working late only a few days into the job, eh?" he asked Michael.

"No choice in the matter." Michael gestured to an empty

chair beside his desk. "Have a seat." Zeke lifted his head and moaned low in his throat, and Michael gave him a soft command. The dog subsided but didn't go back to sleep.

While Sykes settled in, Michael examined his reaction to the man. The way he'd felt last night hadn't been a fluke—he didn't like the guy, but he couldn't put his finger on why. On the surface, Sykes seemed okay. A little overzealous, maybe, but dedicated to his job. And Michael understood overzealous— he'd seen a lot of colleagues in Boston act the same way.

The police chief drew out a slim cigar. He raised his eyebrows, and Michael kept his expression even while he unearthed a used coffee cup to serve as an ashtray.

He had a real hatred of smoke in any of its forms. Most arson investigators didn't feel that way—they actually *liked* the smell of smoke. And many of them were three-pack-a-day addicts, feeling a genuine affection for anything that burned.

"Came by to welcome you to the community," Sykes said after lighting up. "It's great to have someone with your background in town."

"Thanks." Despite his tailored suit and expensive haircut, Sykes had the look of a man who drank too much. The flesh around his eyes was puffy and his cheeks were webbed with numerous small, red blood vessels. Then again, a lot of cops drank.

Sykes settled more comfortably in his chair. "I have to admit, I had an agenda for stopping by tonight. I'm hoping to convince you to join the Big Brothers here in Astoria. The program has a special place in my heart, and I make a point of asking all my officers to spend some time with the more disadvantaged kids in the community, to let them see that we're more than just a uniform, that we're human beings, too."

His request took Michael a little by surprise, though now that he thought about it, it made sense. Given his childhood struggles, Sykes would be particularly sensitive to the

123

problems of children who grew up without good role models at home.

"I don't know." Michael hesitated. "I was an only child—I'm not sure I know how to be a Big Brother."

"Not a problem. I want these kids to start a dialogue with us now, before they get started down the wrong path."

"I'd be of more help after I've been here for awhile, once I have a better feel for the community."

"Once you get your feet wet, you'll do fine," Sykes assured him. "Both as a role model and as a fire chief. Think about it—that's all I'm asking. You can give me your answer later."

Michael nodded.

"People around here *do* take time to warm up to newcomers, though. We've had a lot of folks move out here and then leave within a year or two. So we tend to hold back some in the beginning." He drew on his cigar, then tapped some ash into the cup. "Give it a while—you'll find folks a lot more willing to talk to you."

"I doubt this investigation can wait that long," Michael said wryly.

"Which is the other reason why I stopped by, to suggest you take it easy on this one. Let the police be the primaries. We've got a lot of history with Jorgensen—he's been on my radar for a long time."

Did Sykes want him out of the way? And if so, why? Simple territorial jealousy? Career aspirations? Given what the mayor had told Michael, the career angle made sense.

"I know you're aware that Jorgensen has a police record," Michael said conversationally, not commenting on Sykes' suggestion.

Michael had pulled Jorgensen's police record earlier that afternoon—Gary had a lot of arrests, but the only conviction was for the one assault, and it hadn't carried any jail time. Kaz might've been right about that arrest—there was something that didn't smell kosher about it. And when Michael had asked the bartender at the Redemption about it, he'd clammed up. Fast.

Sykes nodded. "There were a couple of fights on the waterfront, run-ins with my guys on several occasions, and, of course, the assault charge. My opinion? Jorgensen's a tinder keg waiting to blow."

"Still, it's quite a leap from a bar fight to murder and arson. Are you convinced he did it?"

"We found a tire iron with blood on it and a pile of gasoline-soaked rags under a stack of crab pots in the back of his pickup truck. I've got what I need to charge him with first degree murder and first degree arson, and I'll be drawing up the warrant as soon as the lab reports come back."

Michael was silent while he digested this new information. "Do you think that's wise?" he asked finally. "The investigation isn't complete, in terms of the fire or the crime scene."

"We've got enough to move forward." Sykes exhaled an acrid cloud of blue-tinted smoke, and then leaned forward, his expression turning less amiable. "Jorgensen's been a danger to this community for years, and I want him off the streets. If I hadn't pulled him off that fisherman six months ago, he'd have killed him."

Zeke whined. Sykes raised an eyebrow.

"He doesn't like smoke." Michael placed a hand on Zeke's neck to soothe him. "You had any success locating Jorgensen?"

"Not yet, but we will," the police chief said, his tone confident. "He can't hide forever in a community this small. And he'll get in touch with Kaz eventually—he won't be able to help himself. Those two are like peas in a pod."

"I'm new to the community, admittedly, but it was my impression that folks around here like the Jorgensen twins. Wouldn't you be better off, in terms of community relations, waiting until all the evidence is in before arresting him?"

Sykes waved off that suggestion. "Kaz and Gary got a lot of sympathy when their parents drowned, but that doesn't make them saints. In my opinion, this town has been going too easy on them for a long time. Kaz's always been a little too loose with her favors, you know what I mean? She had quite the reputation in high school."

Michael managed to not react, and to stay seated. He'd always disliked men who talked about women as if they were lower-class citizens. But this was the first time he'd had to restrain himself from smashing in a guy's face. "I don't imagine that has much bearing on the case," was all he said, but someone who knew him well would've been wary of the change in his tone.

"Maybe, maybe not. I've always figured that someone with loose morals is capable of anything. There's no doubt in my mind that she'd help that brother of hers get away with this, if we give her the chance."

Sykes's reasoning sucked, but his conclusion was unfortunately valid. Michael started to tell the police chief about the inconsistencies that were cropping up, but for some reason, he stopped himself. He didn't mention the shooting, or that he was worried about Kaz's safety. He realized that he didn't want Sykes anywhere near Kaz, even if he was the chief of police, and even if he had the reputation of being the town's savior. He'd take his concerns to McGuire and her partner.

"I heard that you and Gary Jorgensen have some personal history," Michael mentioned, interested to see if he could get a rise out of the guy.

Sykes' eyes went flat. "You wouldn't, by any chance, be suggesting that I'm letting personal feelings get in the way of doing my job."

"Of course not."

The tension in the room was thicker than the fog that was rolling in off the water. Zeke growled, and Michael tightened his grip on the shepherd's collar.

Sykes' cell phone rang, breaking the silence. Without taking his eyes off Michael, he reached two thick fingers into his pocket and pulled out the phone, flipping it open. "Yeah." He listened for a minute. "I'll be right there," he said, then pocketed the instrument. "You want to be real careful about suggesting things you don't know much about," he told Michael, his tone deceptively soft.

Michael didn't respond. If Sykes was merely another small-town cop acting aggressively for the sake of his career, then Michael was making an enemy he could ill afford. But the remark about Kaz had set him off, and he found it hard to regret his actions.

Sykes leaned over, deliberately dropping his cigar into Michael's coffee. "You're new in town, Chapman, so I'll cut you some slack. This time. But don't ask me something like that ever again."

"Is that a threat?" Michael asked calmly.

"Count on it." Sykes stood, forcing Michael to rise from his chair. "I'll make sure Detective McGuire provides you with a copy of the paperwork on the warrant. In the meantime, I expect to see your report on my desk in the morning."

Michael shook his head. "I don't turn over results of any investigation I'm working on until I'm finished. And I take my orders from Mayor Forbes, not you." He walked toward the door of his office. "McGuire will get a copy of my paperwork when it's ready, and not before."

Sykes followed, stopping at the door. Michael noticed that the police chief was sweating more than when he'd come in, enough to ruin that pretty silk shirt he was wearing. "Jurisdiction over this case rests with the police department, Chapman. I know what goes on around here—I've lived here all my life. If someone sneezes inside a house out on Youngs Bay, I hear about it. And I take murder in my town real personally.

You'd be wise to take that into account before you go mouthing off."

Michael smiled pleasantly. "I'll be sure and give that some careful thought."

After the police chief left, Michael pulled out a plastic baggy and carefully dropped the half-smoked cigar into it. He'd send it to the lab to have Sykes' saliva checked against the DNA found on the boat, just in case the guy had been traipsing all over Michael's fire scene. Besides, it'd give him no small amount of satisfaction when it became known that he'd had Sykes checked out.

Michael stood there, rubbing the back of his neck while his gut screamed at him. On his way home, he'd drive by the Jorgensen house, just to make sure everything looked okay. He wouldn't stop, and he sure as hell wouldn't let himself touch Kaz. Touching would be bad, given the state he was in. But he wouldn't be able to sleep, he knew, if he didn't at least drive by.

He needed to know she was all right.

Kaz awoke with a jolt. Even before she was even fully alert, she was reaching for the baseball bat she'd put next to her bed an hour ago. What had awakened her? She lay still and listened, her heart pounding.

There. A rustle, a floorboard creaking—the one in the living room that they'd never been able to fix.

Someone was in the house.

She slipped out of bed and pulled on her sweats, trying to make as little noise as possible. Then she picked up the bat and crept into the hallway. The moon had come out, its bright light streaming in the window high over the stairs.

She crept forward. At the top of the stairs, she stopped to listen again. The sounds were louder now—intermittent thumps, then the slight *screech* of a piece of furniture as it was shoved across the hardwood floor. Whoever it was, they were opening drawers, pulling books off the built-in shelves...the shelves that her grandfather had built. The shelves that she and Gary had sanded and varnished last week—one of the few projects that she and Gary had worked on together, in harmony, since she'd come back. The bastard had better not be putting any scratches on those shelves.

She gripped the bat tightly and started down the stairs. He'd be able to see her in the moonlight, but who cared? He'd come into their house, was going through their belongings.

Halfway down the stairs, she paused on the triangular landing where the stairway took a ninety-degree turn. The front door was standing wide open. On top of everything else, the jerk was running up her heating bill.

"Hey!" she yelled.

Chapter 13

The intruder exploded out of the living room, running for the front door. Kaz leaped, clearing the last several steps and landing on the area rug in the entry. She swung the bat at his midsection, but her aim was off. It glanced off his shoulder and hit the wall. Plaster rained down.

The intruder rounded on her. A black ski mask covered his face, and he was huge—outweighing her by as much as seventy-five pounds.

She swung the bat again, but he stepped inside the arc and used both hands to shove her, hard. She went flying backwards.

The stair railing broke her fall, but the weight of the bat overbalanced her. She crashed down hard on the risers, her hands flying up to keep the bat from falling in her face. Pain lanced through her, stealing her breath.

Scrambling to her feet, she retrieved the bat, but he was gone—out the door and off the front porch in a single leap. By the time she ran down the porch steps, he'd vanished.

She came to a halt on the front sidewalk, swearing and gulping in the cool night air. Then she made a quick trip around the house, her bare feet turning numb from contact with the cold, damp ground.

He was gone.

Back on the front sidewalk, she searched up and down the street, hopping from one foot to the other. Then she saw him, slouched against the pole of a burned-out streetlight on the opposite side of the street, smoking a cigarette.

She stalked across the pavement, barely feeling the odd bit of gravel digging into the soles of her feet, the bat tightly clenched in both hands. But as she neared, she realized he wasn't who she'd expected.

"Careful with that thing," Chuck said as she reached him. If he thought her state of undress was odd, he didn't comment. Glancing beyond him, she searched the alley between two of her neighbors' houses. Empty. She lowered the bat. Her hair hung in disheveled ropes over her eyes, making it hard to see. She shoved it back with an impatient hand. "Why didn't you stop him?" she asked.

"Stop who?"

"The man who came running out my front door. Black clothes, ski mask?"

Chuck's gaze sharpened, his expression becoming less remote. "Someone was in your house just now?"

"I woke up, he was in the house, and I chased him out." She glared at him. "I can't believe you didn't see anything. What good is all that Super Spy training if you don't even notice a bad guy right under your nose?"

"I just got here," he replied. Grasping her elbow, he half-dragged her back across the street to her own front yard. She had to jog to keep up. "Stay here while I check things out."

"I've already done that..." her voice trailed off as he disappeared around the corner of the house.

He was back in less time than it took for her to complete a few yoga deep-breathing exercises. "No one there."

"I could've told you that." A suspicion formed in her mind. "What are you doing here?"

"Figured I'd keep an eye out, in case there was any trouble."

"Gee, now why would you think there'd be trouble?"

"There's trouble just about everywhere these days. Read the

paper."

She narrowed her eyes. "I could do without any of your cryptic remarks right now."

He glanced down at the bat and raised one eyebrow. "Going after him with that was stupid—he could've had a gun."

"Funny, but I didn't seem to have a gun handy—Gary has it with him."

Chuck didn't even blink. "Can you call Lucy, get her over here to stay with you?"

"I'm doing just fine by myself." Kaz folded her arms. "And you still haven't answered my question about what you were doing here. For all I know, you're the person I chased." Although, she admitted silently, he would've had to pull off the world's fastest change of clothes.

Chuck shook his head.

"Your timing is awfully coincidental."

"Leave it alone."

"Where's Gary?"

At the sound of an approaching car, he whipped his head around. "Cavalry," he said, then melted into the night.

Kaz muttered several choice words and then turned toward the vehicle that pulled up at her curb. Michael Chapman. Her heart rate sped back up. Just great.

Chapman got out of his car, walked around to the passenger side, and unbuckled the seat belt around Zeke. They both strolled over to where she stood, their pace unhurried. Chapman's sharp gaze took in the baseball bat, the sweats she'd pulled on with Gary's Seahawks jersey, her bare feet. She could only imagine the impression she made. "Interesting getup for a late-night stroll."

"I had an intruder, and I took care of him." Her tone was short. "What are you doing here this late at night?"

"Checking up on you, which appears to have been a good idea." He frowned. "You used a baseball bat? That was stupid."

132

Kaz's temper slipped another notch. "Contrary to what people seem to think about us Jorgensens, we don't go around with guns strapped to our bodies or hidden under our pillows. And I haven't spent a lot of time in my life contemplating how I'll handle midnight intruders. This *used* to be a safe town."

He closed the distance between them and grasped her chin, turning her face so that he could see it better. Something cold flashed in his eyes. "Is that your only injury?"

Kaz edged away, unnerved by the effect of his touch. She raised a hand to her head. As if on cue, a lump at her temple started throbbing. "I fell on the stairs when he pushed me. I'll have a few bruises, but nothing serious."

He rocked back on his heels, shoving his hands in his pockets, almost as if he didn't trust himself not to touch her again. "What was he after?"

"How the hell should I know?" She stomped up the front porch steps and through the open door, leaving them to follow. "The break-in probably has to do with the weird phone calls I got today." She started stuffing books back onto the shelves. "Hang-ups."

"Christ." Chapman dumped a pile of paperback thrillers on the shelf and turned to face her, his face grim. "You know they were checking to see if the house was empty."

"Well, it wasn't." She went into the kitchen and filled the teakettle with water, then located some herbal tea bags. He followed her in, and she could feel his pale eyes on her, probably assessing how hysterical she might be. Okay, maybe she was acting a little over the top, but it had been an extremely stressful twenty-four hours.

Zeke sat down beside her and leaned heavily against the back of her left knee, almost buckling it. While she waited for the water in the teakettle to boil, she rubbed the top of his head. The dog moaned and gurgled with pleasure. "This dog thinks he's a person."

"Shepherds have the intelligence of a five-year-old child. He's perfectly capable of reading your moods, reacting much the same as any other human being would. He just has trouble communicating in a language that we humans understand."

"So if he had vocal chords, he'd be telling me that everything's all right, now that he's here," Kaz said, her voice wry.

"Something like that." Chapman took a tea towel off the cupboard door in front of the sink, and then retrieved a handful of ice from the freezer, which he wrapped inside the towel. He held it out to her. "It'll help the swelling."

She held the ice up to her head, wincing at the cold.

He folded his arms and leaned against the edge of the counter. "So far, you've been lucky." When she started to protest, he gave her a hard look. "No, dammit. Let me finish. This morning you were shot at, now you've been attacked in your own home."

"He wouldn't have attacked me if I hadn't attacked him first," she mumbled, earning herself another glare.

"*Next* time, the guy might not be so polite. Now, are you going to tell me what the hell is going on?"

"I don't know." The look on his face was skeptical. "I *don't*."

The kitchen was silent except for the sound of Zeke's tail thumping on the floor. She reached down and rubbed his head some more.

"Why would someone break into this house?"

She chewed her lip. There had to be a connection between the Lundquists' place being tossed and her intruder. Which meant that someone thought either Ken or Gary had something they wanted. It also indicated that Gary might be more involved than she wanted to believe. The risk in telling Chapman her suspicions was that he would leap to the wrong conclusion about Gary. But she was running out of options— she had to tell him.

She filled Chapman in about the break-in earlier that day at the Lundquists' and about Julie's secretiveness. "I think there might be a connection."

His expression was both angry and incredulous. "You *think?*"

"Okay, there's a connection. But I refuse to believe that Gary's behind the break-ins. For one thing, he has no reason to break in here and toss his own home."

Chapman nodded. "All right, I'll grant you that. But what about a partner, a person he might've had a falling out with? Most burglars are hoping to score one of three things: drugs, guns, or cash. Are you sure Gary isn't involved in some kind of drug smuggling?"

She gave him incredulous look. "*Yes*, I'm sure! After seeing what drugs did to men in the military, Gary won't touch anything stronger than aspirin. And he isn't motivated by money—he'd never risk ending up in jail just to score some cash."

"What about the other fishermen?" Chapman asked. "Doesn't Astoria have a problem with heroin smuggling?"

Kaz tried to remember what Lucy might've told her about drug trafficking. "The cops have known for years that heroin is coming through here, going upriver to Portland. But there's never been even one rumor of anyone I know being involved with drugs, and no one in the fleet has ever been arrested."

The teakettle whistled, and she turned to deal with it, but Chapman waved her toward a chair. "Sykes dropped by my office a little while ago." He brought the kettle and two cups over to the table. "They're getting ready to swear out a warrant against Gary."

Kaz reached for the back of a chair, dropping into it, shaking from head to toe. "My God."

"They found what they think is the murder weapon in Gary's truck."

135

"But that makes no sense! Gary's not dumb enough to leave that kind of evidence lying around."

"He could've been in a hurry—or could've been scared off when you arrived."

She shook her head. "He wouldn't have run from me—he would've tried to protect me from whatever was happening." While Chapman poured tea into her cup, a piece of the puzzle fell into place. "Someone's trying to frame him."

"Possibly."

"It's obvious—" she broke off. "What did you say?"

"I said, you may be right."

Kaz stared at him. "Earlier this afternoon, you were hell-bent to convict my brother."

He slanted her a chiding look. "I was leaving open all possibilities," he corrected. "Too many things aren't adding up."

"Like what?"

"I'm not at liberty to discuss that. Let's just say that a few of the findings might be inconsistent with someone killing in a fit of rage, then panicking and setting a fire to cover it up. I'm having the rags from the truck tested to see if the accelerant matches what I found on the boat." He set the teapot down. "But you're right—finding the murder weapon in the truck is just too damn convenient."

His words brought her a huge measure of relief. To have someone agree with her, and to not have them think she was crazy or blinded by her loyalty to her brother...Michael Chapman still wasn't her ally, but he *was* proving to be open-minded.

But why was Gary hiding out, if he was innocent?

She tried to raise the mug to her lips, but her hands were shaking too badly. The hot liquid spilled, soaking through the bandage that covered her burn. She sucked in a sharp breath, her eyes watering from the pain.

Chapman leaned across the table and placed his hands on hers, helping her hold the mug steady while she took a sip. The warmth, both from his hands and from the tea, was a blessed relief. "Thanks," she said, her breath hitching alarmingly. "It's the adrenaline," he said quietly. One corner of his mouth quirked. "You'll be fine in a couple of hours—back to your old, feisty self. Until then, you'll feel like you got flattened by an eighteen-wheeler."

She tried to smile back at him, but failed. Their gazes held for a long, silent moment, then he cleared his throat. Releasing her hands, he got up and rummage through drawers until he found the first aid kit. Sitting back down, he took her hand in his and proceeded to remove the soaked bandage.

Kaz let him, almost paralyzed by his gentleness. His touch was difficult to reconcile with the tough image he typically projected, and it added a new layer of complexity to his personality. If she'd been paying attention, she would've been able to predict that gentleness, based on how he treated Zeke. But she'd blocked out those kinds of observations, trying to convince herself that he was the enemy.

He's not acting like the enemy now, the voice inside her head whispered.

He examined the burn, a slight frown on his face. "It's healing well, but I don't think hot herbal tea is beneficial." His tone was wry as he dug through the jumble of packages in the kit to find some ointment. After spreading it with a light touch, he opened a package of gauze bandages and taped one over the blisters.

She hadn't said anything the whole time he'd worked, hadn't been able to while he had her hand in his. "Um, thanks," she muttered, pulling back and concentrating on her tea.

"No problem," he said, sounding amused. He watched her for a moment, his expression thoughtful. "I want you to take me with you when you go out on the water."

"*What?*" She jumped up to rinse out her cup. Just what she needed—twelve hours in close proximity to the most disturbing man she'd ever met, a man she was starting to feel a real connection with. And wasn't *that* a terrifying thought? "No way."

She had rules, ones that she hadn't broken for fifteen years. Never again was she going to be responsible for taking someone over that river bar. She couldn't take the chance.

"I know what I'm doing, and I won't be in your way," he said, his tone persuading. "I need to get a feel for what goes on out there, listen to the conversations on the radio."

He'd followed her over to the sink, and suddenly, he was standing way too close. Her already stressed system headed toward overload. "I hadn't decided yet whether I was going out," she said, stalling.

"You need to lift your pots, don't you?"

As usual, he was right. She had to get the newly strung crab pots into the water and empty and rebait the others. And it seemed that he'd come to the same conclusion she had—that they might overhear something in the fishermen's chatter that would give them some clues. Of course, the fishermen might also reveal Gary's hiding place, and with a warrant outstanding for Gary's arrest, Chapman would be obligated to tell the police anything he overheard.

"I don't take crew out with me, ever."

He frowned at her. "Why not?"

She shrugged. "Just a rule I have. It's dangerous. And newcomers don't understand what they're getting into."

"I trust you." His eyes gleamed with the irony of his statement. They both knew she was still suspicious of his motives.

She grabbed a washcloth from the sink and started scrubbing a drop of tea that had gotten spilled on the counter.

"Well, you shouldn't. Trust me, that is."

He was silent for a moment. "Funny. I didn't take you for a coward."

"*Excuse* me?"

He leaned forward, his face only inches from hers. "You want this investigation solved, don't you? Your brother cleared?" When she didn't respond, he continued, relentless. "You'll dive into the hold of a burning boat, but you won't take me across the damn river bar. I've got news for you—no one's responsible for me but me. I'm asking you to take me out there, so *I'm* the one taking the risk. You're just driving the damn boat—you're not God."

He was right, and when he put it that way, she felt foolish. But he didn't know the conditions out there, so he didn't really know what he was asking. She started to shake her head.

He moved even closer, placing a hand on the edge of the counter on either side of her, caging her in. "Here's the deal. You're not going anywhere without an escort, not after what's happened today. I won't have you in danger. So if you want to get those crab pots in the water, I'm going out with you. Either that, or I arrest you as a material witness, right here, right now."

"That's blackmail," she snapped.

"Yeah. So deal with it."

She wanted to punch him, and that shocked her. She wasn't a violent person; no one had ever gotten under her skin to the point that she wanted to hit him.

"I'll work for free," he added softly.

"Damn straight you'll work for free," she said faintly, accepting that she'd been coerced—or charmed, she wasn't sure which—into agreeing to his plan. "The business can't afford to pay anyone right now, unless I send you home with a few crabs for dinner."

He smiled, satisfied with his small victory. "When do you

plan to go back out?"

"I must be crazy," she grumbled. "Rule number one—don't take someone you don't trust out on the water with you."

"You trust me. You just don't want to admit it."

"You know, I really hate it when someone tells me how I feel."

He reached out and ran a finger over the bruise that was beginning to form on her temple. His touch was feather-light, but it left a trail of heat on her skin. She started to ease away, but he shifted even closer. She could feel the warmth radiating off his hard body, and she had the insane urge to cuddle against him, to soak up all that heat. She leaned away, lifting her chin.

He looked amused by her reaction. "I'll bunk down on the couch in the living room for the night." His voice had taken on a seductive quality.

It took her fogged brain a moment to process what he'd said. "You want to stay *here?* I don't think so."

"On the couch," he stressed, still smiling slightly. "Unless you prefer otherwise?"

"No!" She swallowed audibly, casting about for an excuse. "I'll be fine. I doubt they'll come back tonight."

He hesitated, clearly not convinced, then reluctantly nodded. "All right. But I leave Zeke here."

"Fine," she said quickly.

His gaze dropped to her mouth, and her pulse headed for the stratosphere. He was going to kiss her. She couldn't decide whether the idea turned her on or terrified her.

He leaned down until his lips were only the barest whisper away from hers, then stopped, his incredible, silvery eyes locking with hers. They questioned her silently.

She used the temporary reprieve to suck in some much-needed air. Laying a hand on his chest, she pushed slightly, testing his resistance. He didn't budge. *"Not* a good idea." Her voice sounded weak even to her own ears.

"Probably not," he murmured, "but I don't seem to be able to help myself." Sliding his warm hands under the heavy fall of her hair, he cupped the sensitive area at the base of her skull, holding her head still while he brushed his mouth gently across hers, barely making contact. His lips were warm, firm, and tasted of the herbal tea they had just drunk.

She shivered. His kiss was as light as his touch had been a moment ago, and just as devastating. Though his grip on her neck was firm and uncompromising, the kiss was an invitation rather than a demand. And that was more of a turn-on than he could possibly know.

She gripped the edge of the counter to brace herself. "Wait," she said, hearing the edge of desperation in her voice.

He trailed his lips along her jaw line to her ear, nipping the lobe and then using his tongue to sooth the small hurt. "I'll stop if you want me to," he whispered, his breath warm on her neck.

Fisting her hand in the material of his sweater, she shuddered. She *didn't* want him to stop—she didn't want to pull away from the seductive promise of what might be developing between them.

Reading her reaction, his eyes darkened. Placing both hands at her waist, he lifted her onto the counter, then parted her knees and stepped between them. Capturing her lips, he kissed her, hard.

The man knew how to kiss. She moaned deep in her throat and parted her lips, inviting him inside. He didn't hesitate, tasting her deeply, his tongue capturing hers and luring her into a duel that hinted of what it would be like if they were to take this to the next level.

It would be good. Incendiary.

She wanted to glue herself to every inch of him. And she wanted that devastating kiss to go on and on.

Think about Gary.

She managed to drag both hands down to his hard chest and push, her body already protesting as she did. "I want you to stop," she managed, her voice unsteady, her breath hitching with regret.

He froze for a long moment, breathing hard and staring at her. Then he sighed and leaned his forehead against hers.

"It's just chemistry," she said, trying to convince herself.

"More like a nuclear explosion," he muttered. He straightened, easing away from her slowly, grimacing at what the movement cost him. Reaching out, he rubbed her lower lip with his thumb, almost destroying what was left of her resolve. His expression was curiously sad. "But you're right—bad timing all around."

He told Zeke to stay and walked over to the kitchen door, then turned back to her, and promise lingering in his gaze. "When this is over—"

"I'll probably be going back to California," she said quickly, though the thought made her slightly ill.

"We'll talk," he said firmly. "And my name is Michael. It's time you started using it, don't you think?"

Once he was gone, she slid down the front of the cupboards until she was sitting on the floor, her knees bunched up. Zeke leaned over and licked her face, then grinned at her, his tongue lolling. Bemused, she raised a shaky hand to pat the top of his head. "I could be in a little trouble, here, Zeke."

"Rawrooo."

She dropped her forehead to her knee and rubbed Zeke's chest. Then on a sigh, she dragged herself to her feet. That kiss had been the knock-out punch for a long, miserable day. She'd deal with the ramifications tomorrow, when she could be more rational about how irrational it was to start a relationship with a man she barely knew. One who could turn her bones to water with just a glance. One who felt like he might be the man she'd been waiting for all these years.

But right now, as she slogged up the stairs to her bedroom, all she could think about was falling into bed.

Sleep. She desperately needed some sleep.

Which wasn't in the cards: At 4:15 AM, she was awakened from a restless doze by Zeke, who exploded into a frenzy of barking and leapt at the darkened silhouette of a man standing in the doorway of her bedroom.

Chapter 14

The man reached in, grabbed the door handle, and slammed the bedroom door shut only a split second before Zeke hit the door, scratching and growling.

"Dammit, Kaz! Call off the dog." The voice on the other side of the door was low and muffled, but she would've recognized it anywhere.

"Gary!" She threw back the covers and scrambled out of bed. Grabbing Zeke's collar, she flung open the door. "It's about time—I've been worried sick." She hugged him.

He held her close for a moment, then moved her aside so he could cross to the window to draw shut the curtains. He then prowled the small space beside her bed like a big, restless cat. Zeke watched him warily, growling low in his throat.

Even in the shadows, Gary's face was haggard, his cheeks hollow. His forehead and jaw were streaked with dark grease paint, adding to the starkness of his features. And he looked gaunt, as if he hadn't been eating.

She knew better than to comment on those facts. "Where've you been staying?"

"I won't tell you that." He rounded on her. "Dammit, I told you to stay out of this, Kaz."

She folded her arms. "What's going on, Gary?"

"Nothing you can do anything about."

"Is that why you've been avoiding me since I came home?"

"Yes." He came over to where she stood, placing his hands

on her shoulders. "I want you to go back to California. Tomorrow. Just pack your bags and go."

She shook her head. "Tell me what's going on," she demanded. "What are they looking for?"

He jerked, startled by her question. "What d'you mean?"

"Someone's been calling here, then hanging up. I had a visitor, around midnight, who was searching through the bookcases in the living room. And the Lundquists' house was tossed earlier today."

"Sonofabitch!" He turned away from her, slamming his fist against the wall.

Zeke snarled, and she knelt to soothe him.

"You've got to go stay with Lucy, where you'll be safe." Gary paced some more, then stopped, running his hands through his hair. "Fuck. I did *not* want you involved. These guys play for keeps. God, look what they did to Ken."

"Who *are* these guys?"

"No way."

"Tell me you aren't trying to handle this alone." The thought terrified her. "That's it, isn't it? You're staying here in town— not up in the backcountry where you'd be safer—trying to find out who's behind this. If the cops find you—"

"I've got some people helping me."

"Chuck," she guessed.

Gary shrugged and resumed his pacing. She hadn't seen him strung this tight since right after he'd returned from Iraq. If Chuck was helping Gary, that gave her some measure of comfort. Still, he and Chuck had no business being vigilantes, if that's what they were doing.

She sat down on the edge of the bed. "Go to Lucy and Ivar, tell them what you know. It's the only way."

He shook his head. "Not an option." He stared down at Zeke, then held out a hand for the shepherd to sniff. "Why do you have that new guy's dog here?"

145

"Michael left him for my protection after the break-in this evening." She bit her lip. "Someone's trying to frame you, Gary."

His laugh was bitter. "You think I don't know that?"

"The cops found the murder weapon in the back of your truck. They've issued a warrant for your arrest."

"Yeah, Chuck told me." Before she could ask how Chuck had found out, Gary shook his head. "Chuck has his sources—I don't ask."

"Clint Jackson is staking out the house—he's been here off an on since this morning."

Gary snorted. "I saw him. He was sitting in his car, half asleep when I came in the front door. He never even saw me." Gary looked momentarily amused. "You don't have to worry about him catching me."

"But there are others out there looking, according to Lucy."

"I just came by to pick up a few things." He knelt, taking her hands in his. "Stay out of this, Sis. For me."

"Not an option," she said, mimicking him.

"You have to trust me on this. If I'm worrying about you, then I can't concentrate on stopping these guys. This Chapman guy, can he protect you?"

"I can protect myself."

"Not from these guys—don't even think that. If you get in their way, they won't hesitate to kill you." He gripped her arms and shook her gently. "Dammit, you're all I've got left."

"Then you know how *I* feel."

"At least go out on the water, act like everything is normal. You'll be pretty safe out there—the guys won't let anything happen to you. And don't go anywhere on your own. Promise me that much, at least."

"What about you?"

"Forget about me—I'm not important." When she opened her mouth to protest, he shook his head and stood, forcing her to look up at him. "You listen to me, Kaz. This time, your stubbornness could get you killed."

"And you don't need to be a hero," she said quietly.

He snorted and let go of her. "No chance of that at this point." His smile was sad, his expression becoming more distant. "But they aren't going to get away with this, not in my town."

He walked over to the window, easing the curtain aside, then swore softly. "Looks like Jackson has actually decided to take a walk around the house. Pity you can't sic the dog on him." Gary pulled a .45 Ruger out of his jacket, chambered a round and flipped the safety on, then handed it to her. "Keep this with you, even when you sleep."

She took the gun reluctantly. She knew how to use it—Gary had insisted on teaching her years ago—but she'd never been comfortable handling it. "Tell me how to get in touch with you."

He shook his head. "If you need anything, find Chuck." He walked to the door and opened it, then looked back at her, his worry evident on his face. "Goodbye, Kaz."

And then he was gone.

Kaz dropped down onto the bed, staring at the empty doorway. She picked up the pillow, shoving the pistol underneath. For several long moments, she stared at the moonlit glow of the white linen pillowcase.

Then she grabbed the pillow and hurled it across the room.

Lucy sat in her living room in her rattiest sweats early the next morning, mainlining coffee, eating cold pizza, and watching a rerun of a World Cup Soccer match while she cleaned her gun. Normally, she slept until the very last minute each morning, then headed into the police station and had her caffeine hit there. But this case was driving her nuts, so she'd gotten up early, figuring that watching the game and sniffing gun oil would help her relax enough to think things through.

In her opinion, soccer was a great sport. Its players exhibited the perfect blend of grace and athleticism, with the right amount of competitiveness thrown in. She snorted. Unlike football players, whom she'd always been convinced got away with culturally sanctioned assault and battery. Most linebackers and defensive tackles were lucky they'd landed a place on a team somewhere—otherwise, they'd be doing ten to fifteen in the state pen.

The United States soccer team scored a goal, and she let out a whoop. Then she removed the firing pin from the Glock, inspecting it closely for wear. The only use the gun had ever seen was on the firing range, but still, a careful cop kept her equipment in top condition.

Sykes had gotten the warrant issued for Gary's arrest in record time, dropping it on her desk the night before. He'd also assigned two more teams of cops to search for Gary, putting Clint Jackson in charge. And that worried the hell out of her, because Clint wasn't, to put it mildly, her first choice for the job. Of course, her opinion might be colored by the fact that Clint was a redneck, chauvinist asshole who got off by objectifying women. The guy made her see red every time he swaggered into the squad room. She didn't mind being treated like she was one of the guys—that's actually what she preferred. But Clint had let it be known more than once that he thought any skills she had were best demonstrated in the bedroom.

Still, no matter what her personal feelings were about him, she was convinced she was right to be worried. She wasn't the only one on the force who thought Clint could be a little too rough on prisoners, not to mention a little too trigger-happy. If Gary decided to put up a fight...she shuddered.

The dumb shit needed to turn himself in. Why the *hell* hadn't he made contact with her? Surely he trusted her. He had to know she'd do whatever she could to ensure that he was treated fairly.

Maybe he trusted her, but didn't have the confidence in her ability to help him. She pondered that while she ran a small brush through the barrel of her gun, scouring it of any gunpowder residue, then shook her head, muttering under her breath. No. She was just being insecure, which was a bad habit of hers. Gary knew she was good at her job, and he also knew she was loyal to her friends. She'd never given him any reason to think she'd let him down.

She sensed rather than heard a movement in the doorway and looked up. Then jumped a foot. "Shit!"

As if she had conjured him out of thin air, Gary leaned against the doorjamb, watching her with an amused expression. "Jesus, McGuire. You clean your gun at 6:30 in the morning?"

"You scared the hell out of me!" she shouted at him. "Don't do that—I could've shot you."

"Your gun is in itty bitty pieces."

"I can have it back together in under seven seconds."

"Yeah, and I can render you unconscious in under two."

She already should've pulled her backup gun, and she cursed the lack of caffeine in her system that was making her brain function like molasses. "You here to turn yourself in?"

Gary grunted and moved out of the doorway. Keeping a wary eye on her picture window, he leaned over and picked up her coffee mug, draining it. When the taste registered, he grimaced. "Christ. What the hell is this?"

She snatched the mug away from him and headed for the kitchen to refill it. "I reheated yesterday's."

"You're hopeless in the cooking department, you know that?" he said, following her. He leaned against the counter, muscular arms crossed, looking tall and lethal in his camouflaged army fatigues and grease paint. "Convince Kaz to

149

lay off. I don't want her mixed up in this."

"*You* convince her."

"I tried—she isn't buying it."

So he'd been to the house and talked to Kaz. Lucy handed him the coffee mug, then palmed the .38 she'd retrieved from the kitchen drawer, pointing it at him. "I've got to arrest you, Gary. I can help you, but I have to take you in."

He shook his head. "Point that somewhere else, will you? I don't want you losing that infamous temper of yours and shooting me."

"Hands behind your head, fingers interlocked. You have the right to remain silent. Anything you do say—"

Carrying his coffee, he walked over to the refrigerator, looking inside. "Got anything to eat besides pizza? I'm a vegetarian these days."

"You can't just ignore me!"

He shut the door, sighing. "You're not going to shoot me, Luce, and I'm not going to turn myself in. So put that thing down, before I feel the need to take it away from you."

"I'd like to see you try," she snarled.

He grinned and winked. "And I'd like nothing better than to try, darlin'. But I've got places to go, people to see."

Pure, hot, sexual awareness arrowed through her, heating her. She swore, de-cocked the gun, and laid it on the kitchen table. Dropping into a chair, she rubbed her face. No way was she going to let him see how much he'd gotten to her with one remark and a sexy smile. "Okay, what d'you want to talk about?"

"Kaz. Convince her to go back to California." Gary's brows snapped together. "Hell, you're the one who called her and told her to come back. So fix it."

"You know about that?" Lucy felt the guilt slide through her.

"Yeah. What a dumbass move."

She bristled at his remark, but he had a point. Kaz was

acting recklessly, and displaying a tenacious stubbornness that was half the reason Lucy had had a sleepless night. And it *was* her fault that Kaz was even involved. "Like Kaz is listening to me any more than to you," she pointed out.

He sat down in the chair opposite her, and she noticed for the first time how exhausted and anxious he looked. Her stomach started to churn as she considered what could make a bad-ass, ex-Army Ranger like Gary so paranoid. "Can't you arrest her or something?" he asked.

"Phil would have her out in an hour, you know that."

"Then put her in protective custody."

"Gee, all our officers are busy out looking for you."

He grunted. "I noticed. Okay, so move in with her."

"Gary..." She shook her head, then folded her arms. "I've heard rumors for a couple of weeks now about the fishermen. Care to tell me if they're true?"

"No."

"Want to confide in me about what you're doing?"

"No."

She gritted her teeth. "Where were you the night before last while the *Anna Marie* was burning down to the waterline?"

"Camping."

"Try again," she shot back. "I saw you in the photos Chapman took of the crowd."

He shrugged. "I went to the mooring basin to spend the night on the trawler, but I hooked up with Chuck instead. Satisfied?"

"Not by a long shot." He wasn't telling her everything, and the knowledge that he didn't trust her to help him hurt so much she was having trouble breathing. She forced herself to pin him with her hardest interrogation stare. "Did you go onto the *Anna Marie?*"

"No." He leaned forward, close enough to pump up her pulse rate. His eyes shone with a feverish intensity. "You know

151

I didn't kill Ken. Quit playing cop for just one damn minute and listen to me. Kaz is in real danger. Did she tell you someone broke into her house last night?"

Lucy swore.

He smiled grimly. "Yeah, I didn't figure she'd raced to the phone to call you."

"Do you know what they wanted?"

"Yeah."

She glared at him. "You going to share with me?"

"No." He stood and walked to the back door. "Figure out a way to keep her safe—that's all I'm asking."

"You can't just waltz out the door! I'm an officer of the law and there's a warrant out for your arrest."

"You never saw me—I wasn't here." He paused in the open doorway. His expression was hard, but his eyes were haunted. She shivered as cool air wafted over her. "Watch your back, Luce."

Two seconds later, he was gone, and she was left sitting alone in her kitchen, listening to the quiet ticking of the clock on the wall and the sounds of the soccer match playing in the background.

Well, hell.

Chapter 15

When Kaz awoke around nine, her first sleep-fogged thought was that she felt like a mummy, wrapped from shoulders to toes. Then she remembered that Zeke was stretched out along one side of her, on top of the covers.

After Gary had left, she'd given in and let the dog sleep on the bed. She had a sneaking suspicion that Zeke was afraid of the dark. He'd been so rattled by their late-night visitor that the only way she'd gotten him to quit pacing, his claws click-click-clicking on the hardwood floor, was to invite him into her bed.

Zeke's forepaw now lay across her stomach, holding her down, and his head lay on her shoulder, tucked into the crook of her neck. He was sound asleep, his hind legs twitching as he chased imaginary prey. She lifted his paw and tried to roll him over. He groaned, snuffling against her neck and licking her ear, then went back to sleep.

It was the same ear that Michael Chapman had licked the night before.

Muttering to herself about the male gender, she lifted the edge of the covers and eased sideways out from under Zeke, half-falling onto the floor beside the bed. She dragged herself to her feet and went into the bathroom to splash water on her face.

After brushing her teeth and throwing cold water on her face, she glanced in the mirror. Big mistake. Two nights of little sleep had left her with purple smudges under her eyes. Worry about Gary had added hollows to her cheeks.

Taking a quick shower, she turned it to a bracing icy cold toward the end, forcing herself to stand under the stream until she felt more awake. Then she tamed her wet hair into a French braid and applied light makeup. Rummaging around in her dresser, she pulled on a clean pair of jeans, a turtleneck, and a heavy cotton sweater.

As she dressed, she assessed the weather. The wind was picking up in velocity, splattering raindrops against the panes of her bedroom window. Another storm was moving in, and it looked like it might have some punch to it. She'd check the marine forecast, but she was certain there'd be gale force winds and at least fifteen feet of storm surge, even close in to shore. No one would be going out crabbing today.

Sighing, she grabbed the pair of running shoes she had drying on the heat register and headed downstairs. Rounding the corner into the kitchen, she came to a halt.

There was a cup of freshly brewed coffee sitting on the edge of the counter, doctored the way she liked it with a small amount of cream, still steaming. It held down a handwritten note. She picked up the coffee and the note, noticing that Zeke was gone. Before she could read it, the phone rang.

She reached for the handset, then hesitated, unsure if she could cope with another hang-up. The phone rang again. She couldn't ignore it—it could be anyone, even Gary. Just this once, she wished her brother was into technology and had installed Caller ID. She sighed and picked up the portable unit.

"So glad you thought to call me about the break-in." Lucy's voice had a distinctly sarcastic edge to it.

Kaz relaxed. "What could you have done? Send the lab guys over to dust for fingerprints?"

"For starters, yeah."

"He was wearing gloves."

She heard Lucy groan. "I don't want to know how you know that."

"I noticed when I swung the baseball bat at him."

"Jesus Christ." There was a pause while Lucy drank something. "Does the word *caution* mean anything to you? The guy could've had a gun."

"That's already been pointed out to me, more times than I wanted to hear," Kaz said mildly. "Did you call for a reason?"

"Where the hell was the surveillance team? Jackson or Brenner should've been right outside."

Kaz shrugged, then realized Lucy couldn't see it. "You tell me. When I chased the guy out the front door, there was no one out there." She didn't add that Jackson had been there later, when Gary had shown up for a visit.

Lucy sighed loudly. "All right. I'll send over a team to check for fingerprints, just in case. And I'll also find out where Jackson was—he should've been out there. Can you *please* stay out of trouble for the remainder of the day?"

Kaz didn't bother to answer. She could hear Lucy shutting a door and walking somewhere outside, her steps crunching on gravel. She was probably leaving for the station. A new thought occurred to Kaz. "Hey. How did you know that someone had broken in here?"

"Your jerk of a brother." Lucy disconnected, leaving Kaz standing in the middle of her kitchen holding a dead phone. She realized her mouth had fallen open, and she snapped it shut.

So she wasn't the only one Gary had visited last night. Interesting. And since Gary wasn't behind bars this morning, that meant Lucy hadn't arrested him. Even more interesting.

It appeared that the men in their lives were giving both of them trouble. Speaking of which—she stared at the note she still held in her hand, focusing on the bold, black scrawl. Michael's handwriting was as forceful as the rest of his personality.

"I assume the weather's too lousy to go out," he'd written in large, slanted letters. "And I didn't figure you'd want me to join you in the shower—at least, not yet." She smiled a little at his cockiness, feeling a trickle of heat as an image of the two of them together under all that steam snuck into her mind. As he'd intended, no doubt.

Then she frowned as she read the rest of the message. "*STAY PUT.* Zeke and I have work to do. We'll be back this evening. *GET SOME REST.*"

That was it—he hadn't even bothered to sign it.

She crumpled the note in her fist and tossed it into the trash. The man had more than his share of arrogance.

Unfortunately, it didn't make him any less attractive.

By late morning, Kaz was pacing her living room like a caged animal. Each wind gust rattled the loose pane in the south window that they'd never gotten around to glazing. Even though she'd closed the damper on the fireplace, puffs of ash floated onto the floor. Rain now came down in drenching sheets, and she could feel the barometric pressure dropping like a stone. The coastal storms had always made her twitchy, and this one was no exception.

She'd already downloaded email and taken care of any outstanding issues from the San Francisco office. That had taken less than an hour—her partner had things well under control. It seemed to be working out fine to telecommute--at least, for now. Which had her thinking about the possibility of a more permanent, commuting-type setup. Of letting her partner handle more of the day-to-day responsibilities.

Though it would've been nice if there'd been enough work this morning to keep her from going stir-crazy.

"Stay put," she muttered, stacking a pile of books in the bookshelf, then adjusting them so that they lay on their sides,

156

then moving them to a different shelf altogether. Like she could just sit around, doing nothing. Another hour of this and she'd need horse tranquilizers.

She couldn't see the mooring basin from this end of town, but she hoped none of the fishermen had gone out before the storm hit. Worry for them had been nagging at her since she'd awakened. Most likely, though, they were camped out in the Workman's Café on the waterfront, waiting to see if the weather let up. Or on their boats, killing the time by knocking out some of the items on their ever-present repair lists.

But her concern for the fishermen was nothing next to the hysteria that threatened to bubble up whenever she thought about Gary. He was out there, somewhere close by, trying to catch people who were capable of murder. *And* trying to evade the cops who, with the exception of Lucy and Ivar, wanted his head served up on a platter.

A nervous widow, fishermen who were too scared to talk, and something that people wanted. What did it all mean? Was it drug-related, as Michael seemed to think? *Were* some of the fishermen running drugs? Could that have been what Bjorn had been alluding to when he'd said that some of them were involved?

But if so, how had Ken gotten mixed up in it? It didn't make sense—he was a family man, not a drug runner. She couldn't imagine him taking those kinds of chances, not with his wife and kids. Then again, Bobby had been horribly sick, and Ken would do anything for him. But Kaz knew beyond a doubt that Gary wouldn't touch drugs, not for any reason.

She stopped fiddling with the books and blew out a breath. *To hell with it.* The least she could do was check up on the fishermen. And maybe one of them would let something slip, provide some small bit of information she could use to figure out what to do next.

Snagging her sou'wester off the hook by the back door, she

157

headed out into the storm.

Halfway to the mooring basin, she changed her mind and pulled a U-turn, heading back toward Uniontown. At this time of the day, the Redemption was mostly deserted. She figured Steve would have time to talk to her and could perhaps shed some light on what had happened two nights ago. Pulling into the parking lot, she set the brake on the Jeep and hopped out, jogging across the gravel to the door.

She paused inside the door, shaking off the rain and letting her eyes adjust to the dimness of the room.

Steve was behind the bar, totaling up last night's receipts. "Hey, Kaz." He smiled, his expression friendly.

Like most of the people in town her age, Steve had gone through school with her. Although they hadn't run with the same crowd, she remembered Steve as being one of the good guys. She'd heard some rumors that he'd gone a little crazy after his divorce a few years back, but the divorce had been particularly acrimonious, so he'd probably had good reason.

If Steve looked the other way sometimes when it came to what went on in his tavern, it was understandable. A bartender heard a lot, knew a lot. And if he made a habit of repeating what he knew, he'd be out of business in a hurry.

Astoria had a healthy rumor mill, but there were unspoken rules about who you should talk to, and about how much you could reveal. Right now, Kaz was counting on those rules, because as the sister of someone who was involved, she was on the list of people Steve could talk to, if he so chose. She also wanted to find out why Gary had felt that Steve had no cause to criticize him that evening.

"I need to know what Gary and Ken were arguing about two nights ago," she said without preamble.

Steve shook his head, his expression turning wary. "It was pretty busy, Kaz. And you know I make a habit of tuning out."

"You were standing right here the whole time—you could hardly miss what they said."

He didn't reply, busying himself with rinsing out glasses.

Her heart sank. She slipped onto one of the barstools and leaned her elbows on the bar. "They've charged Gary with arson and murder. Steve, if you know something..."

He sighed. "I'll tell you exactly what I told Lucy and Ivar, and that new fire chief guy: I didn't hear anything important."

So Michael had already questioned Steve. He was conducting an investigation, she reminded herself--he wasn't obligated to keep her informed. But still, it bothered her that he wasn't being entirely straight with her. "Okay. What did Gary and Ken say that night that *isn't* important?"

Steve shrugged, then glanced around the mostly empty room before answering. "They were arguing about something to do with the crab pots."

She stared at the bartender, perplexed. "That doesn't make any sense. They drag-fish—*I'm* doing the crabbing."

Shooting her an exasperated look, Steve said, "I don't try to reason through what I overhear, Kaz. All I know is that Gary told Ken to shape up or else."

"Was Gary threatening to fire Ken?"

"Not as far as I could tell. It sounded more like a disagreement about how they were handling something."

"Was Ken upset? Or nervous?"

Steve paused and thought about it. "It's kind of hard to tell, with him being so laid back most of the time. But yeah, he did seem to be kind of edgy."

"Who was standing next to them at the bar?"

Steve's face pokered up. "I already answered these questions for the authorities. You're wasting your time, to say nothing of sticking your nose in where it doesn't belong."

"Who was standing there, dammit!" she snapped.

"Karl Svensen, okay?" Steve answered, just as angry. "Now

159

either order something from the kitchen, or get the hell out of here and let me get back to my work."

So she'd been right about Karl. "Was he part of the argument?" she pressed.

"I didn't notice."

She was certain he had but wasn't going to tell her. "Why was Gary so angry with you that night?"

"I wouldn't have a clue." Her disbelief must have shown, because he shrugged. "It was just some crackpot remark your brother made because he was pissed. I'm sure he resented my interference."

He was lying, but for the life of her, she couldn't figure out why. She stood up. "If you think of anything else, please call me, okay?"

He picked up the pile of receipts and put a rubber band around it, then met her gaze, his expression remote. "There's nothing else to say."

"Well, thanks anyway."

He shook his head. "Don't thank me, Kaz. Just mind your own business."

"Why does everyone keep saying that to me?" she wondered out loud.

"Because there are things going on around here that you don't need to know about."

She stared at him, experiencing the same sense of unreality as she'd had the day before when she'd talked to Chuck. Steve looked worried, maybe even afraid. But he'd said all he was going to. She blew out a breath. "I'm beginning to think I have no clue what is going on in my own home town."

"You don't."

"I live and work here, too," she pointed out, sick of the obfuscations.

"Not for the last ten years."

Two blocks away in Uniontown Park, Lucy and Ivar stood in the driving rain in their police-issue slickers, hunched over the body of a small-time local drug dealer. Someone had stabbed him multiple times in the chest, then dumped him in the back of one of the abandoned warehouses on the water's edge. Lucy pulled her collar up, swearing under her breath at the foul weather. Hell of a way to start off the workday.

Rigor had set in, so the guy had probably been killed sometime the night before. "Two murders in as many days." She looked at Ivar. "Just what the hell is going on in our town?"

His expression pensive, Ivar watched Ewald work on the corpse. "Don't like the feel of this."

"Now there's an understatement."

"You think Gary had a hand in this? Or Chuck?"

Lucy frowned. That was *exactly* what she was worried about—that Gary and Chuck were on some kind of vigilante mission. Gary hadn't come right out and said anything that would lead her to think that, but she knew, somehow, that that was what he was up to. And where he went, Chuck followed. Still, she couldn't believe Gary would commit murder.

The murder method—multiple stab wounds—indicated that the killer had been in a rage. And while she'd seen Gary lose his temper and resort to throwing a punch or two, she couldn't envision him losing it and stabbing a man to death. Besides, why would Gary or Chuck be targeting small-time drug dealers?

She realized Ivar was giving her an odd look—probably because he'd never seen her silent for that long. "Nah," she answered. "If Chuck had done it, he would've crept up behind the guy and slit his throat. And this isn't Gary's style, either."

She turned as Clint Jackson approached, dragging a thin, nervous man. "Well, well. Look who we've got, Ivar. Briggs, ole buddy. Why am I not surprised that you're hanging around?"

161

The drug addict shifted nervously in his soiled, torn sneakers, his dilated eyes darting around, landing anywhere but on the body. He seemed oblivious to the fact that he was soaked to the skin and shivering. "I didn't do nothing, I swear."

"Of course you didn't," Lucy soothed. She noted the spittle in the corner of his mouth, the unhealthy pallor, the physical twitches. He hadn't gotten his usual fix, and he was going into withdrawal. Interesting. "So maybe I can help you out a little, Sammy, in return for a little information. Did you see what went down here?"

"I ain't talkin'. It wouldn't be healthy."

Lucy snorted. "Since when do you care about anything but your next fix?"

Sammy threw up two filthy hands, his eyes wild. "Hey, this one's too hot. I tell you what's goin' down, and no one's gonna sell to me ever again."

Even more interesting. She leaned closer, unfortunately close enough that she could smell how long it'd been since he'd had a bath. The rain wasn't even making a dent in the state of his personal hygiene, and if that odor transferred to her angora sweater, she'd make it her personal goal to put him away for a long, long time. "So maybe we'll get a little something out of the evidence lock-up, Sammy, to keep you going while we have our little chat."

The addict's eyes lit up. "Really? You can do that?"

"Sure," Lucy said easily. She ignored Ivar's frown.

But Sammy caught it, and his expression turned angry. "You're lying to me." He spat at her feet. "Cops. You think you're above the law, that you can do anything, get away with anything."

She shot a glare at Ivar, then patted Sammy down, removing a small baggie of grass from his inside pocket. "Look what we have here."

"Hey! That's personal use only."

"Yeah, but Sammy, you've already got two convictions. This little ole bit of weed is going to send you up the river for the rest of your life."

"What? No way, man! I'll get me a lawyer."

"It's called three strikes, Sammy. Maybe you've heard of it?"

"You *bitch!*"

Lucy turned and nodded to Jackson. "Put him in lock-up for now. I'll deal with him later."

As Jackson dragged him away, he yelled, "I ain't telling you nothin', you hear?"

After he was out of hearing distance, she turned to Ivar. "That went well."

Ivar shrugged. "Probably won't tell you anything for a couple more hours. Needs to start really hurting first."

"What do you want to bet that he saw what went down? But he looked more scared about talking to us than he was about being sent up for life."

"Yeah. Wonder why."

Troubled, she turned back to Ewald. "So, preliminary cause of death?"

The medical examiner stood and stripped off his latex gloves. "Unofficially, someone stabbed the life out of him. And enjoyed it."

She shivered.

Kaz had always loved the mooring basin. In some ways, the maze of docks with their neatly aligned fishing boats felt more like home than the bungalow in town did. But what she'd missed most of all, when she was down in California, were the smells—the unique, pungent blend of stagnant water, fish, and diesel, contrasted by the clean, crisp smell of the wind as it blew off the ocean. Cities had their own intriguing odors—the corner deli, the bakery down the block. If she moved away from San Francisco, she would miss that. But up here, the air carried the scents of her past, providing her with a strong reminder of who she was.

She sat in the Jeep on the wharf, staring at the tableaux below her while rain drummed on the canvas roof. Bjorn was on his boat, repairing a net under a hastily rigged tarp that probably wasn't keeping much of the rain out. The rest of the marina looked deserted—not that many people wanted to work in a storm. She told herself to quit woolgathering and hopped out of the Jeep, locking it.

As she walked down the dock, Bjorn motioned to her to join him under the tarp. She climbed on board and sat down on the stern bench, shoving aside a block and tackle. "I appreciate that you told me what you did yesterday, Bjorn."

He shook his head. "I never said anything."

"I had a visitor last night."

His head came up sharply. "You okay?"

"Yeah. He wasn't after me, he was searching for something." She watched Bjorn's face immediately close up. "And I'm betting you know what they wanted."

"If I did, I'd tell the cops."

"Would you?"

He shrugged. "Maybe, maybe not, okay? I've got a family to think about."

He was right. She felt like pond scum for pressing him. "I'm sorry. I'll go." When she stood, he looked relieved. She couldn't stop herself from asking one more question. "Gary paid me a visit. He thinks I'm safer out on the water than in town. Is that what you think?"

Bjorn hesitated, then nodded. "Maybe. Gary okay?"

"He's strung pretty tight. I'm worried about him."

Bjorn glanced around the marina before speaking. "No matter what Karl said yesterday, Gary's got friends around here."

"That's good to hear," she admitted. "But there's a warrant

164

out for his arrest, and unless you guys start telling me or the cops what you know, he's still in danger."

"And if we *do* talk, we'll end up like Ken."

She hesitated. "Bjorn, is this about drugs?"

He shook his head. "No more."

She gave up and turned to leave. "If this lets up, I'll be taking Michael Chapman out with me tomorrow." She tried to dispel the tension in the air. "When he get a good look the river bar, the guy will probably puke all over my running shoes."

As she'd hoped, Bjorn chuckled, then his expression turned serious. "Most of us don't trust Chapman, Kaz. And the fact that you're letting him on the *Kasmira B* won't help matters for you."

"I'll have to take that chance." She jumped onto the dock. "Safe passage tomorrow."

"You too, Kaz."

She was ten yards away when she heard him call her name. She turned.

"Better not come down here again, Kaz, unless it's to take the boat out."

She nodded to indicate she'd heard his warning, then continued up the ramp. Standing next to the Jeep, she let the rain wash over her, so tired she had to hold herself upright with a hand against the hood.

Clint Jackson was parked a block away, watching her. He was probably hoping she'd lead him to Gary. She almost laughed out loud. Fat chance of that.

Ignoring him, she opened the door of the Jeep and climbed in, then put her arms on the wheel and rested her forehead against them. Karl Svensen was standing on the deck of Bjorn's boat, his face set, his gestures angry as he talked. He must've been on his boat, watching while she talked to Bjorn. She closed her eyes, unable to care at the moment.

She had no idea what, if anything, she'd uncovered that

could help Gary, and no clue where to go next. Never had she felt so alone. It was as if people were going out of their way to make her feel like an outsider. She straightened. Well, it wouldn't work. After allowing herself this little two-minute pity party, she'd figure out what to do next. She'd be damned if she'd let Gary down.

The passenger-side door opened and Michael Chapman slid inside, startling her. Raindrops glistened on his dark hair and black Gore-Tex jacket. His eyes gleamed, and his expression was sardonic, but he still managed to look sexy as hell.

"Amateur sleuthing not going as well as you'd like?" he asked.

She closed her eyes, bracing herself against the jolt of heat she experienced whenever he was near. "What are you, some kind of bad penny?"

"I was driving by when I saw you walk up from the dock." His tone turned gentle. "I see you didn't take my advice about staying home. You know, civilians always get hammered when they get in the way."

Was that a glimmer of sympathy she saw in his eyes? Or pity? She stiffened her spine and sent him the coolest look she could manage. "Are you bothering me for a reason?"

He regarded her with a slight smile, as if he were well aware of the double meaning behind her words. The interior of the jeep was suddenly too warm, the cramped space far too intimate. She edged around in her seat, propping her shoulders in the corner, so that she could face him. The last thing she needed was a repeat of last night's idiocy, especially since she now knew that he wasn't being entirely forthcoming with her about the investigation.

"Why don't you think about working with me on this?" he suggested, surprising her. "I could use your insight into the community."

She raised an eyebrow. "And you'll keep me informed as to

the progress *you're* making, right?"

"As much as possible, I will."

She shook her head. "If I can't expect Lucy to do that for me, why would I expect you to?"

"Maybe because, at some point, you have to trust someone. Otherwise, you're on your own. I could be wrong, but I don't see any evidence that your friends are rallying around you, eager to help."

"That's unfair," she protested. "Lucy and Ivar have jobs to do."

"And the fishermen? I don't see them acting any too supportive."

"They have their own worries. Besides, it's possible..." She stopped, realizing what she'd been about to reveal.

"—that they're helping by hiding your brother," he finished for her.

She didn't respond.

He shook his head, reached out, ran a thumb gently down her cheek. "I don't want you to get hurt," he said softly.

Her eyes locked with his, and she saw the truth there. He cared about her, cared about her safety. She started to lean toward him, then straightened when she realized what she was doing. She drew a steadying breath. "I'm okay," she assured him. "The phone calls have stopped, and I seem to have an official escort." She gestured at the police cruiser.

Michael glanced in Jackson's direction and frowned. For some reason she couldn't fathom, he didn't seem to be reassured. He shook his head, rubbing his thumb across her lower lip in a brief caress, as was becoming his habit. "Think about letting me help. Please." He pulled back and opened the door to get out. "I'll drop off Zeke this evening, and you can give me your answer then."

She watched him walk down the dock ramp, her lip tingling where he'd touched it. She shivered. Maybe he was right about the investigation. And maybe, just maybe she really wanted to believe him, to lean on him, if only for a few minutes. But she couldn't take the chance of trusting him.

For Gary's sake, she had to handle things by herself. Which would be easier if she got some sleep. After three visitors in one night, following on the heels of the night of the fire, she was running on empty. She needed a little refueling, maybe a short nap. It wasn't like her to feel sorry for herself. Maybe inhaling all that smoke on the boat had temporarily zapped her drive.

She'd go home, soak in a hot bath. Let her mind wander for a half hour. Maybe something would occur to her, some idea of what to do next.

Then again, maybe she should just go soak her head.

Chapter 16

When Kaz came downstairs at dawn the next morning, Michael was standing in her kitchen, watching coffee drip, and tending an omelet. He'd dropped by late the night before, staying long enough to leave Zeke and bump up her blood pressure, even though he hadn't come within ten feet of her. He was the last person she'd seen before falling asleep, and now he was the first person she was seeing after awakening. Which didn't feel as awkward as it should've.

This morning he wore snug-fitting jeans and another sweater that did illegal things to the width of his shoulders. He looked annoyingly well rested—an effect she had yet to achieve, between her nightmares and her doggy-breath bed companion. She considered snarling.

He glanced at her as he expertly moved the two halves of the omelet onto plates. "Morning."

She grabbed a mug. "Don't you have a kitchen of your own?"

"Still packed."

"How'd you get in?"

"Zeke let me in." She narrowed her eyes at him, and he cocked his head toward the kitchen door. "It was unlocked." He pointed the spatula at her, his expression stern. "That was careless."

"But I locked it," she protested, confused. "I checked *all* the doors and windows before I went to bed. Zeke got restless around midnight and started pacing. But after a few minutes, he settled down. And no one was in the house or he would've gone crazy."

"Maybe he scared someone off before they got inside. Who has keys to this place?"

"Lucy and Gary, that's it." She prayed that he wouldn't ask the next obvious question—whether Gary had been there. She didn't know if he'd come back, and she didn't want to lie to Michael any more than she was forced to.

"You keep a spare key hidden outside?" Michael asked.

"No."

"Would Lucy come in and not tell you?"

She shook her head.

"What about what's-his-name—Chuck?"

An interesting question. Had Chuck come back last night to keep watch? She shivered. "Maybe, I don't know. He's been hanging around."

Michael's expression turned grim. "You didn't tell me that."

She shrugged. "When I confronted him, he said he was looking out for me."

Michael seemed dissatisfied with her answer, but he didn't press her. He brought the plates over to the table, sat down, and nodded at hers. "Eat."

She sampled the omelet and was pleasantly surprised. Okay, so he could cook. She didn't have much luck with omelets, but this one was cooked to perfection, lightly browned on the outside and filled with a fragrant mixture of grilled vegetables and some kind of creamy, tangy cheese. She dug in.

He sipped his coffee, seemingly content to watch her. "Where's Zeke?"

"In my bed," she answered between mouthfuls of food. She shot him a dark look. "Your dog has as much nerve as you do."

One side of his mouth quirked.

"Hey." She pointed her fork at him, irritated. "I didn't ask you or your dog to invade my life. And I sure as hell didn't ask you to stop by and fix me breakfast, or to—to—"

"Show you what you might've been missing all these years?" At her snort, he grinned. "Have you forgotten? I'm going out with you this morning."

She hadn't forgotten. Just what she needed—hours of nerve-wracking work in close quarters with a man whose very presence had her on pins and needles.

"What about Zeke? You can't bring him with you."

"The guys at the station agreed to babysit him. As soon as we drop him off, we're good to go."

Just great. It was going to be a long day.

With Michael's help, Kaz had the crab pots loaded on board the *Kasmira B,* the diesel engines warmed up, and the routine check completed in little more than a half hour. She put the trawler in reverse and backed away from the dock while Michael cast off the lines and pulled in the rubber bumpers that protected the trawler from damage when she was moored. Kaz steered toward the fuel pumps and pulled alongside.

While the computerized pump verified her credit card, a new thought occurred to her. If she were looking for the perfect place to hide something, she knew right where she'd put it. And Gary and she thought uncannily alike—at least, they always had in the past.

She handed the fuel nozzle to Michael and leapt onto the dock. "I'll be back in five. Once the tanks are topped off, go below and change. Use Gary's long johns, the cotton and wool socks, the float coat, and the fur-lined gloves."

Climbing the ramp up to the wharf, she jogged along the east side of it back toward land. Off to her left stood a warehouse containing cold storage units used by the fishermen. She and Gary kept their own unit, using it to hold halibut and tuna until they could negotiate a favorable price.

She fished the key out of her front jeans pocket, unlocked the padlock on the steel door, then yanked on the heavy handle. After checking to make sure the soles of her shoes were dry so that she wouldn't stick to the icy floor, she stepped inside. The cooler was essentially a large freezer with steel walls and a concrete floor, and it was kept precisely at zero degrees Fahrenheit, the optimum temperature for storing frozen fish. Overhead, the compressor hummed loudly, doing its job. On her right, a stack of large tuna lay in a slatted, wooden tray, cleaned and ready for market.

She closed her eyes. *Please, God, let me be wrong.* Because if she weren't, then she would have to admit that Gary was deeply involved in what was going on.

Despite the unnatural chill inside the cooler, she rubbed sweaty palms against her jeans, then forced herself to walk over to the frozen fish. Flipping the top one over, she used both hands to pry the frozen flesh of its belly apart. Inside, she found what she'd been hoping she wouldn't—what someone was so frantically looking for. Carefully wrapped packets of hundred-dollar bills.

Lots and lots of packets.

With shaking hands, she threw that fish aside, then checked the others, several dozen tuna in all. They were all stuffed with money.

She repacked the last tuna and backed away, one hand pressed over her mouth. *Oh God oh God oh God.* She was staring at what had to be several hundred thousand dollars. Gary obviously knew about the money. Had he had it all along and not told her? Was he really tracking down the killer, or was he in on it?

"Everything all right?"

She whirled around.

Michael stood in the doorway.

She swallowed, nodded, and walked toward him. "I thought

Gary might've left some extra pots in here, that's all. Let's go. We're going to miss the tide."

He leaned a shoulder against the doorjamb, blocking her exit. Hands in his pockets, he studied her with that pale, knowledgeable gaze of his, his expression as cool as the dawn air. She held her breath.

Then he shifted to one side to let her past. Had she imagined the flash of disappointment in his eyes? "Whatever you say, boss." His smile held no humor.

Chapter 17

She was lying.

Michael stood in the galley, warming his hands on the oil stove and staring out a portal on the starboard side of the boat. He was eye-level with the surface of the Columbia, which was an odd perspective. The water, which looked smoother from a distance, bounced and lapped past the glass, in concert with the dipping and rocking of the boat. Now and again, a cormorant would float by, startled into flight by Michael's close proximity. In the distance, barely visible through the top half of the small window, he could see forested hills and sand-colored cliffs.

They'd passed through banks of fog, short but fierce rainsqualls, and the occasional bit of sleet. But he wasn't focused on the weather they'd be battling to lift the pots. He was thinking about Kaz and what could have made her face drain of all color in that storage unit.

Something had rattled her. But whatever it was, she wasn't talking. She'd shut herself inside the wheelhouse and hadn't said a word to him since they'd headed out.

He understood he was the newcomer, but dammit, he'd hoped that she was feeling at least some of what he was. They had something special—he *wasn't* imagining it.

Okay, to be honest, he had to ask himself whether, if he were in her position, he would confide in the investigator on the case. And admittedly, it was a tough call. She had to know that as fire chief, he had the authority to arrest her brother. So he probably needed to cut her some slack.

The arson case felt hinky, the murder investigation was full of inconsistencies, and the town fairly oozed with secrets. Add to that his steadily growing, very bad feeling that she was in danger.

To hell with it. Tossing the rest of his cooling coffee into the small galley sink, he filled a mug for her from the thermos and headed upstairs to the wheelhouse to confront her. She had her back to him, consulting the navigational charts that covered the walls. The radio chattered intermittently but was still mostly quiet—they were one of the first boats out.

She jumped a little when he reached around in front of her, the coffee mug in his hand. When she glanced his way, he noted that she was still pale, and that there were deep lines of strain bracketing her mouth.

"Thanks," she said, taking the coffee from him but not meeting his gaze.

He smiled grimly. He had to be six kinds of fool to take this woman on. "Time's up. Tell me what's got you so spooked," he demanded.

She stiffened. "That's exactly what I told the fishermen yesterday," she replied. "Didn't do *me* any good, either."

"Yeah, but if you don't level with me, I'll toss your body overboard to feed the sharks."

"Nothing much in these waters except a few great whites. I'll take my chances."

He grunted. "I am *not* amused." When he reached out to grip her shoulder, it was rigid. "Trust me," he urged.

She turned and searched his face as if she were looking for some kind of reassurance. He waited. Then she lifted a hand in a 'what the hell' gesture, releasing a strained laugh. "I think I've got the 'what-everyone's-looking-for' angle figured out."

As she described what she'd found, Michael felt cold dread

175

settle deep inside him. "That's the kind of money that motivates people to commit murder."

"Yeah."

"Who has keys to the cold storage unit?"

"The guy who owns the warehouse, Gary, and me," she said, her reluctance to answer clear.

"Any chance the owner is dirty?"

"It's possible," she replied, then added reluctantly, "but it doesn't make much sense, does it? Why use someone's locker and risk discovery?"

Michael nodded, waiting while she checked their bearing and adjusted the heading slightly. "You realize this means that your brother is in this right up to his neck."

She stared at the distant horizon, her lips pressed together. "Yes," she said finally. "Though we probably disagree as to his motive. I've been thinking about it, and I believe that Gary found out whatever Ken was into and was trying to extricate him. And maybe that meant helping him hide the money."

The idea had some merit. Michael wondered again whether Gary was being framed. But that didn't explain the money in the locker—no one had access to it.

The trawler began to rock as they neared the breakers, and Michael planted his feet more widely. "What else haven't you told me?"

"Nothing important," she said, too quickly.

"Right," he said, letting the sarcasm bleed through. He ran a hand through his hair, still angry.

She glanced over her shoulder, her expression was pleading. "Look, let's listen to the radio while we lift the pots, then take it from there. Deal?"

"When we get back to port," he ordered, "you're handing the money over to your pal Lucy. And you don't make a move without me—I just became your round-the-clock shadow." She started to protest, and he reached out with both hands,

176

yanking her around to face him. *"No.* You don't get a choice on this one. I'm not letting another person I care about die on my watch. You got that?"

"Don't confuse me with your fiancée," she shot back. "I don't need your protection."

His tone turned hard with anger, his hands gripping harder. "If I have to, I'll have Sykes confine you. I'm sure he'd be happy to oblige."

She paled. "You wouldn't."

"Cooperate, or you're about to see."

She jerked out of his grip. "We're about ten minutes away from the bar. You should get below."

"I'm staying right here."

Their gazes clashed. She was the first to look away, turning her back to him. "Then shut the door. I don't want to be standing in a foot of water while I navigate."

Fifteen minutes later, the coffee Michael had ingested was threatening to make the rest of his day miserable. Huge waves were coming at the trawler from all directions, and remaining on his feet was impossible unless he braced himself against the wall and hung onto the equipment console. In all his summers of crabbing back East, he'd never been this close to being puking.

Kaz stood, feet braced with both hands on the wheel, for all outward appearances cool and calm in the face of what was sheer insanity. But her eyes moved continually—from landmarks, when they were visible, to the navigational maps, and then to her equipment.

He wasn't merely impressed, he was in awe, his respect for her skills having increased ten-fold in just the last five minutes. He knew the Columbia River bar was the most treacherous stretch of water in the Lower Forty-Eight, but until he'd experienced it, he'd had no clue. Waves battered them relentlessly, crashing over the trawler in a crazy jigsaw pattern, tossing the boat about like a toy. A person had to be crazy as a loon to tackle this every day. No wonder she wasn't worried about the occasional intruder in her home—the guy would have to be armed with an Uzi to make her even break out in a sweat.

"You do this every day," he said, breaking the tense silence that still remained between them.

"Most days, yeah." Her response was absent-minded. "This is pretty calm today."

He nearly laughed out loud. The swells were over ten feet. And how long would it take the trawler to break apart if she made a mistake? No more than a few minutes, max. He couldn't even think about what it must've been like for her that night fifteen years ago. He fought down the urge to demand that she turn around and take them back to port where she'd be safe—to demand that she never do this again. To tell her that he couldn't handle it if she went out and never came back. "You need counseling," he said instead.

She shot a quick grin at him. "Nah. I had counseling, right after the shipwreck. It didn't stick."

He shook his head.

She gestured at the horizon with one hand. "This is all part of a tradition—going back, for most of us, at least three generations. I may have left this life behind, and I may have had some bad experiences out here, but I'm discovering that it's still a part of who I am."

He couldn't deny what she was saying—his brothers who fished back East felt the same way. They faced harsh conditions, but nothing like this. "Why not dock the trawler somewhere farther down the coast?"

"All the good mooring basins have river bars." She paused to listen to the radio for a minute, then continued, "Other than the fish processing in Coos Bay, the buyers are all right here in

Astoria. The river bar is an inconvenience—" she rolled her eyes at the understatement—"but it's a fact of life."

"And death."

"Yeah." She pushed the trawler up and over another vertical wall of water. "Gary has always said that you have to be lucky, each and every day you're out here. Because if you aren't, all the skill in the world won't make any difference."

She fell silent, her face unaccountably sad.

Michael's family had been lucky—they hadn't lost anyone in more than fifty years. But he'd seen the effects of such tragedies on the other fishing families back East. He'd always been in awe of their acceptance of the hardships they put up with, year after year.

The waves suddenly lessened in intensity, and the rough water changed texture. They'd left the river bar behind and entered the Pacific. Kaz's shoulders visibly relaxed, and she turned to him with a slight smile that was perhaps a peace offering. "We've got about 45 minutes 'til we reach the pots. Let's use it to get warmed up—it'll be our last chance."

He wanted to touch her, to rub those proud shoulders and soothe the rest of the tension out of them. Looking at her made him ache to help her. But he held back. Instead, he said, "I'll bring you some more coffee—I'm going to wait a bit."

"While you're down there, throw on hip boots and a sou'wester, along with rubber gloves. You don't want your hands icing up when we start lifting the pots."

Hugging the coastline, they traveled south until they came to a string of buoys whose colors matched the black and green stripes painted on the sides of the *Kasmira B.*

The weather, Kaz noted worriedly, was getting nastier. The wind had picked up, and there was considerably more sleet and snow mixed in with the rain. She cut the engines down to a low rumble as they came alongside the first buoy. Then she came out on the deck, dressed in hip boots, pulling on her gloves.

Michael was already kneeling alongside the railing. He glanced up at her. "I'll lift and rebait—you steer the trawler."

She shook her head, moving the hydraulic block that they would use to haul the pots out of the water into position. "It would be better if we had a second crewman, but you're stuck with me. It'll go faster if I help."

They worked in surprisingly companionable silence for the first twenty minutes or so. Michael had slipped easily into the rhythm of the work—lifting the pot while she chopped the frozen bait with a cleaver, working with her to throw back the females and undersized males, then baiting and dropping the pot back into the water, only to repeat the process with the next one down the line. Every so often, she stopped to readjust their position along the lines, then come back out on deck to help.

The catch was looking good, thank God. The business needed the money—this was only their second lift of the season. If production stayed this steady, it might cover some of the repair expenses they'd already incurred. The catch a few days ago had been much lighter; she'd begun to wonder whether she'd have to move her pots to slightly deeper water. They were at twelve fathoms now—a good depth in most years.

She glanced sideways at Michael. He was working steadily and not saying much, evidently content with the screech of the gulls, the lap of the water against the hull, and the sound of the wind. They were both icing up from the freezing spray and sleet, though, and would need to take a break soon.

He was good. Almost as good as Bjorn's son. And they were progressing much faster than she could on her own.

She'd never felt this kind of easy companionship with Phil, not in the three years they'd been together. She'd always had to struggle, to concentrate on making the relationship work. With

Michael, though, everything felt natural. She was starting to depend on him, look forward to the time they spent together. And that was very scary indeed.

It was becoming harder and harder to lie to him, even through omission. He'd been right when he'd told her that she'd have to trust someone. She came to a decision. Once they were back in port, she'd sit down and level with him. Tell him everything.

She stopped chopping bait to listen to the chatter on the radio for a minute. The fishermen had been talking continuously for the last half hour, joking with each other, reporting fake locations meant to confuse the larger, commercial trawlers who might horn in on their catch, and generally keeping each other company. She recognized almost all of the voices—Svensen's, Bjorn's, those of Jacobsen's crew, and others. Svensen was nattering on about something having to do with too many dogfish in his net when she stopped what she was doing to stare intently at the radio.

Michael straightened from throwing crabs over the side. "What?"

She listened for another few moments and then shook her head, perplexed. "Nothing, I guess. It's just that Svensen gave out a location that wouldn't fool anyone—it's too close in to shore. I thought he was smarter than that."

"Maybe not. How well do you know him?"

She shrugged. "We grew up together, but I'm not all that fond of his type."

"Type?"

"The kind of fisherman who only gets into the business for the money," she explained. "He fell into an inheritance, bought up several trawlers from folks who'd tried their hand at fishing and had failed, and put a lot of crews behind hauling big catches, fast. Make the money and get out—that's his attitude. Guys like him don't last through the lean years, because they fail to meet their expected profit margin and there's no love of the work to see them through. From what I hear, no one expected him to make it this long."

"What about the other guy you were talking to earlier?"

"Bjorn?" She grabbed another handful of frozen bait and brought the cleaver down hard. "He's okay, third generation, like Gary and me. He's got a large family—several of his teenage sons are already crewing for him. One of them helps Gary out from time to time."

"Kaz."

The grim tone alerted her even before she turned around. She saw the broken line he was holding up. "Sonofabitch!" She stabbed the cleaver into a hunk of bait and dropped down to look over the side, then along the line of buoys as they stretched out into the distance. She stood and moved into the wheelhouse to run the trawler up to the next buoy.

Michael leaned over the side and snagged the buoy. He connected the line to the hydraulic block and hauled up the first pot. On the other end of the pot, the line had been cut, just like the one before.

"Check the others," she ordered, her anger growing.

For the next hour, they ran the rest of the first half of the pots. Each buoy had one pot attached, then the line was cut. All in all, she estimated that they'd lost well over three quarters the pots. It was a devastating financial blow, not so much the pots but what had been in them. Unless Gary relented and let her invest some of her own savings in the business, it could go under.

Someone had done this, and made it look good enough so that no one would notice. That took time and determination. She returned to the wheelhouse and unhooked the handset for the radio. "This is the *Kasmira B*, over."

"*Kasmira B*, nice to hear from you." Bjorn's voice boomed across the airwaves.

"We've got a problem here. You guys see anyone around my lines the last couple of days?"

"State your situation."

"Lines cut, pots not retrievable." She waited. Michael came to lean against the door, pulling off his rubber gloves and rubbing the ice from his coat.

The radio remained silent.

She clicked to retransmit. "I repeat, lines cut, pots not retrievable. I'd appreciate a report of who y'all have seen over here lately."

Silence.

Her gaze met Michael's. His expression was hard. She swore and tossed the handset onto the console.

"How bad is it?" he asked.

"Bad enough." She rubbed the back of her neck. "Let's take a break, then see what else we can salvage."

She headed down to the galley, and Michael followed. While she was pouring coffee, he came up behind her and put his hands on her shoulders. She tensed.

He overrode her resistance, pulling her back against him and wrapping his arms around her. "All this will be over soon, and these guys will come around." He placed his chin on top of her head. "They probably didn't want to talk because I was on board."

"Maybe." She sniffled once, appalled at how close she was to tears. For something of so little consequence compared to everything else she'd faced in the last week, the cut lines were, for some reason, the last straw. But she knew it wasn't the lost pots, not really. It was the silence on the radio that had gotten to her.

Michael tightened his arms for a moment, then let loose of her. He moved around her, got sandwiches out of a Styrofoam cooler, unwrapped them, and handed one to her. "Eat."

She stared at the sandwich, which looked totally

unappetizing. "Do you always push food as a universal solution?"

"I can think of other remedies, but they're harder to implement when swathed in four layers of foul weather gear."

That got a small laugh out of her. "Valid point." She took the sandwich.

They ate in silence for a few minutes, warming themselves next to the oil stove. The ice on their coats melted and dripped, making a soggy mess of the carpet.

"So what now?" Michael asked.

"We pull what we can, then head for port. I'll see if it's possible to get a diver out here, but with these currents, it's probably a lost cause. Someone knew what he was doing."

"Someone who knew your colors, and who knew what to do to inflict maximum damage. Someone in the fishing fleet."

"Yeah." She tossed down the rest of her sandwich, no longer able to swallow.

Someone not only wanted to frame Gary, but put them both out of business. That took a lot of hate.

Or a lot of desperation.

She'd faced hostile corporate boards, and over the years, she knew she'd made some enemies. They'd undercut her and take her next client maybe, or try to block the merger she was working on. Tit for tat. But that was business.

This felt personal.

It took them five hours to run the rest of the lines. She'd lost the majority of their pots. Tired and discouraged, she turned the *Kasmira B* toward port. The ride back over the bar was a silent one, but Michael never left her side.

They docked the *Kasmira B* well after dark, then went straight to the storage unit to retrieve the money to turn it over to the authorities.

It was gone.

Chapter 18

When Kaz and Michael walked out of the storage unit, several police stood waiting for them. Lucy's expression was grim, Ivar's sympathetic.

Sykes stepped forward and handed Kaz a folded document. "General search warrant," he explained. "Covers your cold storage unit, your boats and vehicles, and your house. We're looking for evidence related to the arson and the murder of Ken Lundquist."

Kaz took the document, unfolding it with shaking hands. The impersonal legalese brought home the gravity of Gary's situation. And hers. "You already have an arrest warrant." She angrily waved the search warrant. "Why are you doing this?"

Clint Jackson, who was standing next to Sykes, smirked at her.

"We've arrested your brother in the past and couldn't make it stick," Sykes said. "This time, I'm personally making sure the DA has all the evidence he'll need to convict."

Kaz rounded on Michael. "Did you know about this?" She'd trusted him, been ready to confide in him. Now she could only choke on his betrayal. Why did it hurt so badly?

He shook his head. "I only knew about the arrest warrant." When he reached out a hand, she shoved the paperwork at him.

She wanted to believe him. But he had to have suspected this would happen. Why hadn't he warned her? For that matter, why hadn't Lucy? The betrayal stung, and her eyes welled with tears.

She held out her key ring to Sykes. He took it, telling her to wait nearby, then he and Clint entered the storage building.

To put some distance between herself and the others, she walked over and sat down on the cold, wet concrete curb of the parking lot. She couldn't shake the feeling that events were spinning out of control. If Sykes and Jackson had searched the unit even a few hours ago, they'd have found the money and been able to use it to build the case against Gary.

It made sense that Gary had moved the money—maybe after he'd seen her go into the storage unit that morning. If so, then he had to be hiding out nearby, perhaps using one of the many abandoned warehouses that were strung out all along the waterfront. The crumbling old buildings were some distance from Astoria's business district—only fishermen would've been close enough to see him coming and going, and they wouldn't say anything. Fear for him made her stomach cramp. He was taking insane risks, moving around in broad daylight.

Lucy came over and dropped down beside her, giving her a hug. "I tried to call you several times today—"

"We were out working the lines."

Lucy's expression turned wry. "So I heard, from just about everyone at the Redemption. No one was happy about you taking a newcomer out."

Kaz shrugged.

"The chief got Judge Banks on his cell phone," Lucy explained quietly. "Banks was out elk hunting and was reluctant to issue a warrant over the phone, but after Sykes told him about the blood on the tire iron matching Ken's, he didn't really have much choice."

Kaz relented a little. It was unrealistic to think that Lucy could've controlled what Sykes did. Glancing toward the storage unit to make certain that Sykes was still out of hearing range, she motioned the others over and brought Lucy and Ivar up to date.

"When there's that much money floating around, it's usually related to drugs," Ivar quietly pointed out.

Lucy clearly agreed. "Which gives us the possible connection to the murder of the drug dealer." She told Kaz and Michael about the body they'd found yesterday morning. "The second murder definitely doesn't look premeditated—more like someone who needed a fix turning violent. We've got a local methadone treatment clinic that was burglarized late this afternoon, what looks like a supply disruption on the street bad enough to escalate to violence, and a huge amount of cash." She shot Kaz a disgusted look. "Floating around God knows where."

"What?" Kaz raised her hands. "How was I supposed to know it would disappear while I was out?" Lucy gave her a look that told her she'd already figured out that it hadn't disappeared on its own, but she didn't say anything.

"It's got to be money that would've been used to buy drugs," Ivar said. "Someone stole drug money, and the drugs it would've purchased never got to the street."

Michael spoke up. "So maybe the fishermen are running drugs. Taking money out to sea for a rendezvous, then bringing the drugs back."

"If so, it's a damn near perfect setup." Lucy blew out a breath. "The Coast Guard wouldn't stop those guys to conduct searches—their boats wouldn't be considered suspicious."

"Gary's not part of this," Kaz insisted, sounding like a broken record even to herself. "There's got to be another reason why he had all that money." She appealed to Lucy. "You *know* he wouldn't be involved, Luce."

"Actually, I agree," Lucy said. Ivar frowned at her, and she shrugged. "I think Gary's being framed, so sue me." But her expression remained troubled. "It's a damn good question, though, what he was doing with all that cash in the storage unit."

"Maybe he got it from Ken," Kaz suggested, thinking out loud. "They could've been arguing that night in the tavern because Ken could've asked Gary to keep the money someplace safe, if he thought someone was after him."

"But if Ken was dealing drugs, why would he need anyone to safeguard the money?" Lucy shook her head. "That's cockeyed—he would've been exchanging the money for the drugs, not hiding it. And we've gone over his bank and phone records. Nada. He doesn't fit the profile."

"Profile?" Kaz looked from Lucy to Ivar.

"He has—had—a stable home life, there've been no dramatic changes in his lifestyle," Lucy explained. "Then again, Gary doesn't fit the profile either, based on our investigation into your financial records."

Kaz glared. "You've been looking at our *bank* records?"

"Yeah." Lucy sent her an apologetic look.

Kaz looked away. All of the sudden, she was sick to death of the whole mess. She wanted this investigation out of the way of her friendships with the people here in town she cared the most about.

A new thought occurred to her. "What if Ken wasn't involved with drug running but stole the money for some reason?"

"That could work," Michael said, looking thoughtful. "He yields to temptation, then gets in trouble and goes to Gary."

"That would also explain the sudden supply disruption at the street level," Ivar mused.

"Didn't you tell me Ken had suffered more than one beating a few days prior to being killed?" Michael asked Lucy. "So he stole the money, the bad guys were onto him, and they beat him up as a warning a couple of times. When he didn't pony

188

up, they got rid of him."

Kaz remembered what Bjorn had said. "The fishermen think Ken was killed to send a message."

"Yeah, I can buy that." Lucy chewed on her lip. "But that doesn't explain why they framed Gary."

"If Ken went to Gary for help and Gary created heat by asking too many questions..." Michael shrugged. "Framing Gary kills two birds with one stone."

"But why would Ken have been stupid enough to steal drug money?" Lucy asked. "I knew him pretty well—he never struck me as being either stupid or suicidal. Anyone with half a brain knows not to steal from drug dealers."

"According to what Gary told me, Ken had horrific medical bills for Bobby's leukemia," Kaz said. "Ken loved Bobby—he'd have done anything for him." She shuddered, unable to imagine what it must have been like to watch your own child suffer that way. "If the rendezvous with the drug supplier is happening at sea, maybe Ken thought he wouldn't get caught."

Lucy shook her head. "We checked out the medical bills. The mother-in-law is paying for them."

Julie had indicated the same to Kaz, but Kaz wasn't so sure. At the time, it had been her impression that Julie was lying. And Kaz had just gotten Ken and his family signed up for health insurance a week ago, which made the cancer a preexisting condition that wasn't covered. The bills had to have been enormous.

"Whatever the scenario," Ivar said, "Gary is in this up to his neck."

"He's trying to find out who's involved," Kaz insisted. She stopped speaking while Sykes and Jackson locked up the storage unit and walked past them toward the docks, then continued. "At least, that's what Gary told me."

Lucy groaned loudly. "And you didn't tell me this earlier?"

Kaz risked a glance at Michael. His expression was set and

189

furious, but she'd deal with him later. "Think about it," she insisted. "Someone else has to be involved, or I wouldn't be getting phone calls. Gary would have no reason to do that."

Lucy looked seriously unhappy. "Dammit, Kaz, you could be in real danger."

"I keep telling her that," Michael growled.

"We need more information," Lucy said. "I can start running checks on the finances of some of the fishermen—look for recent changes in lifestyle, that kind of thing. But we need hard evidence."

"A discussion with Gary right about now would be very useful, to find out what else he knows," Ivar mused.

Kaz stood up. "I'm heading home."

"No," Michael said firmly. "You'll wait right here until I get a change of clothes from my place, then we can go together."

"The cops have a surveillance team at my house, in case you've forgotten." Her voice was cool. "And Sykes and Jackson will be right behind me to search the house. I don't need you."

He strode over to her and knelt, taking both her hands in his. His grip was warm, his expression serious. "I didn't know about the search warrant, I swear," he said, keeping his voice low. "Don't do something foolish because you're upset with me."

Before she could react, Lucy grabbed Michael's arm. "Excuse us." She yanked him to his feet and walked him several feet away. "You're getting too close," Kaz heard her tell him in a low voice. "Back off."

Michael's expression turned hard. "Are you questioning my objectivity?"

"Maybe I am."

He took a step forward, and Kaz rose to intervene, then stopped at his next words. "Bottom line, I'm going to protect Kaz," he said, his voice tight with anger. "And I'll do my damn job." Then he turned to include Kaz. "Don't you two think it's about damn time you trusted me?"

"You're taking my *laptop?*" Kaz asked Sykes, shaking with fury. He and Jackson had arrived just after she'd gotten home. Michael was only a half hour behind, still angry that she'd refused to wait.

She and Sykes were standing in her living room while Jackson carried out boxes of files, printouts, and equipment— all of her records on the fishing business, as well as the records for her consulting business down in California. All of her bank statements, all of Gary's correspondence, all of her *personal* emails to Phil, for God's sake. She reached for the phone. "I'm calling my attorney."

"You'll get it all back, don't worry," Sykes replied, gathering up the loose stacks of printouts that had been strewn across the coffee table. He tossed her keys back to her, looking angry.

He and Jackson had practically torn the house apart, becoming increasingly destructive as they failed to find anything incriminating, yet refusing to answer when she demanded to know what they were looking for. And Clint had seemed to get an almost prurient satisfaction out of going through her personal belongings.

As Sykes walked out with her laptop tucked under one arm, Clint told her, "We're going to nail Gary this time, Kaz. Count on it."

She slammed the front door and stalked into the kitchen, yanking open the freezer and staring at her choices for dinner without really seeing them.

Maybe she was going about this the wrong way. Who in the fishing community was capable of running drugs? Bjorn was one of the more successful fishermen in town. He hadn't taken the government's buyout offer, and he was still operating several boats. But she couldn't imagine that he would be tempted by anything illegal. And if he were in trouble, she

191

would've seen some sign—maybe that he wanted to sell one of the boats. Of course, it was possible the reason he was doing so well was that he had a second, very lucrative source of income.

She shook her head, slamming the freezer door. This was getting her nowhere. Bjorn was the last person she should be suspecting. So far, he was the one who was the most supportive of her, though that wasn't really saying much. After all, what had he really told her? Certainly nothing that could be substantiated. Maybe that was his strategy—sound helpful while keeping her in the dark.

She walked over to the window and stared out at the dark, empty street. Were things so bad that she was wondering whether one of the nicest guys in the fleet—the father of eight children, for God's sake—was a cold-blooded murderer?

When it came right down to it, the only fisherman she could stand to accuse of drug smuggling was Karl Svensen. He *had* refused to press charges against Gary six months ago, but recently, he'd been neither helpful nor friendly. And according to Steve, he'd had some kind of run-in with Ken. She wasn't privy to Karl's finances, but they couldn't be all that great if his boats came back into port on the light side. Of course, that could be said about every fisherman in Astoria, including her.

She sighed. She was going in circles, and those circles were bringing her right back around to Ken. He was the only person who'd had obvious financial pressures. Chemo and hospital stays like Bobby's were expensive, and she'd never been under the impression that Ken's mother was all that wealthy.

On a hunch, she pulled the Portland phone book out of the kitchen junk drawer, looking up the number for the hospital where Bobby was being treated. The clock on the wall above the stove indicated that they were well into the dinner hour, but maybe hospitals kept their offices open later than usual. She dialed the number. When the receptionist answered, Kaz asked for the business office and was informed that it was closed. So she asked to be transferred to the children's oncology ward.

While she waited, she rehearsed what she would say. She jumped when the head nurse answered on the second ring. "Um, yes, hi. This is Julie Lundquist, and I wanted to check on the status of our account. I think I may have paid one of the bills twice, by mistake—"

"I'm sorry," the nurse said, "but it's after hours, and the office is closed. If you could call again tomorrow morning—"

"Um, I knew that," Kaz said. "But it's kind of an emergency. See, I've overdrawn my account, and I know it's late, but I'm trying to reconcile my checkbook while Bobby gets a little sleep—he's having so much trouble sleeping right now—and I'll be getting overdraft notices that I can't afford—"

"Oh, poor thing," the nurse said, her voice instantly sympathetic. "It's so hard to watch children go through chemo."

"Yes," Kaz agreed quickly, feeling a giant twinge of guilt at her deception. "It would really help if you could pull up my records on the computer and take a peek at the last payment I sent you, you know, so I could verify the amount?"

"I'm not supposed to—"

"Please."

"Well, I don't see how it could really hurt..." The nurse seemed to come to a decision. "Hold on and I'll see what I can do." After tapping on the computer keys for a moment, she said, "Please verify the last four digits of your social security number for me."

Kaz froze, trying to remember Julie's number from when she'd filled out the insurance forms for them last week. "8166." She held her breath.

"Okay, here we go. You haven't sent us anything for a long time. Your last check to us was dated four months ago."

"I see," Kaz said hesitantly, amazed that it had been so easy,

193

and then said, "Um, I thought that I might've overpaid. Can you give me the outstanding balance?"

"Well, that's odd. You don't have a balance." The nurse tapped some more. "Oh, right! I remember now. We just received that anonymous donation that wiped out your outstanding balance. Our bookkeeper told us about it. We were so excited that someone would do that for Bobby."

"Anonymous?" Kaz repeated, dumfounded. Then she realized the woman had to be talking about Ken's mother. "Oh, you must mean the payments from my mother-in-law."

"Nooo," the nurse said, sounding confused herself now. "The payment was anonymous, and there's a notation right here in the file that they called you to give you the good news about your unknown benefactor. Your mother-in-law hasn't paid anything in quite some time."

"That's right," Kaz said quickly. She started to end the call, then thought of one more question. "When was that payment made again?"

"Hon, you must really be out of it. They called you this afternoon."

Kaz recovered quickly enough to laugh nervously. "You know, I am. I've been losing so much sleep—well. Sorry to have taken up your time." She hung up before the woman decided to get suspicious, then stood in the middle of the kitchen, lost in thought.

So Ken had probably been using the drug money to pay for Bobby's treatments. It made sense. And Julie must've known about it and lied to cover it up. She'd *known* that the burglary wasn't real, that they'd been looking for the money. That explained her edginess when Kaz had been at the house, and her unwillingness to talk to the police.

Kaz had no doubt, though, who had made the anonymous donation. Absently setting the portable phone down on the counter, she acknowledged the full import of what she'd just

194

discovered. The anonymous payment was *exactly* the type of gesture that Gary would make, especially in light of Ken's murder. Of all the information she'd unearthed to date, this had her the most freaked, because it meant that whoever killed Ken would now be after Gary.

Kaz paced for another moment, trying to control her anxiety, and then pulled a frozen meal at random from the freezer. She popped it into the microwave. She had to get in touch with Chuck, right away. Gary's only hope of staying alive was to turn himself in, telling the police everything he knew. And that meant she needed to drive out to Chuck's that evening.

She opened the junk drawer to rummage for a pad and pencil. She'd leave a note for Michael. He'd be angry, but there wasn't any help for it. If Michael was with her, there was no way either Chuck or Gary—

Her only warning was a slight shifting of the air behind her. She started to turn, but he was on her too fast, a gloved hand encircling her neck, cutting off her air.

Chapter 19

Before she reacted enough to struggle, her assailant's arm locked hard around her waist, trapping her. He jerked her backwards so that her feet were dangling in the air. Then he half-carried, half-dragged her, kicking and squirming, into the darkened living room.

Gasping, she clawed at the hand at her throat, unable to do more than scratch the leather of his glove. The hand tightened, and her vision grayed.

She flung her other hand up and back, trying to claw his face, but all she got was a handful of some kind of soft wool material.

A ski mask.

He yanked her higher against his body. She tried to kick backwards, but she couldn't get a good enough angle to inflict any real damage. Her ears started roaring.

She threw her head backward as hard as she could, hitting him in the face. He howled, and his grip loosened slightly. Gulping in air, she curled her body over his arm, forcing him to bend forward, then threw herself backward, causing him to lose his balance and fall to the floor.

They crashed into the coffee table, then fell sideways, landing in a heap on the area rug with him underneath. She rolled away, scrabbling to get the distance she needed to kick him—his knees, his groin, his ribs—anywhere she could inflict enough damage to slow him down. But he recovered faster than she'd anticipated.

In one swift move, he was on her, slamming her against the hardwood floor with enough force to knock the air out of her lungs.

He was heavy, and strong. *But not fit.* Even as she struggled to drag air into her lungs, she dimly registered the softness on his chest and stomach.

She kneed him, but he dodged to the side, deflecting her aim. A lamp crashed to the floor beside her, shattering. She jerked her head sideways to avoid the exploding shards of glass.

Using both hands, he rammed her head hard against the floor. Pain exploded, stars swimming on the blackened edges of her vision.

Sliding both gloved hands around her throat, he squeezed, cutting off her air. She glared at him, defiant, but couldn't see anything except his eyes gleaming at her through the holes in the mask.

His hands loosened slightly, and she gulped in air to scream. Then they tightened again, choking off any sound she could've made. She bucked and squirmed, but he had most of his weight on her, and she couldn't move more than a few inches. Over the thumps they were making in their nearly silent struggle, she heard the pinging of the microwave as it finished cooking her dinner.

She continued to fight him, using her hands to punch and scratch him, anywhere she could reach. He never spoke, just eased the pressure on her larynx once in awhile so that she could draw in enough air to keep from passing out. Then he'd cut it off again, his teeth flashing at her in a grin. He was toying with her, and he was enjoying it.

She subsided, exhausted and trembling.

And heard his soft, low, laugh.

"That's better," he whispered. "This was a demonstration of

what will happen to you if you don't give us the money. You won't know when I'll come back, and you won't be able to stop me any more than you could this time. Nod your head if you understand."

She nodded reluctantly, straining to memorize details, anything that she could later use to identify him. He had to be someone she knew. Somehow, she was certain of that fact. A sob of frustration worked its way out of her throat.

"Good girl," he whispered. "You've got twenty-four hours to return the money. We'll be in touch."

He grabbed her hair and used it to yank her head up, wrenching her neck. Then he slammed her head down.

The last thing she remembered was the floor rushing up at her left eye, and pain exploding in a flashing prism of color.

Then everything went black.

Chapter 20

"Kaz? Come on, sweetheart, wake up. Talk to me." The voice, deep and filled with urgency, came at her out of a fog of pain.

Someone held her hand and gently stroked her cheek. There was a light above her; its brightness hurt. She made out the shadow of someone leaning over her.

She moaned and gulped in air. Breathing hurt, she discovered.

"You're safe," Michael reassured softly.

She thought she could hear sirens, but the pounding inside her head overwhelmed all other sound. Beside her, a dog whined. Zeke. He licked her hand. Raising it, she touched her temple, which seemed to be the source of the pain. It felt funny—wet, and the wrong size, somehow.

"Easy. Let's have the EMTs take a look at that, okay?"

"What—"

"When I drove up, the kitchen door was standing open. Zeke found you on the living room floor, out cold."

The man in the ski mask. *The threat.*

Twenty-four hours. She had only twenty-four hours to find the money.

She struggled to rise, but gentle hands held her down. "Don't move, sweetheart.

"Help...sit up."

"Not until the EMTs check you over."

She could focus a little better now with one eye. Michael's

expression was fierce, at odds with the soft, crooning quality of his voice. "I'm okay," she insisted. "Help me up."

He grumbled something and rose, scooping her up off the floor in one fluid motion. Walking over to one of the easy chairs, he settled her in his lap, keeping his arms tight around her. The abrupt movement made her dizzy, and she laid her head against his shoulder, closing her eyes.

Her throat was sore, and she placed a hand on it.

Michael's brushed her hand aside, saw the bruises, and his expression became even grimmer. "Did you see who attacked you?"

Two EMTs arrived, cutting off her reply. One of them knelt beside their chair and grinned at her. "Hey, Kaz. How ya feeling?"

"Like someone...flattened me."

He nodded and looked at Michael. "Sir, if you'll set her down and move out of our way—"

"Not a chance," Michael replied, his voice implacable. "Check her right where she is."

The EMT eyed him and decided not to argue. She continued to lean against Michael while the EMT checked her pupils, took her blood pressure, and asked her simple questions to determine if she was alert. He cleaned her face with an antiseptic wipe and placed a temporary bandage over the cut on her forehead.

"Pupils are okay," he said, packing up his instrument case. "But let's take a ride to the hospital, Kaz. You'll need a CAT Scan and some stitches."

"No, I'm all right." She shrugged out of Michael's arms and got shakily to her feet, gripping the arm of the chair for support as a new waved of dizziness attacked her.

She felt someone catch her as she fell.

Four hours later, Kaz lay on a bed in the hospital emergency ward, waiting. They'd stitched up the cut on her forehead, then strapped her to a table and run her through a giant tube to take pictures of her head. Someone was supposed to come by with a verdict as to whether she would live.

She wanted out. Right now. She hated hospitals. The last time she'd been here, she'd been in the basement morgue to identify her parents' bodies.

Her whole body hurt, all the way down to the cellular level. Getting slammed into a hardwood floor a couple of times—then landed on by a 200-pound gorilla—did that. But she'd just have to take large quantities of aspirin.

Twenty-four hours. That's all she and Gary had, if she believed her attacker. And call her crazy, but she didn't think he was the kind of guy who'd be very flexible.

Michael and Lucy chose that moment to come through the curtains surrounding her bed. They were arguing, as usual. Lucy's expression when she glanced Kaz's way was worried, her eyes full of regret.

"Where the *hell* was your surveillance team?" Michael asked. "She was a sitting duck."

"Jackson called them off. They received some kind of tip on Gary's whereabouts that they're following up on. I didn't find out until just a few minutes before I heard your call come in."

Kaz shivered, her sense of urgency worsening. Were they closing in on Gary?

The emergency room nurse popped her head in. "The doctor wants to keep you overnight for observation," she announced cheerfully. "We've got a room all set up."

"No way," Kaz said in a hoarse voice. "I'm leaving." She swung her legs over the side of the bed, then had to wait a moment for the dizziness to recede.

The nurse rushed over and pushed her firmly back onto the bed. "That requires the doctor's signature, and he's not available. Why don't you lie down—"

Kaz leaned sideways on one elbow, squinting at Lucy through her good eye. "Show her your gun," she said, sotto voce.

Lucy rolled her eyes.

Using one hand to keep the nurse at bay, Kaz slid until her feet touched the floor, then grabbed the edge of the bed in an effort to stand up. The nurse tut-tutted and waved her hands.

Michael cleared his throat. "There were no cracks in her extremely hard head, right?" At the nurse's reluctant nod, he continued, "I'll keep an eye on her for tonight. Hunt up the doc and get him to sign the release papers." When the nurse opened her mouth to protest, he added, "Do you really think she'll stay put?"

"Where're my clothes?" Kaz demanded, glaring at her.

The nurse threw up her hands and left.

While they waited, Lucy commandeered the only available chair, pulling it up to the edge of the bed. "Talk," she ordered.

As best she could with a throat still refusing to work, Kaz told them about the attack. "He was convinced that I knew where the money was."

Michael's eyes were on the bruises beginning to form on her neck. "Did he try to strangle you?"

"I don't think that was his intention. He was controlling me by cutting off my air supply."

Michael turned abruptly on his heel and walked over to the window, standing with his back to them.

Lucy watched him, a worried frown on her face. "Can you describe the guy?" she asked Kaz.

"Not really—he was wearing a ski mask."

"Height? Weight?"

"He was heavier than me—I'd say by at least seventy pounds. And he was tall enough to lift me off my feet, so he has to be over six feet."

"So six-two, maybe three, around one-ninety to two-ten.

What else?"

"He was strong, but...he had a gut." She couldn't stop the shudder that went through her. "He used his weight to subdue me."

Michael turned to look at her.

"He had brown eyes, I think," she continued, forcing herself to think back to those moments when Ski Mask had had her pinned. "But it was dark, so that's just an impression. Thick wrists, pale skin...and dark hair, fairly thick, on the back of his wrists."

"What about smells? Aftershave? Was he a smoker?" Michael asked.

"Sweat," Kaz remembered, wrinkling her nose. "His clothes were...damp with it." She closed her eyes.

She'd been helpless—completely helpless—for the first time in her life. She'd rather face down another thirty-foot storm surge than cross paths with that guy again. "I think he was the same guy who was in my house two nights ago. This time, though, I did some damage."

"Of course you did." Lucy grinned. "Any rings on his hands?"

Kaz shook her head. "He had on leather gloves." She folded her hands in front of her in an effort to stop their trembling. "He said I had twenty-four hours to return the money."

Michael swore, walked back to the foot of the bed, and gripped the metal railing. "That's it. You're out of it, from here on." He turned his fierce gaze on Lucy. "I want her in protective custody—that's a formal request. I want someone with her every damn minute until we catch this guy. And I want her in a safe location."

"No," Kaz said, and raised her hand when he would have roared at her. "Don't you see? We don't have any time left. Sykes thinks he's closing in on Gary. I have to get to him before they catch him. We have to find out what he knows."

"He can talk to Lucy. I want you out of it."

"He won't talk to anyone but me," Kaz insisted.

"Tough," Michael said, his voice rough. "I won't have you hurt, not again."

"That's not your call," Kaz said evenly.

"She's right," Lucy said, and Michael swore. "If Gary's willing to talk to anyone, it would be either Chuck or Kaz," Lucy insisted, not looking any happier about it than Michael. "I questioned the junkie we found at the scene of the second murder again, and he's not still talking. I even threw the three strikes prison sentence at him as a threat, and he won't budge. After you two left the mooring basin, I also talked to several of the fishermen at the Redemption. *No one* is talking—they're scared out of their wits. I don't have any suspects, dammit, and Kaz is my only hope of finding some leads I can pursue." She turned back to Kaz. "I assume you're going to contact Chuck."

Kaz nodded.

Michael heaved a sigh and scrubbed a hand over his face. "What's your plan?"

"To drive out to his place and talk to him."

"Won't work," Ivar said, appearing at the edge of the curtains. His long face was somber. "We found Chuck about a half hour ago in your backyard. The EMTs are bringing him in right now, but they aren't optimistic. Whoever got the drop on him beat him almost to death."

Chapter 21

Kaz shooed everyone out and pulled on her clothes, gritting her teeth against the pain and dizziness that kept threatening to swamp her. She walked slowly toward the waiting room where Michael was waiting, just as Chuck was being wheeled down the hall on a gurney. She froze, taking in his blood-soaked clothes. One side of his face was purple, and his lips were swollen and split in several places. Splints immobilized his left arm and leg.

When she made a sound of distress, he opened his eyes. He lifted his free hand. "Sorry..."

She rushed over to him, holding his hand in both of hers. "Don't talk."

"...let Gary...down...promised..."

"No," she said softly, tears blurring her eyes. "You *didn't*. He understands."

The emergency room doctor who had sewn her up came around to move her out of the way. "That's all—we've got to get him into surgery. *Now.*"

But Chuck gripped her arm hard, his expression fierce under the pain. "Get...away from...here."

She leaned closer. "Where's Gary, Chuck? I have to talk to him."

"*No...*" He shook his head back and forth, agitated.

The doctor placed a firm hand on her shoulder and pulled her away. "I said, that's *all.*"

Chuck whispered something, then started mumbling.

"Wait," Kaz said urgently, then bent down, putting her ear next to his mouth. "Say it again, Chuck."

"...boats..." he whispered, then lapsed into unconsciousness.

"Shut up. Just...shut up and let me take care of you for a little while." Michael eased Kaz into the passenger side of his car.

He'd almost lost her. It had been so close. From the back seat, Zeke licked the side of her face, whining, and she raised a hand to pet him. Michael leaned across her to fasten her seat belt. "For once, quit trying to handle everything yourself."

"We have to go to Bjorn's," she said.

"No, we don't. We're going back to your house, where we've got a police presence, and you're going to let me put you to bed. You have a head injury, and I can tell you're hurting..." He stopped and shook his head.

She laid a hand over his on the seat belt fastener. "Twenty-four hours," she said quietly. "That's all I've got."

He was so close he could see every small scrape and abrasion the bastard had put on her. Unable to respond without snapping, he straightened, slammed the car door, and walked around to the driver's side. If the guy had simply hit her a little harder...been a little rougher...

"Why Bjorn's?" he asked as he got in.

"I think he might know where Gary is."

"If I take you there, *then* will you come home with me?"

"After we talk to Gary," she insisted.

He wanted to rage at her for taking so many chances. But the blame lay squarely with him—he hadn't been there when she'd needed him.

But he couldn't think about that now—that was exactly what the killer wanted him to do. He wanted Michael to act irrationally and emotionally. To panic, so he lost his edge, so he'd miss something. Starting the car, he put it into gear. "How

206

do I get to Bjorn's?" he asked more calmly.

She gave him the directions, and five minutes later, they were parked in front of Bjorn's house. She climbed stiffly from the car on her own—that damned independence again. She seemed grateful, though, when he put his arm around her to help her up the walkway.

She moved slowly, almost shuffling her feet. She had to be hurting bad. Although they'd filled a prescription for pain medication at the hospital pharmacy, she'd refused to take it, worried, she'd said, that it would keep her from thinking clearly. He'd let her get away with acting tough for another hour or two, but eventually she'd take the pills, even if he had to grind them up in her food.

Bjorn answered the door on the first ring of the doorbell—he'd probably seen them drive up. He took in her injuries and bruises. "What happened?"

"I was attacked," Kaz said. "Chuck's in the hospital—we don't know if he'll pull through."

Bjorn slumped against the doorjamb. "I can't do this anymore." He ran a hand through is hair, then seemed to remember his manners and held open the door, showing them into a large living room cluttered with comfortable chairs and children's toys.

Michael gently eased Kaz into the nearest chair but remained standing. "If you know something," he told Bjorn, "now's the time to tell us."

"You know where Gary is, who's hiding him, don't you?" Kaz asked.

"How do I know you won't arrest him?" Bjorn asked Michael. "He isn't part of this, you know."

Before he could speak, Kaz said, "You can trust Michael." It was the first time, despite all they'd been through, that she'd given him any concrete indication that she believed in him.

Bjorn kept his gaze on Michael. "Gary doesn't want her

207

involved."

"She's already at risk," Michael said. "Her attacker gave her one day, then he's coming back."

Bjorn looked from one to the other of them, squared his shoulders. "Gary's been staying on the boats—mine, Jacobsen's—moving a couple of times a night, then hiding out in the abandoned warehouses on the days we're out on the water."

"Where is he right now? Which boat?" Michael asked.

"Jacobsen's 70-foot trawler, the *Alliance.*"

"Thank you," Kaz said softly, getting up to walk over and give him a brief hug.

He gently hugged her back, his eyes sad. "I hope I've done the right thing. You'll be careful?" With the last question, he looked to Michael for confirmation.

Michael nodded. "I'll take care of her. She's not getting out of my sight until this is finished, not again." He'd handcuff her to her bed if he had to. Her days of risk-taking were over.

Bjorn saw his determination, heard the emotion in his voice, and frowned. "That thing back in Boston—you let that guy die in that fire?"

Michael raised an eyebrow, but shook his head. "No, but I'll never be able to prove it."

Bjorn studied him for a long moment, then nodded. "Just handle this honorably, that's all we ask."

"You have my word."

They drove straight to the mooring basin, but the *Alliance* was locked up tight, its portholes dark. When they spied two search teams a couple of blocks down, Michael noted the sick look on Kaz's face.

They spent another forty-five minutes searching other trawlers in the vicinity, as well as the closest warehouses, but there was no sign of Gary. If he *was* nearby, he wouldn't reveal his hiding place, not with the cops so near. Seeming to give up, Kaz allowed Michael to drive her back to the house.

Zeke trailed them into the kitchen, hovering close to Kaz. Michael made her sit in one of the kitchen chairs while he rummaged around in her cupboards, finally coming up with a can of chicken noodle soup. Standing at the stove, he kept an eye on her while he stirred the soup. When she got up to help, he exploded. "For God's sake, just let me do it!"

"It wasn't your fault."

"I should've been here—I shouldn't have let you come back here alone. My gut was screaming at me, and I didn't listen to it." He set the saucepan aside and came over to her, kneeling down to put his arms gently around her. "I can't stand that you've been hurt, that you won't let me handle things for you."

She rested her head on his shoulder. "I'd like nothing better than to check out, but there's no time."

His arms tightened for a minute. "At least let me feed you."

He felt her smile against his shoulder. "Your specialty."

"Yeah."

He served the soup and they ate in silence for a few minutes.

"I should've been paying more attention," she said between spoonfuls. "He must've come in while I was on the phone to the hospital in Portland."

He gave her a curious look and she related what she'd discovered. "So Ken was using the drug money to pay for Bobby's treatments," she concluded. "And I think Gary may have made the anonymous payment." She looked frustrated. "I *have* to get to Gary, but I can't figure out how."

The swelling in her cheek and eye was going down a bit. He got up to add more ice to the cold pack. Then he refilled her soup bowl and placed it back in front of her.

"I want you to take a time-out for the night," he said quietly. "Get a good night's sleep—let your body heal a little." She started to shake her head, and he leaned across the table, taking both of her hands in his. "Just listen to me. I don't think there's anything you can do tonight. You have no way of knowing where Gary is or how to get hold of him. And you need the down time. Hell, *I* need the down time."

"I've got some places I can check—"

"Places you can get to in the dark?"

He watched the emotions flit across her face—the worry, the frustration. And finally, the resignation. "Okay, for a few hours."

He squeezed her hands. "Thank you," he said simply.

Kaz hadn't been asleep long when the sound of Zeke's tail rhythmically thumping on the hardwood floor woke her up. As she opened her eyes and tried to move, she realized Michael was in bed with her, and that he was holding her close, both arms wrapped tightly around her. He must've come back upstairs after he'd tucked her into bed, to sleep beside her and protect her. She'd unconsciously curled into him in her sleep, her head resting on his shoulder, her arm on his chest.

She raised her head to peer into the darkness, hoping to identify what had awakened her.

Michael was instantly awake. "What?"

"Someone's in the house, I think," she replied softly.

"Damn straight." The voice came from the bottom of the bed.

They both bolted upright, Kaz moaning at the quick movement Michael reached under his pillow for a gun.

She placed a hand on his arm. "It's Gary."

"Hell of a way to keep my sister safe, Chapman." Gary cursed as he tripped over Zeke. After making sure the curtains were closed, he switched on the lamp on the night stand.

"Are you okay?" Kaz asked him, her eyes squinting in the sudden glare. He looked even worse than he had forty-eight hours ago. His clothes were filthy, and his eyes held the feral look of an animal who knew it was being hunted.

"Seems like I should be the one asking that question. Bjorn told me what happened." He knelt by the side of the bed, taking her chin in his hand and turning the bruised side of her face toward the light. His lips tightened. "Dammit, Kaz, I told you to stay out of this."

She shook her head. "You aren't safe here. You know about Chuck?"

Gary nodded, his expression angry and frustrated. "The hospital has him listed as critical."

Michael had climbed out of bed and was pulling on a sweater over his jeans. "You're well informed for someone on the run," he told Gary in a mild tone.

"I haven't been on the run." He gave Michael a hard look. "You get Kaz out of town, *now*. This mess is about to blow wide open."

Kaz made herbal tea and scrounged together a sandwich for Gary. When she entered the living room with the tray, Michael and Gary were talking quietly.

"It's our speculation that the fishermen are running drugs," Michael was saying.

Gary accepted a mug from Kaz and nodded. "Ken figured it out before I did."

"Did he steal drug money to pay for Bobby's treatments?" she asked.

"Yeah, the fool. And he paid the consequences. I tried to talk him into giving the money back, although I wasn't sure it would save his sorry hide. But he'd already used some of it. After the second time they beat him up and threatened to go after his family, he gave the rest of the money to me to put in the locker." He shot an exasperated look at Kaz. "And then you had to go looking for it."

211

"I figured if you had something they wanted, the locker was the logical place to hide it."

"Yeah, and that analytical mind of yours put you right in the line of fire." He took a bite from his sandwich. "Cutting the lines on the pots was a warning. They'll threaten your life, next."

"They already have," Michael said and told him about the ultimatum she'd been given. "Who else besides Bjorn in the fishing community knows about my background?"

Gary paused from wolfing down the rest of the sandwich to give him a curious look. "Pretty much everyone. Why?"

"Because I think someone's counting on your instinctive distrust of me as a newcomer to slow down the investigation." He shrugged. "And it's not the first time someone I care about has been targeted."

Kaz frowned. She hadn't even considered that angle. Lucy hadn't told her the real source of the rumors about Michael— just that the cops had been talking about him. But Bjorn had clearly known the details of Michael's background; he'd indicated as much when they'd talked to him earlier in the evening.

Gary's expression was speculative. "Even if you're right, it doesn't help us unless you can figure out who's been checking you out."

Michael nodded. "I've got a call in to a buddy of mine back East. I should hear back from him in the morning. Who told you about me?"

"Bjorn." Gary frowned. "But he could've heard it from any number of people."

Michael shrugged. "I'll find out, sooner or later. In the meantime, I won't have Kaz at risk because you get off playing the vigilante. You need to turn yourself in, tell the cops everything you know."

Gary set aside his empty plate. "If I do that, I'm as good as dead."

"I can get you protective custody," Michael insisted.

Gary shook his head. "That won't stop them."

Kaz placed a hand on his knee. "At least tell us who's involved. Give us something to go on."

"No." Gary got up and started pacing. "I'm close. I only need one more day to put it all together."

"Is Karl Svensen involved?"

Gary rounded on her. "You stay away from Svensen and his crews. They don't have any loyalty to us, and they won't lift a finger to help you."

"So that's what the fight was about six months ago, and why Svensen never pressed charges. Ken had found out what Karl was doing, and Karl threatened him. You stepped in to protect Ken."

"I didn't know what was going on, but yeah. Svensen took a swing at Ken, and I stopped him. At the time, it surprised the hell out of me when he refused to press charges." Gary growled in frustration. "Dammit, Kaz, haven't you heard anything I've said? They'll kill you without even flinching."

"Who else is in on it?" Michael demanded. "Either tell us what you know, or I call the cops now. Jackson is right outside."

Gary abruptly sighed and sat down. "I'll talk if you promise to take Kaz out of the equation."

"Done."

"Hey!" They both ignored her.

"They're using the Redemption as their meeting place," Gary told Michael. "The back room. And yes, before you ask," he said to Kaz, "Steve is in on it. I don't know what they have on him, something that happened around the time of his divorce. He's turning a blind eye to the meetings. He could finger every damn one of them if he wanted, but I can't get him to talk. I searched Svensen's boat, but I didn't find anything,

213

other than some notations in the ship's log that could've been drop-off points."

He shook his head. "Bjorn's in the clear, but I think he knows what's going on. If he does, he's not saying, and I don't blame him. He's got his kids to think about. The supplier is someone off shore, probably a Triad offshoot. The buyer's right here in Astoria. Most of the drugs are going up-river, only a small amount is staying here in town."

"Who's the buyer?" Michael asked.

"No one you can do anything about. He's set up so well no one can touch him—at least, so far, but Jacobsen and I are planning to follow Karl and observe the hand-off, then take the information to the right people. And that's all I'll tell you. Now will you please get Kaz the hell out of town? I can't finish this unless I know she's safe." He pinned Michael with a hard glare. "If you're sleeping with her, the least you can do is take care of her."

"You're jumping to the wrong—" Kaz started, but Michael cut her off.

"My intentions are honorable," he said evenly. "And I resent the implication that I would use her in any way."

"You moved in awfully fast after I split. I'm not happy about that."

"Get used to it," Michael suggested. "I'm not willing to let her get hurt again."

Gary hesitated, then nodded. "Fair enough. But if you've taken advantage of her in any way—"

"Oh, for God's sake," Kaz exploded. "Will you two listen to each other? You sound like we're living in Regency England. I've been taking care of myself for a long time. If someone doesn't recognize that, and damn quickly, I'll throw you both out of the house."

The men exchanged a "see what I have to put up with" look.

Gary stood and handed Kaz his empty mug. "Twenty-four

hours, that's all I need." His expression turned wry. "At least try to keep her out of my way during that time."

Michael nodded, then added, "I still think you should go to the cops."

"Not yet."

Michael closed the back door and leaned against it, watching her clean up the dishes with an expression she couldn't fathom. Unaccountably nervous, she grabbed the dish towel and dried off the counter around the sink.

He pushed away from the door, walking slowly toward her. She backed up, saying the first thing that came to mind. "I can't believe you two, thinking you can make a plan to 'take care of me' without even asking me what I want."

He shrugged, but kept coming toward her. "We know what's best in this situation—you don't."

"Bullshit." She backed up another step, her retreat abruptly stopped by the edge of the counter. Lifting her chin, she said, "I make the decisions concerning my life."

"Not this time." He came to a stop in front of her and looked down at her, his silvery gaze heated. "Quit using the issue of your independence to dodge the real issue here."

She swallowed. "What real issue?"

"Whether I'm taking you back upstairs."

In an instant, she went cold, then hot. She could think of a thousand reasons why this wasn't a good idea. They had a killer closing in, maybe even waiting nearby for the perfect moment to strike. Chuck was in the hospital, in critical condition. And Gary was out there somewhere, laying a trap, taking God knew what kind of risks.

Michael took one more step, invading her personal space. Her mind blanked. All she could think about was the strength and heat of his body, and how much she wanted to explore it. It was pure insanity, but she couldn't seem to make herself

215

care.

Leaning over, he braced his hands on either side of her. His face was only inches from hers, his expression rigid from tension. "Am I?"

"Are you what?" she breathed.

"Taking you back upstairs."

"I—"

He captured her lips, cutting off any protest, however weak, that she would have uttered. His kiss burned through her remaining resistance, its fire streaking through her, all the way down to her toes, curling them. Her hands fisted in the soft wool of his sweater, her mouth softened and molded itself to his.

Stepping back, he left her wanting more, much more. They were both breathing hard.

"Kaz." He took her hands in his. "I want more than this one night."

It was crazy, what he was proposing. She lived in San Francisco and ran a consulting firm. He was a firefighter who'd seen unimaginable violence and human evil, who might have to arrest her brother. They had almost nothing in common. And yet, it felt so right.

She didn't make decisions lightly, but this one seemed so natural, so easy. She lifted her chin and looked him square in the eye. "All right."

He let out a slow breath, smiling a little for the first time. But she could still sense a hesitation in him. "Are you sure you're up for this?" he asked softly, running his hand lightly over her bruised face.

She rose on her toes and linked her arms around his neck. "Make love to me, Michael."

Chapter 22

Michael bent and picked her up, carrying her upstairs. He laid her down gently in the center of the bed, taking care with her injuries. The small lamp on her bedside table was still on, casting a soft glow throughout the room. He made no move to turn it off.

He unbuttoned his shirt, revealing a broad, muscular chest sprinkled lightly with dark hair narrowing to a vee at his waist. Her fingers gripped the bed covers, itching to run her hands over those hard planes and ridges of muscles. Her breath hitched as his hands moved to his jeans, unbuttoning them.

He was magnificent—all muscle and sinew, all hard lines of masculine elegance. She couldn't breathe.

He smiled, then placed one knee on the edge of the mattress and leaned over her, tugging the football jersey over her head and tossing it onto the floor. He lay down, the bed dipping under his weight.

Seemingly content to just look at her, he took his time, driving her wild by doing nothing more than touching every part of her body with his incredible eyes. No one had ever done that, just looked at her as if she looked exactly the way he wanted her to, as if he wanted to experience the anticipation of what would come next.

"You're so beautiful," he murmured.

She trembled, and reached out to lay her palm against his chest.

He caught her hand in his, kissing her palm in a way that made her shiver. "Let me."

The shadows of the darkened room closed around them intimately. He drew her closer, warming her with the entire length of his body. Reaching up to smooth her hair, he finger-combed the silky blond strands so that they flowed over her shoulder and down over her right breast. His fingers lingered there for a long moment, his touch unbearably light and teasing. Heat built, and she arched involuntarily into his touch, but his hand moved on.

Down, over the slight swell of her lower stomach to the edge of her panties, never even hesitating as he slid them off, dropping them on the floor beside the bed. Then to the sensitized insides of her trembling thighs. His fingers trailed fire, all the way up to her core.

He cupped her. She moaned aloud, dampening his hand. His gaze flew to hers, the silver of his eyes darkening to a stormy gray.

"Michael—" she panted, fighting against the building pressure, surging against his hand to try to ease the ache. She was ready, so fast it almost frightened her.

"Shhhh." He soothed her, leaning down to kiss her softly, then with more insistence, taking her with his tongue, mimicking the movements of his hand as he stroked her, explored her.

Her hips bucked off the bed. When she thought she couldn't take any more, he slid two large fingers all the way into her, finding the bundle of nerves and rubbing rhythmically.

The climax hit her hard, bowing her body, scaring her in its intensity. She tried to pull away, but he held her gently, stroking her through it. Waves roiled through her, great rushes of heat, starbursts of pleasure. He wrung every last spasm out of her, then brought her slowly, gently back down to earth. She collapsed against the tangled bedcovers, panting.

He leaned down and kissed her lower belly, then moved up to her breast. Taking it into his mouth, he tugged on it softly with his teeth, nipping, and she felt the need start to build all over again. She gasped and sobbed.

He laughed softly. Moving away for a moment to deal with protection, he slid over her, settling heavily between her thighs.

The delicious weight of him galvanized her and she reared up, hooking her hands around his neck and pulling his mouth down to hers. Their hearts beat crazily against each other, but in unison.

He fought the urge to rush, to possess. She tasted as he'd imagined she would, only better. She felt as he'd imagined as he settled over her, all soft and yielding, only better. He wanted her at such a gut-wrenching level that he was afraid to let himself go, afraid he'd just go all caveman and take and take, consuming her until there was nothing left.

Holding onto his control by a thread, he slipped inside her, letting her adjust to him. He saw her eyes widen with shock, their soft brown glazing over with pleasure. She murmured against his lips, tightening her hold on him, cradling him.

He was big, bigger than she realized. For a moment, she wasn't sure she could take all of him, and she pulled back slightly, but his grip on her kept her tightened, allowing her no retreat. He withdrew a little, then surged forward again, seating himself deep inside, touching the core of her, making her arch mindlessly.

After a long moment, he started moving. Pulling back, then pushing, long, slow, deep strokes that drove her wild. She'd never known a man to take such care, to give so generously. She watched his control slip away in his fierce gaze as he settled into a strong, powerful rhythm that rekindled a driving need deep inside her, taking over her very self, flinging her into a world she'd never known, never even had a glimpse of.

Her vision grayed, every cell in her body building toward an explosion more powerful than the last one. Her pulse galloping and roaring in her ears, she dimly heard his hoarse calling of her name, then his long moan. Then she peaked and exploded, crying out as, arms wrapped around each other, they slid down through crashing waves of pleasure.

He settled heavily on top of her, his chest heaving. For several long moments, Kaz lay there, reveling in the feel of him covering every inch of her, listening to his heart as its beat eventually slowed in concert with hers.

She rubbed her face against his shoulder, inhaling the damp, musky, already familiar scent of him. Never before had she felt this connection, either during or after sex. She'd surrendered a part of herself that she hadn't even known existed, that had been lying dormant all these years, waiting for the right man to come along.

Lying there in the quiet of the pre-dawn, she listened to the sound of Michael breathing, and she worried. About what they'd experienced, about how either of them could ever casually walk away from it, about how much she already was in love with him. Then she thought about Gary and where he was right now, while she was lying there, guilty in her sated pleasure.

Michael stirred and turned on his side, taking her with him, wrapping his arms around her. Cocooning her from the outside world, if only for a few more hours.

"Don't think about it," he soothed, his voice a murmur. "We'll sort it all out."

Chapter 23

Kaz awoke to the sound of Michael talking softly on the phone, his voice low. "Yeah, I understand. They'll keep him there for now?...Right. I'll let her know."

She threw back the covers and sat up—slowly. The throbbing in her head was down to a dull ache, probably because she'd been able to sleep for the first time in days. But the rest of her body was, if anything, stiffer and sorer. She tentatively stood up, wincing, and used one hand to hold onto the headboard. Funny how she hadn't felt any of this while Michael had been making love to her a second time last night. Or again this morning, their whispered words and low moans gently disturbing the pre-dawn quiet. She smiled at the memory.

"What are you doing out of bed?"

She turned to find him standing in the doorway, a coffee mug in one hand. His hair was damp, his face freshly shaven. Even with a scowl on his face, he was adorable. And all hers. At least, for now. "What time is it?" she asked, smiling at him.

"Early afternoon."

"What?" She gaped at him. "Why didn't you wake me up?"

"Because you needed the sleep," he replied evenly. "Don't expect me to do things that aren't good for you."

She grumbled at that as she walked unsteadily across the room. "What are you supposed to let me know?"

"It's not good news."

She stopped, searching his face. "Gary?"

He nodded. "They've taken him into custody."

She put out a hand, leaning heavily against the dresser. "Is he okay?"

Michael hesitated. "According to Lucy, he resisted arrest. She says he's roughed up but refusing treatment. They're holding him at the station until he's arraigned later this afternoon."

"I want to see him." Kaz pulled open a drawer and starting yanking clothes out at random.

"That may not be possible—"

Her head whipped around. "I *will* see him." She bumped the drawer shut with her hip and grabbed the pile of clothes on top of the dresser. "If I can get him to tell me who the Astoria connection is, then we can take over his investigation."

"We?" Michael folded his arms, one eyebrow raised.

"Yes," Kaz said, and waited.

"All right." He nodded. "As long as we work together on this."

She sighed with relief, falling a little more in love with him. "I'll take the world's fastest shower, if you'll hunt up the world's largest bottle of aspirin."

An hour later, Michael dropped Kaz off at the station, extracting a promise from her to call him at the fire station when she was ready to leave. The light was already starting to fade. She couldn't believe she'd slept away most of the day. There was almost no time left.

She opened the door and, catching Joanne's eye, pointed at the interior security door. Joanne released the lock and waved her on through.

Lucy and Ivar were both at their desks, going through the stacks of papers that Sykes had taken from her house yesterday. Ivar had her laptop open in front of him, and he was tapping on the keys, a frown of concentration on his face. As she approached, he looked up, his expression relieved.

"What's your password?"

Kaz shook her head. "If anyone else was asking, I'd tell them to go to hell." She walked around to his side of the desk and typed it in for him.

"Someone's been accessing the fishermen's bank accounts, posing as Brenner, giving out his badge number." Lucy scrubbed a hand over her face. She looked like she'd been up all night, and she clearly wasn't happy about it. "When I called the bank first thing this morning, the manager's comment was, 'But I gave all this information to your officer yesterday afternoon.' " She sighed. "Never mind that the guy didn't think to ask for a subpoena. I don't suppose that was you?"

"I didn't think of it, but I wish I had," Kaz replied, earning a glare. She perched on the edge of the chair beside Lucy's desk, reaching out to pick up the muddy snow globe that was sitting there. Shaking it, she watched the snow drift down around the fishing trawler while she considered. "Could've been Gary, though."

"Yeah, that was my second thought."

Kaz set the snow globe back down and leaned forward. "Where is he? I want to see him."

Lucy hesitated, the expression on her face scaring Kaz. "What's wrong? Is he all right?" she asked.

Lucy nodded. "For now. The Chief has him on suicide watch, though."

"For God's sake, *why*?"

"He's despondent, refusing to talk, and refusing to eat." Lucy leaned back in her chair, looking truly defeated for the first time since the investigation had begun. And a little desperate. "I can't get through to him, Kaz. He just keeps repeating that I need to convince you to leave town."

Kaz leaned forward. "Take me to him."

"He's only allowed to see his lawyer." Lucy bit her lip. "But he's refusing legal representation."

"Then let me talk to him. Tell Sykes that I'm standing in for Phil until I can get him to fly up here."

Lucy shook her head. "A family member can't stand in for a lawyer. Anything he told you would be admissible in court."

"Then put me in a room with him and turn off the intercom," Kaz insisted. "Five minutes, that's all I'm asking."

Lucy glanced at Ivar, who made a production out of ignoring them both. Then she checked the rest of the squad room before nodding. "All right—five minutes. But if Sykes shows up, you're out of there. This is irregular as hell—I could lose my job over a stunt like this." She rose. "I'll have him brought out to one of the interrogation rooms."

"Thank you."

"Don't thank me yet. And Kaz, be prepared. He put up a hell of a fight. It took four of our guys to subdue him, and they weren't too happy with him by the time it was all over. Two of them are in the emergency room right now, getting stitched up."

Kaz waited impatiently at Lucy's desk until she returned, then followed her into a room that was halfway down the hallway at the back of the building that led out to the parking lot. When she entered, Gary was sitting in one of the chairs, his hands and legs in shackles. Clint Jackson was standing guard in the corner. Lucy motioned for him to follow her, and after a moment's reluctance, he did.

Once they were alone, Kaz took Gary's face in her hands and gently turned it up to the light. His nose was bloody and slightly crooked, his lips split and ballooned to twice their normal size. Small cuts and areas darkening to bruises covered his face.

She unbuttoned the three shirt buttons that hadn't been ripped off and inspected his ribs. Black and purple splotches

224

covered them. A small sound of distress escaped her lips. Who could've done this to him? What right did they have to cause this much damage?

He'd barely moved when she touched him, but his eyes slowly focused on her. He licked his lips and tried to speak, but she shushed him. To see him this way, in shackles, made her want to throw up. She swallowed hard. "So," she said, keeping her voice as light as she could. "I guess I should see the other guys, huh?"

One side of his mouth lifted slightly. "Kaz..." The word came out slurred, almost garbled. He closed his eyes and grimaced.

"Talk slowly and quietly." She glanced around at the closed door and the window, then moved so that anyone looking in wouldn't be able to read his lips. "They can see us but Lucy said she'd leave the intercom off for a few minutes to give us some privacy. Tell me everything you know, and Michael and I will take it from here."

He shook his head. "Get...out of...town."

She stooped to look directly at him. "Listen to me, Gary. We can find the evidence to clear you."

"I...don't matter..."

"Yes," she said fiercely, "you do. Don't you dare let them win, damn you. You *tell* me, and then you *stay alive* until I can get you out of here."

He stared at her for a long minute. "Trap door," he managed. "Svensen."

Kaz thought rapidly. "The trap door in Steve's office?" All the old waterfront bars had shanghai trap doors—doors in the floor that led to the water below the pier. In the old days, sailors had regularly been shanghaied, or kidnapped, and taken out to sea to serve as indentured crew on ships. "So Svensen goes to the tavern, picks up the money, then drops into a boat below the pier?"

Gary nodded, then sucked in a breath. "Svensen takes

225

out...to be swapped for drugs." He tried to wet his lips with his tongue, and she rose to get him some water out of the cooler. She held it to his battered lips and trickled it into his mouth. He gave her a grateful look as he swallowed.

"Who is Karl's contact?"

Gary shook his head abruptly, then winced. "No...no way....Too dangerous."

Kaz let that go while she paced and thought it through. So how did Karl get away with regularly meeting someone out on the water and not being seen by the other members of the fishing fleet? The last piece of the puzzle fell into place. It was the obvious solution, and she'd even heard Karl say it herself. She hadn't put it together until now. And, she realized, no one else would've either. It would've escaped everyone's notice. Only a fisherman would've caught on, and only over time.

"You said you found notations in Karl's ship's log. Did any of them match to this?" She repeated what she'd heard Karl say over the radio when she and Michael had been out. Gary nodded.

She resumed her pacing. Okay. So she had the list of drop-off locations, and she also knew which one was for the next rendezvous. She had to find Svensen, follow him. If they could catch him in the act, they'd have enough leverage on him to get to whoever was in charge. Was today a day that they'd make a drop? It was Friday—a day most fishermen were superstitious about going out on the water. Which made it ideal—less people would be out there to observe what was going on. She'd bet Svensen was going out tonight.

She hugged Gary again, carefully, trying to will some of her strength into him. "I want you to rest, and to not worry. But most of all, I want you to *stay alive* until we get back."

"Sure."

Kaz frowned at him. Something wasn't right. She opened her mouth, but just then, she heard a commotion outside the door.

The door opened, and Sykes strode in, trailed by Lucy. He leaned over the table, his expression angry, one eye showing bruising underneath. "What the hell is going on in here?"

"Why hasn't he been treated?" Kaz demanded right back, not answering his question. "He could have internal injuries."

"That's a damn good question. McGuire?"

Lucy stared at Sykes, speechless.

"Do you mean that you didn't know about this?" Kaz asked, confused.

"Of course not. I've been out of the office since we apprehended him, putting ice on this black eye," he said. "You shouldn't be in here, Kaz. There's no way I'm giving you an opportunity to tell the judge that we compromised the legal process. Gary can see a lawyer, and that's it." He turned to pin Lucy with a hard look. "Was this your idea?"

Kaz deflected him, answering for her. "I was concerned about Gary's condition and demanded to see him. Clearly, he's in no shape to be making his own decisions. I will be immediately calling a lawyer to represent him, and I'd like you to delay arraignment until he can arrive."

Sykes shook his head. "We'll temporarily assign him a public defender. The DA won't agree to bail, anyway, not after the fight he put up when he was arrested. So all he has to do at the hearing is plead 'Guilty' or 'Not Guilty.'"

Kaz didn't like it, but she knew she couldn't stop him. "Why do you have him on suicide watch?"

Sykes stared at her for a long moment. "This is the first I've heard of it—I'll check it out." He came around the end of the table and gripped her elbow hard enough to leave bruises. "You're leaving, now."

Lucy, who was standing slightly behind Sykes, cocked her head toward the squad room, indicating that she wanted to talk.

Kaz glanced at Gary, who was watching the exchange with intense concentration. When he realized she was looking at him, though, he immediately dropped his gaze back to the floor. Something was horribly wrong, she could feel it.

"Go." Gary said, the word almost a whisper. He had slumped back in his chair, pain clouding his expression.

She jerked her elbow out of Sykes' grasp, walked back over to him, bending down. "What?"

Gary drew a long, shaky breath. "I'll be all right," he said, his voice stronger. "Just...*go*."

Back in the hallway, she walked over to Lucy's desk to retrieve her jacket. "I'm headed for the marina, then the Redemption. I'll call Michael on my cell phone—"

Lucy was already shaking her head. "You know he wanted you to wait for him."

"There's no time, he can catch up with me." Kaz glanced at her watch. Slack tide was in just under two and a half hours. She turned to leave, then stopped. "Wait—was there something you wanted to tell me?"

Lucy hesitated, then shook her head. "Not yet. There's something I need to check first. But Kaz—be careful."

At the fire station, Michael stapled the last of his notes together and placed them in the arson investigation file. His cell phone rang. Dropping the file folder on the desk in front of him, reached for the unit, flipping it open. Recognizing the Caller ID, he smiled. "Mac. You ship me those coffee beans yet?"

"Sent them out yesterday. Tasha at the coffee shop sends her best. How the hell you keep them sniffing around when you don't put out, buddy, is a mystery to the entire staffs of the fire and police departments of the Greater Boston Area."

"Right." Michael's smile widened, remembering the events of last night. Mac didn't know that he'd finally broken his long run of celibacy.

He'd forgotten that making love to the woman you'd fallen *in* love with was a completely different, shattering experience. He felt like he'd been turned inside out, that he'd crossed some invisible threshold and was now looking at the world with an entirely new perspective.

"Yo, buddy. You still there?" Mac's voice held a note of curiosity.

Michael forced his mind back to the present. "Any word back on who's been checking me out?"

"The mayor of your cute little burg called a few of the higher-ups, including your surrogate papa, but that's no surprise. And someone from the police department evidently talked to Geoff Whitford who, as we all know, loves you just the way you are. The son of a bitch probably blabbed everything, out of spite."

Michael wouldn't be surprised. Mac was right—Whitford had resented Michael for more than a decade, stemming from an incident during Whitford's rookie years. Michael had been the one to write him up, and to point out to the brass that Whitford wasn't good management material. If Geoff could make Michael's life difficult, he'd leap at the chance. "You know who placed the call?" Michael asked.

"Couldn't ferret that out. So, when are you moving back?"

"Not in this lifetime."

"Says the person with the addiction to quality caffeine."

Michael's phone beeped, indicating another incoming call. "Gotta go. Say hello to Sharon for me."

"You're behind a little, pal. That's what living in the boonies gets you. This week, it's Susie."

Michael shook his head, smiling, and ended the call, picking up the next one. It was the state lab. "Tell me what you've got."

The lab technician, for once, sounded dead serious. "You'd better get over here. *Now.*"

229

Chapter 24

Lucy watched Sykes go down the hall to his office, enter, and close the door. She stood and wandered over to the vending machine against the far wall, fed quarters into it, punching the button for a can of soda with more force than was necessary.

Okay, think. Something wasn't adding up—what she'd just overheard didn't compute. And dammit, if she just had more caffeine in her system, her fuzzed-out brain would be able to sort through this mess.

Clint Jackson had told her that Sykes had been the one to put Gary on suicide watch. But Sykes was acting as if this was news to him. So someone was lying. And when she put that together with Gary's refusal to talk to the cops all along, then the way he resisted arrest...*hell*. Somewhere, there was a dirty cop. And the obvious choice was Jackson.

Could he be the in-town buyer of the drug smuggling ring? The fishermen were just the runners, she was fairly certain. But a *cop*? She knew these guys. She had trouble believing that any of them would be in on drug deals.

Then again, who *better* than a cop? A cop would have the inside track on investigations and undercover narc work. She remembered what her snitch had said the other morning at the warehouse. *You cops, you think you're above the law.*

A shiver ran down her spine. Jackson made sense—he'd been in the right places all along. He'd been assigned surveillance on Kaz's house, yet suspiciously absent when she'd had break-ins. Hell, he'd even been in on conducting the search warrant. He'd been in the vicinity and easily could've attacked Kaz afterward. And he'd been present at Gary's arrest. How many of Gary's injuries were *really* the result of resisting arrest?

She slapped the wall beside the vending machine, then leaned her forehead against her arm, closing her eyes. If she was right, then Gary was in real danger. He knew too much to be left alive. *And a cop could make it look like suicide.*

She gulped down soda. Although she didn't like her options, she had no choice—she had to take her suspicions to Sykes. If she were wrong, well, then she'd look like a fool. So what else was new? It wouldn't be the first time she'd jumped to conclusions and then had to live down the consequences.

No question that the guys on the force wouldn't trust her from here on out. Cops didn't rat on each other. But stand by and watch Gary possibly be murdered? *No way.*

She turned and walked down the hall to Sykes' office. His door was still closed—she could see through the window that he was on a phone call. When he finished, she tapped on the door and opened it, entering.

Eyebrows raised, Sykes motioned for her to sit. "What's on your mind, McGuire?"

"Sir, I'd like you to delay the arraignment."

He leaned back in his chair, his hands behind his head, a scowl on his face. "I've already been through this with Kaz. Jorgensen doesn't need his own lawyer to stand there for five minutes and enter a plea."

"That's not what I'm talking about." Lucy leaned forward in her chair. Her best strategy was to convince Sykes that the case wasn't yet solid enough. "I've uncovered some information that indicates that Gary might've been framed."

Sykes went abruptly still. "What makes you think that?"

"Well, for one thing, Gary's not stupid enough to leave the

231

tire iron where we could find it. And," she continued before he could argue, "the timeline doesn't work. I got the lab results back, and given the match of the concrete and mud samples with the bridge, Gary wouldn't have had time, after leaving the tavern, to meet up with Ken, kill him, then transfer him to the boat and set a time-delayed fire. Kaz was right on his heels—"

Sykes held up a hand. "Look, McGuire. I understand that you haven't worked that many homicides, so you wouldn't necessarily be aware that, in cases like these, not all the evidence lines up neatly. There's always some detail that doesn't seem to make sense. But that doesn't mean that Jorgensen is innocent. The man ran, and he resisted arrest."

"I think I can explain that," Lucy said urgently. "If I'm right about a theory I'm working on, one that I'd like your permission to pursue."

Sykes took his time pulling out a cigar and lighting it. After a couple of puffs, he motioned for her to continue.

She drew a breath and plunged in. "You said, a few minutes ago, that you didn't know that Gary had been placed on suicide watch."

Sykes stared at her through a cloud of smoke, his expression blank. "So?"

"So Clint told me before you got here that *you* were the one who had put Gary on suicide watch." Lucy waited for a reaction, but he said nothing. "Don't you see? If Clint is in on this, and Gary knew it, he'd be afraid to turn himself in."

"Whoa." Sykes sat forward abruptly. "McGuire, you can't just go around accusing your fellow officers of being dirty."

"But what if Clint put Gary on suicide watch because it would make a good explanation if he winds up dead?"

Sykes didn't say anything for a long moment, and she resisted the urge to shift in her chair. Finally, he nodded thoughtfully. "Interesting theory. Do you have any proof?"

"Not yet, but I'm working on it. And Kaz could have plenty

later this evening."

"Oh?" He pinned her with a hard look. "You letting a civilian get mixed up in this?"

She fell back on the excuse that he would understand. "Do you think I could've stopped her? Her brother's in jail, accused of a crime he probably didn't commit—"

"We don't know that," Sykes said, his tone firm. "I'm still inclined to believe that he's guilty. But he may not have been working alone—almost certainly, he wasn't. Where is Kaz right now?"

Lucy hesitated. She'd opened the door—she could hardly refuse to answer. "The mooring basin."

He stubbed out his cigar in the ashtray and stood, indicating that their meeting was over. "I'll look into what you've said. I don't want one cop investigating another on my force. Until I have more proof, I'm not formally investigating one of my own detectives. If you pick up any other information, you need to tell me right away, is that clear?"

"Yes, sir." Lucy stood and turned to go.

"McGuire?"

At the door, she turned back. "Sir?"

"Good work."

At the Redemption, Kaz sat in the darkened corner of the same booth that Michael had occupied that first night, sipping a glass of beer and watching the other patrons in the bar. She'd tried Michael at the station, but there'd been no answer. Then she'd left a message on his cell phone. So far, he hadn't shown up.

Steve hadn't been happy when he'd seen her arrive, but she doubted he suspected why she was there. Svensen was standing at the bar along with Jacobsen and others. It was now two hours before the end of slack tide. If Karl was planning to make a move, he had to make it soon.

Karl drank the last of his beer and paid his bill, then headed for the back hall, his actions exhibiting a casual purposefulness. Anyone watching him, though, would assume he was simply going to the men's room.

After a minute, Kaz stood and followed him. The back hall was dimly lit, like the rest of the bar. Several doors, all closed, led off it, and at the very back, a door led outside, probably to the pier. Svensen was nowhere to be seen.

Kaz walked down the hallway to Steve's office door. She turned the knob quietly, opened the door a crack, and glanced inside. The room was empty. She stood there for a moment, perplexed. Then she heard a toilet flush in the men's room, and footsteps. She ducked into the office, closing the door behind her.

That had been close. Evidently, Karl really *had* come back here to relieve himself of all that beer. Then the footsteps got louder, coming down the hallway.

The knob of the office door turned. She hurriedly glanced around for a hiding place, then she dove underneath the desk, curling herself up as best she could inside the cavity and pulling the chair back into place.

The door opened, temporarily letting in the noise from the bar. The bar noise abruptly muted as Karl closed the door, locking it from the inside.

Kaz concentrated on breathing shallowly and quietly.

The light came on, and she watched boot-clad feet walk over to the file cabinet. He opened a file drawer. The plastic of folder frames clacked as he shoved them together. Then she heard something thud down on top of the cabinet. As quietly as possible, she shifted so that she could put her head down on the floor and look out from under the edge of the desk.

Karl stood with his back to her, unwrapping some kind of package. She heard a rustling sound, then he slammed the drawer shut, picked up the package, and turned around. Just before she ducked back under the desk, she saw that whatever he had was covered in black plastic. Her movement brought her butt up against the other wall of her hiding space. The wood of the desk creaked ever so faintly.

He stopped, turning back toward her hiding place. She stopped breathing.

After a long moment, his boots shifted out of sight. The light went off, plunging the room into darkness. Then, silence.

He wasn't leaving. Her air was running out, her heart pounding so loud she couldn't believe that he couldn't hear it.

Finally, finally, he crouched in the far corner of the room, pulling back the carpet. Reaching for something in the flooring, he flipped it, then used it to pull open the trap door. The dank odors of the pilings and stagnant water flowed into the room. She heard the waves lapping against the pier. There was a shuffling noise, then he dropped through the door, pulling it closed after him.

Kaz sucked air into her deprived lungs.

She climbed out from under the desk. Gary's information had been dead on—Karl was probably on his way upriver to the mooring basin. She had only minutes to spare if she wanted to follow him.

Rounding the desk, she cautiously opened the door. The hallway was clear. She slipped out, closing the door behind her. Smoothing her clothes and hair, she walked back into the bar. Steve gave her a sharp glance, his eyes worried. She smiled reassuringly.

Casually walking over to her table, she sat down and drank the last of her beer, unhurriedly setting down the mug, then placed some folded bills under the edge of the glass. Standing, she walked calmly out the door.

Outside, she broke into a run.

Chapter 25

After losing a battle with herself, Lucy walked back toward the interrogation room to talk to Gary one more time in the hopes of getting him to cooperate. She needed to stay out of it, let Sykes handle it. But where Gary was concerned, well, she might as well get used to it—she had no objectivity.

As she reached out to open the door, she glanced out the window at the end of the hallway. And froze her in her tracks.

Sykes was standing in the parking lot next to a police cruiser, talking to whoever was inside. He said something, threw his head back and laughed, then reached inside the window to clap the cop on the shoulder. Then the cruiser backed out of the parking spot, turning and giving Lucy a clear view of who was driving.

Clint Jackson.

She leaned against the interrogation room door, closing her eyes. Sykes hadn't believed her. She made a sound of self-disgust. And why would he? She was the rooky detective, the one who had no experience. The one with the rep for jumping to conclusions.

She stood in the hallway, debating. Gary was in grave danger, she wasn't wrong about that. She *had* to buy him some time.

She glanced toward the squad room. Ivar was sitting where he'd been for the last two hours, still working on Kaz's computer. Should she tell him what she was up to? *No.* She didn't need to take his career down along with hers.

Squaring her shoulders, she opened the door to the interrogation room and told Brenner, who'd been standing guard, to leave. Gary looked down at the floor, refusing to acknowledge her presence, just as he had since they'd brought him in. She had only minutes to get through to him. Once he was arraigned and locked up for the night...

Pulling up a chair, she sat down, her knees touching his. "So," she said with a casualness she wasn't feeling. "I'll bet you don't have any way of knowing, since you haven't spent a lot of time in our cool new police station, that the men's room is right by the back door."

Gary's head slowly came up. He stared at her with his good eye.

"The back door that leads directly to the parking lot, and beyond that, to those old warehouses," she added.

He shook his head. "What...are you doing, Luce?"

She leaned forward and lowered her voice. "I don't think you'll be alive, come morning. Am I wrong?"

He just stared at her, his expression giving nothing away.

Anger bubbled up, edged with panic. "And I don't think you resisted arrest. They beat you, just like they beat Ken. Didn't they?"

No response.

She kept going doggedly, determined to get through to him. "You know, rumor has it that you have a weak bladder."

After a long moment, he reluctantly nodded.

Relief flooded through her. "Then you'll need to go to the men's room after all that water Kaz just let you drink." She stood up and took hold of his elbow. "Let's go. *Now*. There's no time."

He shuffled along beside her docilely enough. To anyone glancing her way, it looked like it was supposed to look—that

237

she was escorting the prisoner to the restroom. Once inside, she quickly checked the rest of the stalls, then took a key out of her pocket and unlocked his hand and leg cuffs.

"Okay," she said, standing back and assuming a fighting stance. "Make it look good."

Gary shook his head. "Can't...hurt you."

She rolled her eyes. "It has to look like you overpowered me. That is, if I'm going to stand a chance of keeping my job when this is all over."

He shook his head again, and glanced at the closed door. "Find...another way."

She blew out an exasperated breath and angled her chin at him. "Just knock me out, dammit. I've taken worse on the mat at the gym. Do you want to live, or not?" She glared at him, then went for the taunt that might make him angry enough to do what was necessary. "Or is that it? Wouldn't want you acting out of self-interest, now would we?"

He growled and reached for her, placing his hands on her shoulders, cupping the curve of her neck. His thumbs caressed the sensitive skin behind her ears. She tried to control the shiver that went through her at his warm touch but wasn't quite fast enough.

One corner of his mouth quirked. "So I...still...get...to you."

"Oh, just shut up—"

His hands tightened just slightly. The darkness came quickly, swamping her.

The last thing she remembered was being gently lowered to the floor and the whispered words, "Sorry, love."

"Like you thought, the accelerant was gasoline," the lab technician confirmed.

Michael stood in the basement lab at the State Police facility in Warrenton, glancing through the paperwork the technician handed him.

"And it matches what was found on the rags in the back of Jorgensen's car." The tech pulled out the report, then pointed at the two gas chromatograph readings. "That's not definitive, since most of the gas around here comes from the same refinery, but along with everything else..."

Michael glanced at his watch, worried about the passing time. He needed to get back to the station and pick up Kaz. He wouldn't put it past her to get impatient and strike out on her own. The woman needed a keeper. And so far, the tech hadn't given him any reason for his demand that Michael drop everything and drive out there. "Why the hell—"

"And I've got a match on the DNA," the tech interrupted. He rummaged around on his desk, then held up two DNA diagrams which, sure enough, looked identical. He was shifting from one foot to the other, acting nervous.

Michael's heart sank. It had to be either Gary or Kaz. Which didn't prove that either one of them had committed the murder, but it left him with no way to prove that they *hadn't*, either. When would he catch a break on this damn case? "Whose sample matched?" he asked, resigned.

The tech shuffled his feet again. "That's just it. I re-tested two times, because I thought I'd made a mistake. Then I checked your labels again, and I was wondering if you'd mismarked the samples—"

Michael ground his teeth. "I didn't screw up the fucking samples! Just spit it out. Which one matched?"

"The cigar."

Michael froze. "Pardon?"

"The cigar's a match to the hair follicle. Where'd you find the cigar, anyway? We didn't find anything like that on the boat, or...*hey!*"

The paperwork fluttered to the floor as Michael sprinted for the door, taking the basement steps three at a time.

Sonofabitch! Sykes had been playing him all along. And Kaz

239

was at the police station. Surely Sykes wouldn't try anything in front of the other cops—he wouldn't be that brazen. But who knew how many of them were working with him?

Racing across the parking lot to his car, he used his cell phone to dial the station. Ivar answered Lucy's phone. "Where is she?" Michael shouted.

"In the interrogation room with Gary," Ivar answered. "Why?"

"No time to explain. Tell Kaz not to move. I'll be right there."

"Kaz isn't here." Ivar sounded confused.

Michael skidded to a stop at the car door, one hand in his pocket, reaching for his keys. Zeke barked at him from inside the car, jumping up and down. "*What?*"

"Yeah, she left about half an hour ago."

"Fuck! Where was she headed?"

"She said something to Lucy about heading to the mooring basin and then to the tavern."

"Is Sykes there?" Michael asked, terror's grip making it hard for him to form the words.

"Hold on." Ivar put the phone down for a few seconds, then came back online. "He must've gone home already, I don't see him in his office."

"Keep me posted." Michael disconnected and yanked open the car door. He started to toss the cell phone on the front seat when he saw that he had a message. Why hadn't it come through? Because he'd been in the basement at the time, dammit. No coverage. He started the car and pulled on his and Zeke's seatbelts, listening to the message from Kaz. Then checked the time stamp.

Kaz cut the *Kasmira B's* running lights and stayed back so that Karl wouldn't notice her in the approaching darkness. With the wind picking up and conditions becoming choppier, she found

240

it hard to keep him in sight. If he crossed the river bar faster than she did, or if she made any navigational mistakes, she could easily lose him on the ocean side. Then her only option would be to head for the location he'd given out over the radio the day before and pray that she was right.

Once out of the Redemption, she'd driven along Marine Drive, keeping Karl's small skiff in sight as he took it upriver to the mooring basin. By the time she'd gotten there and parked, he was fueling up at the pumps and hadn't seen her sneak down the docks and onto her own boat.

The *Kasmira B* bounced harder than usual, sending alarm skittering along her nerves. The weather report coming across the marine channel wasn't good—a storm surge of up to fifteen feet was predicted just offshore, with more than thirty feet out at sea. Add to that winds up to thirty knots, and it would be a hell coming back across.

If she made it at all.

Being caught out for the night wasn't an option. Whatever she learned out here she *had* to be able to communicate back to Lucy—she didn't believe Gary would survive until morning. And that scared her far more than crossing the river bar under the wrong conditions.

Keeping closer to shore, she paralleled Karl, staying as far back as she dared off his port stern. Only half an hour after turning south, he cut his engines to an idle and ran alongside a buoy. His location matched the position he'd given out on the radio yesterday. He'd employed the fishermen's habit of broadcasting false locations, but his intent all along had been to inform the drug suppliers which crab pots he'd used as the drop location. She had to admit, it was a clever idea. Someone had once said that the best place to hide something valuable was right in plain sight. This was just a fisherman's variation on that theme.

Karl's running lights provided just enough illumination so

that with binoculars, she could watch him pull the crab pot out of the water, open it up, take out a package, and then drop in the plastic wrapped package he'd taken from the office back. He lowered the cage back into the water.

Grabbing a pen and paper, Kaz noted the longitude and latitude, as evidence for later. Karl had brought himself down by following every ship captain's habit—writing down everything in the ship's log. With her notes as corroboration, they had him. Now all she had to do was follow him back to port and then on to his meeting with his in-town contact.

"Gotcha," she murmured out loud. She was one giant step closer to proving Gary's innocence.

"No," the voice behind her said. "We've got *you.*"

Chapter 26

As Michael's car skidded onto the wharf, his cell phone warbled. He picked it up and flipped it open. "Talk."

"I found Lucy," Ivar said. "Knocked out cold in the men's room. Gary's escaped."

Michael started swearing. "Were you able to revive her?"

"Yeah, she says Kaz planned to observe the hand-off of the cash at the Redemption and then follow Karl Svensen from there."

"Follow him where?"

"That's not clear, but I'd bet out on the water somewhere. Makes sense."

Michael got out of the car and searched the boats on the docks below. "Both boats are gone, Svensen's and Kaz's. *Goddammit*! What did she think she was doing, taking this on by herself?"

"My guess is she didn't have a choice. They both were at the mercy of the tides," Ivar pointed out.

He was right, but that didn't make Michael's heart pound any slower. "Yeah, okay. Listen to me. It's Sykes."

There was momentary silence on the other end.

"Sykes is behind this, dammit. You and Lucy notify the Coast Guard, have them put a rescue boat out on the water."

"You're wrong, man. Lucy says it's Clint Jackson. And Steve called from the Redemption just now, worried about Kaz. He didn't say a thing about Sykes."

Michael told him about the DNA samples. "I don't know whether Jackson is in on it, and I don't know what Steve knows, but Sykes is the killer." He could hear Lucy shouting in the background. "I can see Bjorn from here—I'll convince him to take me out. Let's just hope to hell we're fast enough. Sykes' Lincoln Navigator is parked a block from here, locked up tight."

He threw the phone onto the car seat and locked the door, leaving Zeke whining unhappily inside with the windows cracked for air. He cleared the ramp down to Bjorn's trawler in one leap.

Kaz stared at Jim Sykes, who stood on the top step of the stairs leading to the engine room, pointing a large, black handgun at her. His smile was humorless. "You Jorgensens. You never did know when to mind your own business."

"You're in on this?" she asked stupidly. "Jim, *why*?"

His tone turned derisive. "You think a police chief's salary in a Podunk town like Astoria will ever get me where I want to go? Money is power, Kaz. You know that from all those consulting gigs you had."

"But, Jim. Murder?"

He shrugged, seemingly unmoved. "Ken would've blabbed, sooner or later. I had to shut him up. All my life, I've done what had to be done."

Kaz shivered. "It was you who shot at me out by the Elk Preserve."

Sykes chuckled. "Couldn't have you running around proving Gary's innocence, now could I? He was a necessary part of my plan—my scapegoat." Sykes leaned toward her, his expression coldly satisfied. "It gave me great pleasure to frame him. I've hated both of you ever since we were kids. The great fucking Jorgensen twins—smart, popular, and with parents that every kid envied. That night your parents drowned? I goddamn cheered. The only bad part was that *you* survived." He nodded and leaned back, pleased with the effect his words had on her. "Now where's the fucking money?"

Kaz cleared her throat, hoping her voice would be steady. "It's gone—you'll never get it back. Gary used it to pay off Bobby's medical bills."

Rage flashed across his face. "Well, now," he said softly. "I was going to spare you by knocking you out, but I guess after hearing that bit of news, I'll just let you burn alive. In fact, killing both of you is going to be a real pleasure."

"Why kill Gary?" she protested.

"Plans have changed. Clint'll handle that little task for me, later this evening." Sykes looked amused. "Your brother was always unstable. His suicide will be just one more tragedy for your family." He stepped to the side and motioned her out onto the deck. "Let's go."

She needed to keep him talking while she came up with a plan. A quick glance around the wheelhouse told her there was nothing that could be used as a weapon. "Listen, Jim—"

Lightening fast, he backhanded her.

Pain exploded. She cried out, stars glittering in the periphery of her vision.

"That's for damn near breaking my nose last night in your living room, you *bitch*," he said. "Now, *move*. No more games."

Michael stood on the bow of Bjorn's trawler, staring intently into the gathering darkness and gusting wind. When they were riding high on a crest, he could just make out the *Kasmira B.* His gut churned, his hands so slippery with sweat he could barely grip the binoculars.

Sykes had played him, using his newcomer status to control the investigation so he could frame Gary. And the mayor was no saint in all of this, either. Forbes had to have suspected Sykes, or he never would've visited Michael that morning on

245

the docks. Michael had thought he was merely worried about old loyalties getting in the way of the investigation—he hadn't really given his talk with the mayor a second thought.

That had been Michael's first mistake. His second had been underestimating Sykes.

Sykes had chosen arson as his method on purpose, and he'd planned on having the power to block Michael's jurisdiction over the case. Well, he'd planned wrong. But he'd still managed to slip under Michael's radar long enough to put Kaz in grave danger.

Not again, not again. The refrain played over and over in Michael's mind. Kaz was paying the price for his stupidity. He'd been too slow to figure it out, too slow to put the details together. All along, Sykes had run the investigation from behind the scenes. He'd had access to the boat and to Gary's truck. He also had enough SWAT team training to handle shooting at Kaz that day from the Elk Preserve.

"If someone sneezes out on Youngs Bay, I know about it," he'd told Michael.

He probably knew all those old logging roads like the back of his hand. Michael swallowed bile-filled rage. And Sykes had been at Kaz's house last night, executing a search warrant. All the son of a bitch would've had to do was leave, wait a couple of minutes, then come back and attack her.

So where was he? He had to be out with Svensen. And Kaz was following them, trying to gather evidence. If either one of them saw her...

Michael walked back to the door of the wheelhouse. "Cut your running lights. I don't want anyone seeing us."

Bjorn complied without comment, and Michael held up the binoculars. He could make out Kaz in the wheelhouse of the *Kasmira B,* along with the shadow of someone else.

His heart simply *stopped.*

Fiddling with the focus, he brought the man into sharp

246

relief. As he watched, Sykes pistol-whipped Kaz, putting the weight of his body behind the vicious blow. She hit the far wall and slid out of sight.

An icy calm settled over Michael. His heartbeat slowed to a strong, steady rhythm. He carefully set down the binoculars, turning to Bjorn. "Do you have an inflatable raft?"

"Yeah, but in these conditions—"

"Get it."

Chapter 27

Kaz pulled herself up from the wheelhouse floor and walked past Sykes out onto the deck on shaky legs, her right hand pressing against her throbbing cheek. As the storm moved closer, the *Kasmira B* started to pitch in earnest. She stumbled once, then regained her balance.

Sykes motioned for her to stop just outside the door. Keeping the gun trained on her, he braced his feet and switched on the radio, then picked up the handset. "Karl."

"Yeah."

"Give me five minutes, and then come alongside."

"Make it ten—we've got storm surge."

Sykes switched off the radio and then yanked out the cord of the handset, tossing it on the floor. Then he came out and motioned Kaz toward the stern. She staggered, almost tripping over the can of gasoline that was sitting against the winch.

Keep him talking. "What did you do—stow away?"

Sykes' expression was smug. "I figured you wouldn't check the head. I was in there the whole time."

He motioned to her to sit on the stern bench, then took out a roll of duct tape, taping her hands and feet so tight that her circulation was cut off. He gave her a hard shove, and she fell onto the deck.

Pain shot through her shoulder. She swallowed a yelp. "So you were the one who broke into my house and attacked me. I knew there was something familiar about you."

He laughed. It was an ugly sound. "Yeah, I enjoyed that. It's a shame I was in such a hurry, or I could've had some real fun with you." He picked up the can of gasoline, opened it, and started pouring it on the deck. The acrid smell burned Kaz's nose as the liquid flowed across the planking toward her. She rolled as far away from it as she could.

He walked toward the bow, pouring the gasoline as he went, then put the can down and stepped inside the wheelhouse, pulling a small timer and some rags out of his pocket.

He was going to burn the boat, with her on it. If she didn't do something, and quickly, she would die. She thought of Michael. By now, he had to be frantic.

Trying not to alert Sykes, she felt along the edge of the stern compartment, but she found nothing she could use as a weapon. She kept her bait cleaver in a slot behind the winch. Could she get to it? She would have to scrabble across the deck, through the gasoline, which would soak into her clothes. And if the fire started before she freed herself, she'd burn to death in seconds.

She pushed herself along the deck toward the winch, using the rubber edges of her running shoes to fight the rolling of the trawler. Spray slapped her down, soaking through her clothing. She closed her eyes, now stinging from the salt, and kept going.

When she heard a slight thump on the decking, she jolted. Was someone else on board? Or had it just been the wind moving the gear around? Craning her neck, she glanced at Sykes. He was busy pouring gasoline and hadn't seemed to notice the sound.

Quickly, she used her feet against the stern bench to shove herself the last several feet. The pooled gasoline was slippery, making her progress easier. She maneuvered around so that her hands and back were to the winch, feeling frantically for the cleaver.

249

There. Her hands closed around the handle. She slid it under the edge of her sou'wester just as Sykes came back out of the wheelhouse.

He stared down at her in her new position, and his expression clouded with fury. He raised his gun.

"Drop it!" Michael appeared around the corner of the wheelhouse, his feet braced, his gun trained on Sykes.

Sykes kept his gun trained on Kaz and glanced over his shoulder. "I don't think so. You shoot me, and I shoot her."

Michael shook his head. "You don't want to die, Jim."

Sykes tightened his finger on the trigger. "Drop your gun, Chapman, or she dies. Now."

Michael's lips tightened, and he shot a tormented look at Kaz. Then he complied, leaning down and placing his gun on the deck.

"That's better," Sykes said, turning and aiming his gun at Michael. "Kick it away."

Michael did as he was told, and the gun slid across the deck and over the edge, disappearing into the waters below.

Kaz closed her eyes, her shoulders slumping. They were going to die if she didn't do something. Sykes' finger tightened on the trigger, and he took careful aim at Michael.

"No!" Kaz raised her bound feet and kicked the back of Sykes' knee. The shot went wild as Sykes lost his balance. Michael launched himself through the air, taking Sykes down with him.

They rolled, grappling for the gun. The gas can toppled, spraying gas in all directions, some of it hitting Kaz. She shook her head to clear the burning liquid out of her eyes, trying to focus on the two men. They rolled toward the stern, fighting silently, viciously.

Sykes landed a punch, then managed roll on top of Michael and slam his head into the deck.

Kaz whimpered. Positioning the cleaver, she sawed it back

and forth against the edge of the tape, her hands now so numb that she couldn't control the angle of the cleaver or what she was cutting. She felt something warm flow ever her fingers, but she kept sawing.

Michael scissored his legs, throwing Sykes to the side. Sykes raised his gun. Michael gripped his gun hand, deflecting his aim. A second, deafening shot went wild.

Kaz felt the tape on her hands give and she wrenched them apart, then sat up to work on her feet. She was almost finished when the gun went off again. Her head flew up, terror locking her throat.

Michael fell back, and Sykes shoved him out of the way so that he could get to his feet, gun in hand. "Nice try, Chapman." He was panting heavily.

Kaz got to her feet stealthily, the cleaver still in her hand. She advanced on Sykes quickly, the cleaver raised. But he turned, and seeing her, kicked her feet out from under her. On a deck covered with a mixture of seawater and gasoline, she never stood a chance.

She went down hard, the cleaver flying out of her hands. Rolling onto her back, she looked up. He pointed the gun at her head, his finger on the trigger.

She glared defiantly, daring him, and he laughed.

Then he jerked, his face registering surprise. Lurching awkwardly, his fingers sagged, nerveless, as he dropped the gun. Twisting around, he tried to grab the fishhook that was embedded in his back. Staring at Michael, he started to fall, his arms flailing wildly. Landing on the deck railing, his momentum carried him over the side.

Kaz got to her knees and crawled to the rail and peered over, but there was no sign of him in the churning waters.

She slid and scrambled toward Michael. He lay where he'd fallen, his eyes closed. A dark, rapidly spreading pool of blood stained the decking beneath him.

Chapter 28

"Michael!" Sobbing, she grabbed the front of his shirt. "Don't you dare die on me, dammit!"

"Okay," he said calmly, not opening his eyes.

"What do you mean, *okay?* You're bleeding!"

"Yeah, but I got the bastard." He opened an eye and tried to smile at her, then frowned at the blood on her hands. "Are you okay?"

"You're the one who's been shot!" She started pulling at his clothes, ripping open his shirt, feeling along his rib cage.

"My leg," he managed. "I think he got lucky and hit the bone." He tried to rise up on one elbow, but the effort was too much and he sank back, closing his eyes. "Go into the wheelhouse and disconnect the timer before this damn boat goes up."

She glanced back at the wheelhouse, then at Michael. She didn't want to leave him. Taking off her coat, she quickly pulled off her sweater, then her cotton turtleneck. Folding it into a pad, she pressed it to the bloodiest area on his leg. Then she laid her coat over him to conserve his body heat. "Hold the pad in place until I get back."

Getting to her feet, she slipped and slid into the wheelhouse, clad from the waist up only in her bra. She might be freezing, but at least she had less gasoline on her. Grabbing the timer and the pile of rags, she leaned out the door and threw them overboard. Then she started searching for something, *anything* she could use as a tourniquet.

The *Kasmira B* rocked to port, hard. She glanced out the window. They'd drifted north, putting them closer to the river bar. The swells were getting huge. Restarting the engines, she turned the trawler into the oncoming waves. Leaving the engines on idle, she ran back out onto the deck.

Spying a length of line, she fetched the cleaver. Kneeling beside Michael, she drew the line around his leg, above the bleeding area, and tied it tight.

"Tighter," he said, his voice more faint than it had been a few minutes ago.

A wave crashed over the railing, its icy foam hissing and bubbling as it engulfed them. Michael sucked in a breath. His body started to shake. He was going into shock. She had to get him out of the water, or he'd die before she could get help.

She used the cleaver to rip his jeans to take a better look— there was a small entry wound about midway up his thigh, and an exit *crater* on the opposite side. She let out a sob. The leg looked funny—it was bent at an awkward angle. "Is it broken?" she made herself ask.

"Yeah, I think so....feels like it." He managed to get up on one elbow and look at it. "You'll have to tie it tighter, love, or I won't make it back to port."

Ripping her turtleneck in half, she fashioned two pads out of it, then rolled him to press the second one to the back of his leg. She positioned the line over each pad pulled it tighter. He let out a groan. The bleeding slowed but didn't stop. Her makeshift bandages were already turning bright red.

"I've got a better idea," she said. The deck was pitching hard, but if she could manage to get him below... "Come on."

She put an arm around his shoulders and helped him sit up. His face was white, his teeth chattering, his skin clammy with sweat. She had to move fast—he wouldn't be conscious much longer. "Okay, on the count of three, we're going to stand up.

You're going to use me as a brace to get down the stairs."

"You're insane, you know that? I've got a perfectly good deck I can lie on right here—"

"A deck that you'll slide right off of when we go over the bar. Plus, I can get your leg elevated down below, and tie you in, in case you conk out."

"Make that cruel and insane." But when she counted, he heaved himself up, leaning heavily on her. "Here you are almost naked," he panted, "and I'm in no shape to follow through."

"I am not amused, Chapman."

They almost lost balance twice before she got him to the stairs. Bracing her body below his and using the stair railing to hold herself upright, he leaned across her as they hopped down the stairs. Once in the galley, she laid him down so that half of his body was on the dining table, then hauled his legs up until he was lying flat. Then as gently as possible, she propped his injured leg on the hanging spice island. The platter was designed to move with the boat's motion, and it would keep his leg immobile.

She raced back up on deck, fetching the roll of duct tape Sykes had left behind. She taped Michael to the table, then taped his leg to the hanging platter. Through it all, Michael kept his eyes closed. His face had lost all color.

Finally, he was immobilized. "Are you still with me?" she whispered.

"...Yeah."

The elevation had slowed the bleeding, but not enough. "I have to tighten the rope again. Hang on." She re-tied it as a slip knot, and tightened the rope by degrees. When he groaned, she cringed but kept going. She tied the rope in a double knot, then yanked a blanket off the berth and threw it over him.

"I've got to get us over the river bar." She rummaged in the locker for a sweater and pulled it on.

"Lucy and Ivar called the Coast Guard....They should be looking for us..." his voice faded.

"Yeah, but Sykes ripped out the handset; I can't get off a signal. And with the weather like this, our best bet is to cross the bar and hope to meet them on the other side." She took a precious moment to lean down and kiss him, then lay her cheek against his. "Try to stay conscious, okay?"

"...yeah." He grimaced, then leered half-heartedly at her. "Liked you better...just the bra."

She laughed softly. "Another time, I promise. I'm going to get you back over that bar, you hear? So no wimping out on me."

There was no response.

"Michael?" She felt for his pulse. It was too rapid, and his breathing was too shallow.

"*Kasmira B*, come in. *Kasmira B*, can you read?" Bjorn's voice crackled through the radio.

Kaz took the stairs two at a time, grabbing the radio mike off the deck. She twisted the ripped wires together, praying that the radio would work, then flipped the switch. "This is the *Kasmira B*. Bjorn, Michael Chapman is on board, badly injured." She gave him their position. "Do you copy?"

"*Kasmira B*, do you read? We have you in sight. State your condition."

Kaz stared at the mike, flipped the switch again, retransmitting.

"*Kasmira B*, do you copy?"

She threw down the mike in frustration. Searching the churning waters, she couldn't see anything. Climbing to the flying bridge, she searched again.

Nothing.

Jumping back down to deck level, she threw open the stern seat cover and searched for a flare. Breaking it apart, she held it up as high as she could for a few moments, then tossed it into the waters off the stern. Hopefully, Bjorn would see it.

She returned to the wheelhouse and waited. After an agonizingly long minute, the radio crackled to life.

"*Kasmira B,* we have the flare in sight and have transmitted your position to the Coast Guard. They are currently just east of Sand Island. Kaz, you have to cross the river bar—they can't get to you where you are. If you have navigational capabilities, set off a second flare to confirm."

After complying, she waited for the next response. "Confirmed, *Kasmira B.* We will follow you through the bar. Over and out."

Quickly, she assessed the conditions. The storm surge was still building, the winds now howling through the rigging. She pushed the throttle bar forward and heard the trawler's engines roar to life.

For a split second, she thought about that night fifteen years ago. Then she shoved the memories down deep and forgot about them. Failure wasn't an option. Losing Michael wasn't an option.

Taking a deep breath, she climbed up to the flying bridge where her visibility—what was left of it—would be best. Her feet planted wide, her body braced against the wild pitching of the trawler, she turned the trawler into the oncoming breakers.

The boat labored up the steep crest of a wave and then slid sickeningly down, bottoming out with a bone-jarring thud in the next trough. The trawler's timbers creaked, and for just one second, Kaz lost her nerve.

She couldn't do it, she didn't have the skills. Maybe she was better off turning around, heading back out to sea. Bjorn could notify the Coast Guard; maybe they could get a helicopter up in this...

Gary's voice was suddenly there with her. *You've got to know what you're doing to get lucky on the river bar, Sis.*

First thing, get your bearings. Then steer based on your instinct, on the feel of the water beneath you.

She took several deep, calming breaths. Trembling hard, she took a reading off the whistle buoy at the mouth of the river, then adjusted her course.

Cold rain fell in sheets, obscuring the channel markers, the faint outlines of land and blurry halos of lights on shore disappearing altogether.

Hold her steady, Kaz. Don't panic. Wait for the next lull in the storm to get your bearings again, then correct your position.

Number 4 Buoy bobbed past, off to starboard, its beacon so pale that she almost missed it. The *Kasmira B* shuddered as the next wave hit, her rigging clanking against the boom. As the trawler pitched hard to starboard, she gave a second's thought to Michael down below, praying that her makeshift setup was keeping him strapped in.

"*Kasmira B*. You're looking good." Bjorn's voice came to her faintly. "Adjust one degree to starboard. Kaz, you're gonna make it. Hang in there." Tears streamed down her face, mixing with the rain.

As she neared Clatsop Spit, huge breakers slammed into the trawler, their giant, white-foamed crests obscuring the buoys. She wrenched the wheel to the right with all her strength, forcing the trawler to sluggishly change course again. A spate of icy sleet hit her numbed face like hot needles.

The roar of the surf was so loud now that she could barely hear her own thoughts. The radio crackled again, and Bjorn said something, but it was lost on the wind.

She eased her way toward the Lower Desdemona Shoal, where shifting sands made safe passage a game of Russian roulette. The trawler's diesel engine coughed, and Kaz froze, terror sliding sickeningly along her nerve endings. If she lost power...

The engine coughed again, then resumed its ponderous chugging. She steered for the next buoy.

Another wave crashed over the trawler, slapping her down, washing her halfway over the railing of the bridge. She clung to the wheel as it spun wildly under her weight, dragging herself back to her feet. Struggling against her waning strength, she willed the trawler back on course.

She caught a glimpse of another buoy, enough to adjust her course again, just before fog enveloped the boat. Concentrating on keeping her course and speed even, she released another trembling breath when the next buoy loomed out of the murky darkness in front of her, right where it was supposed to be.

You're almost there, Sis. Home free.

Instinct caused her to glance to stern. A sneaker wave slid with deadly intent under the trawler, tilting the stern up high, pointing the trawler straight down.

Kaz swallowed the scream at the back of her throat, waited three seconds for the bow to start back up, counting them off inside her head, then yanked the throttle full open. The *Kasmira B's* engine growled under the strain, fighting the river current. She felt the full power of the wave catch the boat and heard the roar of the water under the hull as the boat surged forward, surfing the flood. Moments later, the waters smoothed out.

She was across the bar. Braced against the console, she stood with shoulders slumped and head down, gulping air.

Out of the darkness the running lights of a large ship suddenly blinded her, washing bright light across the trawler's decking. "*Kasmira B,* this is the United States Coast Guard. Prepare to be boarded."

Chapter 29

Kaz and Lucy backed up the stairs from the engine room, ahead of the two medics carrying the stretcher with Michael on it. Lucy cursed, her feet slipping on the treads made treacherous by the rocking of the trawler and the spilled gasoline.

Kaz hadn't wanted to let go of Michael's hand, but there wasn't enough room in the galley for two EMTs, the stretcher, and her. She'd had to stand off to the side and watch, terrified, while they pushed plasma into Michael's veins in an attempt to stabilize him.

They'd finally managed to raise his blood pressure and were now preparing him to be airlifted to the hospital. The Coast Guard helicopter hovered overhead, its deafening rotors flattening the waves.

"Creative use of duct tape," Lucy shouted as they moved into the wheelhouse to let the men by. "I'll bet you didn't learn that in that fancy MBA program down in California, did you?"

Kaz tried to smile, but tears leaked out, and suddenly, she was crying again. She'd been crying off and on for the last half hour.

Lucy put both arms around her and held her tight. "He's going to be all right, you know," she said. "You saved his sorry hide by elevating his leg." Then she straightened abruptly, sniffing Kaz and then her own clothes. "Ewww. Do you have *gasoline* all over you?"

Kaz nodded, wiping the tears off her cheeks with the palms of her hands. "Sykes poured it everywhere, and I had to roll through it to get to the cleaver that I used to cut myself free."

"Dammit! I just bought this jacket—you could've warned me." Lucy's disgust was comical as she surveyed the damage to the camel hair blazer she had on under her life vest. The EMTs had given Kaz a blanket to hug around herself, and it was the only item on her that didn't reek of gasoline and seawater.

"Sykes went overboard." Kaz watched the medics navigate the wildly rocking boats to attach the hooks to the basket in which Michael was lying.

"Probably for the best," Lucy replied. "I don't think this town could've stood the stress of the trial." Then her face crumpled. "God, Kaz. This is all my fault. I was the one who told him everything, including where to find you."

Kaz shook her head. "You couldn't have known."

"I *knew* there was a dirty cop, but I thought it was Jackson. I never even considered that the chief might also be involved. I blabbed everything to him, trying to get him to hold off on arraigning Gary until we could check out Jackson."

"Jackson *was* in on it, according to Sykes." Kaz hugged herself. "Gary's okay?"

"He's fine." Lucy started pacing in the cramped space. "The jerk! I ask him to knock me out—just a small tap to my jaw is all it would've taken—but does he do it? No. He uses some kind of Kung Fu crap to put me out for about fifteen minutes. I'll never live it down."

"Gary escaped?" Kaz asked, confused.

Lucy looked embarrassed, then shrugged. "I was worried about him, so I cut him loose."

Kaz started laughing. "You purposely engineered a prisoner's escape."

"Well, shit. What *else* was I supposed to do?" Lucy glared. "I was afraid—"

"You don't have to explain," Kaz interrupted, snickering. "Really."

"Gary radioed in a little while ago," Lucy added grudgingly. "He and Jacobsen nabbed Svensen, along with the money and drugs as evidence. They're on their way back in. And Ivar is questioning Jackson, to see what his involvement was." Lucy looked even more disgruntled. "So far, this evening is *not* helping my career. A prisoner escapes on my watch, and then my friends apprehend the bad guys."

"You'll get over it." Kaz patted her shoulder.

One of the EMTs stepped into the doorway of the wheelhouse and crooked a finger at Kaz. "You're going with us. We've got to get that gasoline off you before you have a toxic reaction, and we need to check you out for hypothermia."

Kaz's heart leapt at the thought of being allowed to go in with Michael, but she stayed where she was, shaking her head. "I have to bring the *Kasmira B* in to port."

"I'll handle her—you go on," Lucy said. "What the heck—it beats filling out paperwork, which is all you guys have left for me to do."

Chapter 30

Michael woke up in a hospital room. Machines beeped incessantly, making his head ache. His leg felt like someone had jammed a hot poker into it, then wrapped the poker inside some kind of huge, immobile casing. A bag hung overhead, dripping clear liquid into his left arm, and his other arm wouldn't move.

He slowly angled his head so that he could see what was on his arm. Kaz sat in a chair beside the bed, both her hands wrapped around his right one. Her head lay on their joined hands, and she was sound asleep.

Her hair was a mess, half pulled out of the braid she'd put it in the afternoon before. He could smell a faint odor of gasoline, overlaid by some kind of hospital detoxifying agent. Her face was scrubbed clean, but the purple bruises from Sykes' beatings were a garish contrast to her pale complexion.

Someone had brought her clean clothes—Lucy, probably. She'd obviously gathered them in a hurry. The football jersey Kaz wore was wrinkled, the jeans so ratty they were almost indecent.

She was the most beautiful woman he'd ever seen.

He must've shifted slightly. She woke with a start, her sleep-softened brown eyes staring into his in momentary confusion. She straightened abruptly. "How do you feel?" Her voice was raspy. "Are you in any pain?"

"I'm okay." Her expression became more anxious, and he

smiled to reassure her. "Any chance you can break me out of here any time soon?"

She shook her head, her eyes closing briefly. "I thought I'd lost you."

He reached up to run hand over her hair. The movement caused pain to shoot through his leg, but he needed to touch her. "Same here," he said, his voice gruff. "When I saw Sykes hit you..."

"You saw that?" she asked, surprised.

He nodded. "From Bjorn's boat." That image haunted him and, he suspected, would give him nightmares for some time.

"I'm fine," she reassured him, accurately reading his expression.

"...Chuck?"

"He's still listed as critical, but improving. He lost his spleen and one kidney, but the doctors are hopeful that he'll pull through." She shook her head. "He was trying to protect me."

"It's a good thing that Sykes is dead." Emotion clogged his throat. He cleared it, then said lightly, "Since we've—"

"So you're awake." The voice came from the doorway, interrupting them, and they both turned. Wallace Forbes stood there, looking tired. "May I come in?" the mayor asked, pointing inside the room, clearly not sure of his welcome.

Kaz stood on stiff legs and moved toward the door, giving Michael a small smile. "I'll be back in a few minutes."

He shifted, and the fire that traveled up his leg made his vision blur. He gritted his teeth and rode it out. "Where are you going?" he asked, not wanting her to slip away.

"There's someone who's anxious to see you. I'll go get him."

Michael motioned the mayor in. "You used me to flush out Sykes."

Forbes nodded, his eyes somber. "My town was sick, Michael. I had no choice." He put the stack of magazines he'd been holding on the table next to Michael's bed. "When your

263

resume came across my desk, I knew I'd been given my only chance to bring in someone who could take Jim on. But I didn't think you'd have to move so quickly, or that Jim would be clever enough to turn the situation around on the Jorgensens the way he did."

"Kaz damn near got killed." Michael's voice was arctic cold.

Forbes sighed and reached into his pocket for his cigarette case, then realized that he couldn't smoke in the hospital room and grimaced. "I never meant to put her in danger."

"You had to know that she'd do whatever she had to, to protect Gary."

"Yes, but I didn't know he was involved, not until the fire." Forbes shook his head and sighed. "Jim was more ruthless than I gave him credit for."

But Michael wasn't ready to let Forbes off the hook. "Why didn't you tell me about your suspicions that morning after the fire?"

"Because that's all they were—suspicions. I had no proof, and I didn't want to influence your investigation one way or the other."

"No one influences me. You should've said something."

Forbes looked out the window into the hospital parking lot for a minute, considering. Then he turned back, giving a quick nod. "My mistake. But we can move on now, as a community."

Michael pinned him with a hard stare. "If you ever lie to me again—"

"There won't be a need." Forbes frowned. "I don't suppose you have any suggestions on filling my new vacancy in the police department?"

After thinking about it, Michael replied, "I might." In fact, the idea of luring a certain friend out here from Boston had some appeal. He grinned a little, envisioning Mac's reaction to Astoria.

"Good. Have his resume on my desk by next week." Forbes

walked to the door, then turned back. "I know you think less of me because of this little affair, and I'm sorry for that. But answer me this, Michael. What's a little manipulation by an old man who wanted to save his town really worth when you stack it up against a chance for personal redemption?"

Michael said nothing.

Forbes shrugged and turned to leave. "You think about it, son. In the end, I did you a hell of a favor."

Unfortunately, the bastard had a point.

Kaz entered Chuck's ICU unit and found Gary sitting in the chair beside the bed. One of the ER nurses had obviously convinced him to let them treat his injuries—his cuts had been cleaned and stitched, and through the open neckline of his shirt, she could see the edge of the white tape bandage around his ribs. The swelling over his left eye had gone down slightly. He turned and smiled slightly at her.

"How is he?" she asked softly, approaching the bed where Chuck lay still and silent, his face pale beneath the bruises.

"He made it through the night—the nurse says that's a good sign." Gary shook his head. "I figured I'd better hang around, though, just in case he wakes up. He'll try to drag himself out of here—he can't stand hospitals."

Kaz sympathized. "You okay?" she asked Gary softly.

He shrugged. "The bastards are either dead or behind bars. I figure that makes it a good day." He straightened and stretched, grimacing at the pain it caused. "But I'll be better when Chuck wakes up."

"I hear Lucy busted you loose at the station."

He grinned a little. "Yeah. Right about now, I don't think she's talking to me. I was pretty sneaky when I put her out."

"You sure as hell were."

They both turned toward the doorway where Lucy stood there, looking tired but calm.

"Everything under control?" Kaz asked.

Lucy nodded. "Svensen's crew is behind bars, along with Jackson. Clint is talking a mile a minute, hoping to use the information he has as a bargaining chip for a lighter sentence." She dragged another chair from the adjoining cubicle and fell into it. "Like Gary told you, the buyer was offshore—we'll probably never be able to lay a hand on him. I've notified the DEA, but..." She sighed. "Sykes was the in-town contact, running everything from behind the scenes and moving the drugs upriver. Svensen was making the drops and pickups for a cut of the profits. Jackson was the muscle, when needed. He's the one who beat up Ken."

"How did Ken find out about them?" Kaz asked.

"According to Jackson, by pure dumb luck. He saw Karl remove something from a crab pot, right after he'd spent that day baiting and laying pots in a different location. That didn't make sense to Ken, so he asked Karl about it. Karl reacted badly, which made him suspicious. He started watching more closely, put it all together, and confronted Karl that night six months ago in the tavern. Karl exploded." Lucy glared at Gary. "Which is where you came in."

Gary shrugged again. "I didn't know what it was about—just that Karl was threatening Ken for some reason. And I wasn't about to stand by and let that happen." He shook his head. "I should've been suspicious, though, when Karl didn't press charges. It wasn't like him to let something like that go. And he had no reason to be nice to me—he's never liked me. But I didn't have a clue until Ken turned up at the boat ten days ago, badly beaten. That's when I made him tell me what was going on."

Kaz pursed her lips. "So Karl broadcast a 'fake' location, which was the signal to the sellers that he was leaving the money in one of his pots with a buoy attached. He goes back out when no one is around and leaves the money, picking up the drugs. He probably figured that anyone who saw him would think he was either stealing some crabs for dinner, which happens all the time, or repairing a line." She frowned. "Why did it take six months for Ken to put it together?"

"I wondered the same thing," Lucy said. "But crab season only runs for six months—they had to have a strategy for the rest of the year. Karl said whenever he was drag-fishing off-season, they simply met in international waters when no one was around."

"So they had the advantage of using two different types of drops, which would confuse anyone who was on to them."

"Yeah."

"*And,*" Kaz realized, "right after the fight, the season ended and they switched over to meeting in international waters, so it was awhile before Ken could steal the money. Meanwhile the medical bills probably piled up..."

Lucy nodded. "There you go."

"What about Steve?"

"Jackson says Sykes had something on him from the time of his divorce, but he didn't know what it was, and Steve isn't talking. I'm not going to push it—other than turning a blind eye, Steve wasn't involved. And he did call the station last night, worried about you."

Kaz was relieved. She liked Steve; she hadn't wanted to hear he was under arrest.

Lucy stood. Her demeanor was subdued—not at all like her. "I'm going home to get a few hours' sleep, then I have to return to the station. Morale is real low in the squad room—two of our own involved in a drug ring and one man dead. And Ken—a good family man—murdered because he was just trying to keep his head above water but making bad decisions." She took a deep breath. "But we'll get over it."

They were all silent for a moment.

Lucy seemed to shake herself out of her brooding. "I left

Ivar with all the paperwork, which means he's in hog heaven. I still have the murder of the drug dealer to handle—but my snitch is finally talking. It looks like Sykes took the dealer out in a fit of rage when the guy threatened to expose him after the drug supply was cut off. But there are a few more details to nail down." She headed for the door, avoiding Gary's eyes, then cocked her head at Kaz. "Six o'clock at the tavern. If I don't get a chance to cream you at pool tonight, I might just slit my wrists."

Kaz smiled. "Deal." Lucy left, and Kaz turned toward Gary, her eyebrows raised.

Gary grunted and stood. "Looks like I have some explaining to do."

"I think there's more to it than that." She watched the panic come and go in his eyes.

"Maybe." He started down the hallway after Lucy, then hesitated, hanging his head. After a moment, he squared his shoulders and headed in a different direction.

So Gary brother was back in martyr mode, unwilling to take a chance. This was one battle Kaz couldn't help him with—he was on his own. But she hurt for both of them, and she hoped they could work it out.

She sat down in the chair he'd vacated and reached for Chuck's hand. She held it for a long moment, trying to will some of her strength into him. Was it her imagination, or was his color better than it had been when she'd come in? She hoped so.

She used both hands to warm his. "Thank you," she whispered.

For a brief moment, his hand tightened on hers.

Zeke burst through the door of Michael's room with Kaz in tow, scrabbling on the linoleum as he leapt across the room. He launched himself at the bed. Monitors jerked and beeped, and the IV line swung wildly, almost ripping out of Michael's hand. With both paws on the bed, Zeke slathered Michael's face with dog saliva.

Michael laughed and scratched his ruff with his free hand. "Easy there, boy. I'm okay."

"Mawrooo, rooo."

Zeke then tried to climb into the hospital bed, and Kaz grabbed his collar, hauling him back. "Sit," she told him firmly, trying to avert disaster.

He grumbled, his expression accusing, but sat. He slapped a giant paw against the edge of the covers and grinned, his tongue hanging sideways out of his mouth.

"Zeke hasn't slept a wink, worrying about you," she told Michael. "I promised him I'd sneak him up here as soon as I could."

Michael grunted. "Good. Maybe the hospital staff will discover him and it'll get both of us expelled."

"Fat chance," Kaz said, but she secretly commiserated. "You're in here for awhile, at least until the pin they put in your leg starts to knit with the bone."

She could see that he didn't like the sound of that. "So," he said, his voice casual. "Since we've now slept together—"

"I beg your pardon?" Kaz interrupted, her eyebrows arched, a slight smile on her face. "I don't remember getting a lot of sleep."

"—how about, when I get out of here, I take you out on a date?"

She made a production out of hesitating. "A real date, huh? Like dinner, and maybe a movie?"

"Yeah," he said. "I could put the moves on you after the lights go down."

"*That's* appealing." Her heart turned over. "I haven't necked in a movie theater since high school."

"Then you've been missing out," he said firmly. He reached

out, took one of her hands and kissed the inside of her wrist. A small jolt of desire ran through her. "You'll stick around?"

"Of course. I've got the work on the *Anna Marie*, and Gary still needs help with the business. We'll have to recoup from our losses—" She shivered, heat flashing through her when he used his teeth on her palm. The man knew how to turn her into mush, thank God.

"I meant," he growled, "will you stay around for us? Because otherwise, we're trying out a long-distance relationship. I'm not letting go of you anytime soon."

A feeling of contentment washed over her. She smiled tremulously. "Yes."

She'd work out whatever she needed to with her business partner. She'd probably have to commute back and forth, but it would be worth it. There was no way she was going back to California on a permanent basis. This was where she belonged now.

"Yes, what?" he demanded.

"Yes, I'm sticking around." She leaned down and kissed him, placing her hand on his cheek. "For us."

The End

About the Author

New York Times bestselling author P. J. Alderman is one of fifteen Indie authors to break into the Top 150 *USA Today* bestsellers for 2011. She has spent more than two decades in the Pacific Northwest port towns that inspire her romantic thrillers and mysteries.

Alderman's contemporary Columbia River thriller, A Killing Tide, was a RITA finalist and recently climbed the charts to stay on the New York Times and USA Today bestselling lists for eight weeks. Her Port Chatham cozy mysteries, also bestsellers, take readers on a journey back in time to a lawless nineteenth century waterfront, blending history, murder, and present-day supernatural sleuthery.

Visit PJ at www.pjalderman.com, or follow her at http://twitter.com/#!/PJAlderman

Books by P. J. Alderman:

Columbia River Thriller Series:

A Killing Tide
Phantom River

Port Chatham Mystery Series:

Haunting Jordan
Ghost Ship

From *Phantom River*, **coming soon:**

Prologue

Astoria, Oregon
Tuesday, midnight, late winter

John MacFallon wrenched the steering wheel to avoid the sudden drop-off into howling black at the bottom of the hairpin curve. The pickup's rear wheels spun on the gravel shoulder, then found purchase. He kept his grip white-knuckled, his gaze glued to the narrow ribbon of pavement winding along the bluffs of the Columbia River. Not for the first time that night, Highway 30 struck him as an irresistible temptation for anyone looking to commit suicide.

The road's white fog lines, demarcating safety from oblivion, had become a distant memory just west of Longview. Rain hammered the windshield, restricting visibility to a few yards beyond the truck's hood. Though he had the wipers on high, it was as if he'd never turned them on at all.

When he'd flown out from Boston a few weeks back to interview for the job of Chief of Police, his longtime friend, Michael Chapman, hadn't seen fit to warn him about the weather. They'd met at a fishermen's hangout afterward to catch up over a few pints before Mac headed back.

Chapman had shrugged. "Yeah, it can get a little wet out here in the winter. But hell, Mac, you're ex-Navy. What's a little wet to you?"

What Chapman failed to mention—and Mac learned in one

Internet search—was that Lewis and Clark had nearly gone insane their first winter at Fort Clatsop on the Columbia River, battling the darkness and the damp that never went away. Even the NOAA precipitation charts hadn't provided a clear picture. This was a fucking river pouring out of the sky.

The road abruptly straightened, but Mac knew the respite wouldn't last. He rubbed his jaw, three days of stubble pricking his palm. The smart move would've been to stop in Portland for the night, then tackle the last leg of his journey during daylight hours. But he'd pushed all the way across the country, his own private demons nipping at his heels, and he hadn't wanted to stop an hour short of his goal.

Don't think, keep moving. That had been his mantra for weeks now.

Not that he'd had any luck outrunning the images in his head.

Leaning forward, he kept one hand clamped to the steering wheel while he held down the Scan button on the radio. He'd heard nothing but static since he'd left Portland—grating white noise that blended with the impenetrable gray mist enshrouding the truck.

Surely he could find some local station. People lived out here, didn't they? Right about now, he could use a bit of human contact. A voice coming out of the night—any voice at all—would suffice. He'd take whiny, brassy, or slick and salesy, he really didn't give a damn. At this point, anything would be a comfort—

"If my grandmother were alive, she'd tell you I've never had much use for men who covet money and power."

The smoky voice flooded the dark interior of the truck, muting the hiss of tires on wet pavement. Mac froze, the tip of his index finger a hairbreadth away from the radio button.

With a husky, contralto laugh, she continued. *"Actually, my grandmother would tell you I haven't had much use for men lately,*

273

period. But that's not up for discussion this evening, fellas, so don't go heading for the phones, trying to change my mind."

Mac snorted. There wasn't a man alive who could resist that challenge—the call lines had to be lighting up. His Boston S.W.A.T. buddies already would've had their laptops open, attempting to triangulate the signal.

"When I was eight, my grandmother told me a story that has stuck in my head even to this day. It's the Northwest legend of how Coyote stole Fire, but I think you'll agree with me when I say that's not what it's really all about..."

Mac stared at the radio console.

"You see there was a time when people were always cold and hungry. Fire, which could have kept them warm and fed, burned high up on a mountaintop, jealously guarded by three greedy men. And those men weren't about to let anyone steal Fire, because then everyone could be as powerful as they."

"But Coyote wanted all men, women, and children to have Fire. Sounds like a modern-day populist, doesn't he? Anyway, Coyote crept up that mountain to watch and to wait for his chance.

"Along about dawn the next morning, the man on guard stood and went into his tent, leaving Fire momentarily unattended. Lightning quick, Coyote seized Fire and leapt down the mountainside.

"With a shout, the man gave chase, catching the tip of Coyote's tail. Which is why the tip is white to this day. Coyote ran to Squirrel, who leapt from branch to branch down the mountain with Fire on his back..." Her voice faded on a surge of static.

Mac leaned forward, straining to hear as he gunned the truck around the next curve.

"...so hot it burned the back of Squirrel's neck, and to this day you can see the black spot there...to Frog, who spit fire onto Wood..."

"...After a while, the man abandoned the chase and climbed back up to his camp on the mountaintop where he felt safe. Coyote then gathered all the people around and showed them how to rub two

sticks of wood together, releasing Fire.

"As they do to this day."

Mac heard dead air, then a long, soft sigh.

"I'll leave you to ponder and dream on that one...it's time for us to wrap it up for the night.

"According to my friend Gary, all you fishermen made it across the river bar safe and sound on the flood tide. So I'm happy to report that we've got us another win against the Columbia River ghouls. And Caitlyn will have the ship report for you bright and early tomorrow morning, so don't forget to tune in."

The ghostly hulks of three elk appeared out of the mist, trotting across the road. Mac slammed on the brakes, swearing when the truck fishtailed. Unfazed, they disappeared over the side of the bank, heading down to the river.

"Oh, and for any newcomers or tourists who are crazy enough to be driving down Highway 30 right about now, try to miss hitting the elk herd around Milepost 94. We don't know you yet, so we don't know whether to regret your passing. But Elk has been our friend and neighbor for as long as Coyote has. We wouldn't take kindly to you hurting him.

"You've been listening to KACR, Astoria's community radio at 90.7 on your FM dial, dedicated to helping all men, women, and children learn how to get Fire out of Wood."

There was a moment of silence, then a return to static as the station went off the air. Mac was left with only the faint glow of the radio dial, the drum of rain on the roof, and the unsettling echoes of his own bleak thoughts.

His palm slapped the steering wheel, hard.

She hadn't mentioned her name.

Several miles to the east in an elegant Queen Anne home overlooking downtown Astoria, a man hurled his radio, shattering it against the basement wall.

She *knew.*

275

He fell to his knees, chest heaving, heels of his hands pressed against his eyes.

She'd poked her nose where it didn't belong, asking too damn many questions. Refusing to *let it go*.

She'd signed her own death warrant.

Chapter 1

Thursday, 2:40 P.M., aboard the helicopter Seahawk

"Wind's out of the south today."

The tinny voice screeched at Jo Henderson over the static in her headphones. In the background, the staccato whump-whump of the helicopter's rotors sounded like sub-woofers on amphetamines. Her feet were already numb from engine vibration.

Only moments ago, they'd lifted off from Astoria Regional Airport, flying blind. Thick fog streamed past the Astoria Bar Pilots Association helicopter as they headed toward a freighter waiting in the Pacific, fifteen miles northwest of the CR buoy.

"Got a little fog, though." The pilot, Tim Carter, tapped the instrument panel with the blunt end of his finger.

Jo exchanged a look with Erik, their winch operator. Master of understatement, that was Tim. She rubbed the salt-etched glass of the window with her cuff, wishing she was back at the radio station broadcasting another Northwest legend. Wishing she was anywhere but strapped into a helicopter.

Given their current heading, the forest-green ridges of Saddleback Mountain would be over her right shoulder, the river and the town's steep hillsides dotted with Victorian homes directly in front of her. That is, if she could see them.

She forced herself to relax her grip before she dug holes in the leather armrests. The helicopter pilots contracted by the Association flew in almost any type of weather, and Tim, whom she'd known all her life, was one of the best. She knew that.

They hit an air pocket, and her teeth snapped together.

"Oops."

Oops?

"Sorry." Tim frowned at the controls. "She's acting a bit sluggish today."

...